THE RESURRECTION OF WILDFLOWERS

THE RESURRECTION OF WILDFLOWERS

MICALEA SMELTZER

PAGE
&
VINE

Page & Vine
An Imprint of Meredith Wild LLC

Paperback ISBN: 979-8-9871901-1-1

For anyone who has had to live through unimaginable pain and had to become stronger because of it.

"Flowers grow out of dark moments."

—*Corita Kent*

PROLOGUE

Salem

It took me a while to learn that sometimes no matter how much, or how hard you love someone, or something, you have to let them go. You can't save a sinking ship.

Sometimes, you have someone else you have to be strong for, who needs you more.

You make a choice.

A devastating one.

And you hope, maybe one day, they'll come back to you.

CHAPTER ONE

Salem

Spring in Hawthorne Mills is my favorite. I haven't spent any time here since I left six years ago. I came back a few times that summer, hoping the man I loved next door would snap out of it and see me, come back to me, but he never did.

Thayer Holmes was lost to me, so I tucked my tail and moved on.

Got a job waitressing at a diner close to Lauren's apartment. I stored away every penny I could. Caleb and I started talking more, and then we started dating again. It was almost a year to the day of Georgia's wedding that he asked me to marry him, and I said yes. We married two months later. He finished college and we moved to California. I loved it there, almost as much as here, but he got a job offer a year ago in Boston, so we returned.

And still I never set foot back here at my childhood home.

He knew why and it hurt him.

All I've ever done is hurt him.

So, I let him go.

Our divorce was easy, just like everything with us. I know he'll always be in my life, but now he's free to find the kind of love I knew once. Once you've had it, nothing else compares no matter how much you try and how much work you put into it.

It's like trying to fit a puzzle piece in a space it doesn't belong.

Opening the car door, I step onto the driveway.

As much as I swore I'd never come back here, to this place, to *him*, only one thing could bring me back. Letting myself into the house, I find my mom in the makeshift bed set up in the living room.

"Hi, Mom." It takes everything I have in me to stave off the tears. I don't want her to see me cry.

"There's my girl," she smiles, beckoning me forward with a swish of her pale thin hand.

My mom's dying.

The cancer found its way back and nothing has worked this time. No matter how hard she fights, it's stronger, and now she has two months, perhaps not even that, left to live.

My steps sound so loud to my ears as I make my way into the living room and bend down to hug her.

"You just missed Georgia," she tells me, her hug weak. There's not much muscle or fat on her body. She's withering away right before our eyes.

"I'm sure I'll see her later."

"The kids were asking about you guys."

I smile, brushing my fingers over the papery skin on her cheek. "They'll see us soon." Georgia and Michael have two kids now and another on the way. To say they have their hands full is an understatement, but they're happy. "Do you need anything?"

"I'm okay right now. Maybe we could watch a movie or something after you bring your stuff in?"

"That sounds good, Mom."

Caleb and I have remained living together since the divorce. It just made sense while I figured out my next step, but with my mom's condition deteriorating I knew it was time to return home. To take care of her in her final days, give Georgia a break, and when the inevitable happens, clean out the house and figure out what comes next.

It's hard, knowing my future is a big question mark at the moment. I'll be twenty-six later this year and just like at eighteen, I still don't have shit figured out. But maybe that's the truth of adulthood no one wants to tell you—we're all out here winging it.

Outside, I steadfastly ignore the house next door. I know he still lives there. My mom mentions him from time to time. Sometimes I wonder if she does it trying to gauge my reaction. I've never told her about what happened with Thayer. With my heart so broken, and accepting that he and I were truly over, I didn't see the point.

I manage to get all of my stuff brought inside without stealing a peek next door.

That's a lie.

I take a small one.

Just long enough to see the completed treehouse in the backyard and the hint of the roof of a greenhouse.

"Did you get everything?" My mom's croaky voice sounds so small from the living room.

"I did. I'll carry some of it up now."

"All right. I think I'll just ... rest my ... eyes ... for a bit."

She can't see me in the kitchen, but tears spring to my eyes.

She's slipping away. What could've been a long life is now measured in weeks, hours, minutes, seconds, and every single one is precious.

CHAPTER TWO

Salem

My room is a relic.

It's literally exactly the same. For some reason, I expected my mom to have changed it in some way. It's clean since both Georgia and I pitch in to pay a cleaning lady to come by weekly. There's not a speck of dust anywhere. The bed is freshly made, the corners of the covers crisp.

Since my mom is sleeping and not going to be ready to watch a movie anytime soon, I unpack my clothes and toiletries, then call Caleb.

"Hey," he says, his voice deep. "Did you make it in all right?"

"Yeah, thanks for asking."

"How's your mom?"

I sigh, rubbing my forehead. "Sleeping. She's frailer than I expected."

"I'm sorry." I can hear the genuineness in his voice. Despite us falling apart, Caleb remains to be one of the kindest people I know.

"It is what it is," I reply softly, sitting on the end of my bed facing the window I used to sit out on, often with Caleb himself.

"Someone's trying to steal the phone from me," he chuckles.

I laugh too. "Put her on."

"Mommy!" My daughter's voice is like a balm to a wound. With just one word she makes me feel better, more grounded.

"Hi, baby. How's your day been?"

"Good. Daddy picked me up from school and we went to the grocery store. I got a lollipop."

I hear Caleb laugh in the background. "That was supposed to be our secret."

"Oops," she giggles.

Seda was the unexpected surprise Thayer left me with. She's been the gift I didn't know I wanted or needed. Being her mom makes me feel like a superhero.

"I miss you already," I tell her.

"I miss you, too, Mommy. Give grandma kisses—you always say kisses will make it better."

Oh, fuck. I'm going to cry. I wish tears would make my mom better, but I don't think magical kisses can fight cancer off.

"I will," I say to my daughter. "I love you."

"Love you, Mommy!" She hangs up the phone, the line going quiet.

When I make my way back downstairs, my mom is still asleep so I decide to go ahead and start on dinner. Georgia says Mom isn't eating much these days, but I have to at least try.

Searching the cabinets I come across a bottle of wine, probably something Georgia stashed before she got pregnant again, and open it. Filling the glass, I drink as I cook. I'm not a huge drinker, but today calls for a little wine to soothe my nerves.

"Salem?" My mom calls and I turn away from the simmering pot.

"Yeah?" I call back, surprised she's awake. I expected to

have to wake her.

"Could you bring me some water?"

Filling up a cup with a straw, I carry it in to her and hold it to her lips. She drinks greedily, her eyes grateful. Setting the cup down, I ask her, "Do you need anything else? I'm making dinner."

"No, the water was all." She pats my hand lovingly. "I'm sorry I fell asleep before we could watch a movie."

"It's okay. I'll put one on while we eat."

She watches me, her eyes sad, and I wonder what she's thinking about. "Are you happy, Salem? You don't look like it."

"I'm as happy as I can be right now."

"I guess that will have to do."

I smile sadly at her, backing out of the room to finish dinner.

When it's ready I carry two plates of spaghetti and garlic bread into the living room. Propping her up, I fix a tray across her lap and get her comfortable before I sit down myself to eat.

The movie plays but I'm not paying attention.

I leave it going while I clean our dirty dishes. My mom barely touched hers, but I know she tried to eat as much as she could.

By the time I return, only a handful of minutes later, she's fallen asleep again.

It's getting late anyway, so I switch off the TV, cover her more fully with the blanket, make sure she has water, and that her phone is where she can easily access it if she needs me.

"I love you, Mom." I kiss her forehead.

A tear leaks from the corner of my eye. Swiping it away, I quietly take the stairs and shower before heading to bed myself. It's been a long day and I need my rest.

***

Returning from my morning run, I let myself in the side door into the kitchen and smile when I see my mom at the table. There's a little more color to her skin this morning, more pink than gray, and I hope that means she got a good night's sleep.

"Hey," I smile, adjusting my ponytail. "Are you hungry?"

"I had some cereal," she explains, flipping through a magazine.

"You know," I say gently, "you're not supposed to walk around without someone to help you."

She's a fall risk and she knows this.

But I guess if I was in her situation, I might be a little stubborn too at times. It has to be difficult coping with needing another person to help you do basic things like use the bathroom or wash your body.

"I had my non-slip socks on."

"Mom," I say in a warning tone, starting a pot of coffee. "You know that's not going to cut it."

She sighs. "I felt okay this morning. I wanted to move on my own."

"Just be careful," I beg.

"Salem," she says my name softly, carefully. My back is to her, grabbing a mug for my coffee so I turn around. "You know I'm going to die, right?"

I lower my head. I know. Georgia knows. We all know.

"Yes."

"I just want to still feel like me with as little time as I have left. All right?"

I give a tiny nod in understanding, damming back the tears that beg to burst forth. It's the worst feeling mourning someone while they're still alive.

"I was thinking," she continues, "that we could bake some cupcakes together today. Since I'm feeling okay."

My shoulders stiffen. I haven't baked cupcakes since whenever the last time was I made them for Thayer. Afterwards, it hurt too much. They only make me think of him.

"We—uh—we can do that."

I'm not about to tell my dying mother no.

"I thought we could make cookie dough. They were always your favorite. Thayer, next door—they're his favorite too. I always took some over when I made them, you know, before I got too sick to bake anymore."

My shoulders tighten with tension.

"Y-Yeah," I stutter. "I remember he loved those."

She's watching me carefully, with this assessing look, and I stare back. "He's a nice man. It's a shame what happened all those years ago. His poor son. I think I would've had to leave, but he hasn't moved."

"Mom," I try to change the subject, "do you want a drink or something?"

"Not really." She closes the magazine and slides it away from her on the table. "He mows the yard for me, you know?" She continues on, still talking about Thayer. I don't want to hear about him. I don't want to know. It hurts too much, but I can't say that to her. With my back to her, I add some cream and sugar to my coffee. My hands shake, but from where she's sitting I know she can't see. "He comes over sometimes. I think he's lonely, and we'll have a drink—"

"Are you into him?" The question rushes out of me before I can stop it and I immediately cringe.

I don't even want to consider the possibility of Thayer and

my *mom*. I might throw up.

"God, no." She laughs, but it turns into a cough. I sit down across from her, watching with a careful eye to make sure she's fine. "But it was nice to have someone to talk to. You moved clear across the country and Georgia was busy with work and her family. I needed a friend."

"Well, I'm glad you had each other."

Fuck Thayer Holmes. He can talk and be friends with my mother, but he can't talk to me?

I think of all the time I spent trying to get him to open up to me. I knew he still loved me like I loved him, but it wasn't enough apparently, and I gave up trying. I couldn't be the only one trying to fix what was broken. He needed to put in some effort too and he wouldn't.

"When we finish the cupcakes, you can take some over to him."

I tap my fingers on the table and force a smile. "Sounds great."

It's been six years. I should be over him. Moved on.

But I'm not sure you ever really move on from your one true love.

CHAPTER THREE

Salem

The kitchen smells of cupcakes, and I'd be lying if I didn't admit I'm weak and cave to the need to eat one. They taste just as good as I remember, and baking felt good too. It was like riding a bicycle. I don't think I let myself realize how much I missed it.

"I need to ... go sit down for a while." My mom sounds out of breath, the weakness creeping back in.

"No problem." I rush around the counter to her side, giving her my arm to hold on to. I guide her into the living room, feeling her rest more of her weight against me as we go. "Do you want to sit on the couch or the bed."

She thinks for a moment. "Bed."

"Okay." I help her into the hospital bed and cover her with blankets. "Rest, Mom." I kiss her forehead.

"Don't forget to take cupcakes to Thayer."

I stifle a groan. "I won't."

I send up a silent prayer he won't be home when I take them over.

Her eyes grow heavy and she's already dozing off asleep before I leave the room.

My phone rings and it's Georgia.

"Hey." I put her on speaker so I can clean up the kitchen as we talk. "What's up?"

"How's Mom today?"

"She had some energy this morning but she's taking a nap now. We made cupcakes."

"Oh." I hear the smile in her voice. "That's good. That's really good."

"I thought so too." I load the dishwasher.

"Thank you for coming and staying with her. I know you didn't want to, and I don't blame you. I understand not wanting to have—"

"Georgia, she's our mom. You don't need to thank me. I want to be here. I need to be."

She clears her throat and I know she's getting a bit choked up. "I have to get back to work. I'll call you later."

"We're fine." I know my sister's the nurse and I'm not, but I'm not incapable of taking care of our mom and she has enough on her plate without worrying about what's going on here.

"Maybe I could drop by after my shift with some fast-food or something."

"Just let me know."

We say our goodbyes and hang up. The kitchen is spotless once more, so that leaves me with no choice but to take the plate of cupcakes over to Thayer.

I know it shouldn't, but it annoys me learning he's been friends with my mom. He spoke to her and never reached out to me.

Asshole.

I plate the cupcakes and cover them with saran wrap. The frosting gets smashed a bit, but I don't care.

Taking a deep breath, I prepare myself to face Thayer for the first time in years.

I can do this.

I'm a strong, powerful woman. I won't let any man make me feel down.

Only, when I go around the side of the fence, there's no vehicle in his driveway.

That's good ... I guess.

But as long as I'm staying at my mom's place it doesn't matter. I'll run into him eventually and I'm not sure how that makes me feel.

***

Georgia comes in the side door with bags of food. Her scrub top is stretched over the swell of her belly, and I can't help but smile.

"Oh, look at you," I coo. "Can I feel?" I ask, taking the bags from her and putting them on the table.

She sighs, jutting out her belly. "Go for it. This one is just like his dad. Never still. I'm exhausted. He keeps me up all night kicking."

"You found out it's a boy?"

She grins from ear to ear. "Yeah, just the other day. Three boys, can you believe it? I always thought I'd be a girl mom, but you know, I wouldn't have it any other way." She places her hand on her stomach by mine. "Don't you want another?"

"I think I've got all I can handle right now."

"I don't know how you can stand being away from her," she goes on, "I know your reasonings, but⬚" We both look to where our mom still sleeps in the living room. She's slept ever since she laid down.

"It's killing me being away from her, but she doesn't need to see her grandma like this." I motion to all the medical equipment and our mom's sleeping, frail form. "She's too young. I know she's in good hands with Caleb anyway and we FaceTime any chance we get."

Georgia shakes her head and pulls out a box of fries from Wendy's shoving around five in her mouth at once. "I was shocked when you said you guys were getting a divorce. I always thought you had it together so well. I mean, that boy stepped up to the plate and married you when you had someone else's kid."

I lower my head. It was no secret to any of our families that my daughter wasn't Caleb's. We didn't want to lie to them or to her either about her parentage, but no one except Caleb and Lauren know who her real father is.

I still remember the hate Caleb's mother spewed at him when we told her. She couldn't understand him taking me back, *marrying* me, when I was having a child that wasn't his.

She stopped talking to him right after that. Didn't even come to the wedding.

I've never forgiven myself for that. I was never her biggest fan, but she's Caleb's mom. I haven't had the heart to ask him if she's contacted him since our divorce.

"Caleb's a good man," I tell her, rifling through the bags of food. "But he's not the right man for me."

She shakes her head, clucking her tongue. "Forgive me, but you're stupid."

I laugh, pulling out a wrapped burger. "I know."

Believe me, I'm all too aware of my mistakes and sins. Caleb being at the top of the list. The worst part is, he's still my best friend. But I guess that makes things easier in a way with Seda involved. My daughter is just as much his as she is mine. It's not only DNA that makes a parent, it's how you behave, and Caleb is the best daddy to our little girl. He's never, not once, treated her like she's not his.

She lowers her voice to a whisper, "Do you think you'll stay here or move back to Boston after mom...?"

"I won't stay in Boston," I answer quickly. I've never been a city girl, and I've had enough of them in the past few years. "But I don't know if I'll stay here either."

She looks around, pondering. "This is a good house. If you decide to stay."

"I don't think I could live here."

It's not just about Thayer, though he's a factor, but this is our mom's house, and I don't think I'd ever feel like it was mine.

"Yeah." She lowers her head sadly, eyes flicking to where our mom slumbers in the next room. "I understand. I'm not sure I actually could either." Pulling her hair over one shoulder, she says, "Christy, one of my nurse friends said she could stay with mom for a day and night this weekend. I thought you might want to use the time to see Seda, but I wanted to run it by you first before confirming with her."

"That would be great," I tell her honestly, feeling relief flood my chest.

I know Seda is in great hands with Caleb, but I hate being away from my little girl. I didn't want her to be around my mom while she's dying. Death is inevitable, but no child should see someone they love disintegrate right before their eyes. It's not that I won't let her see my mom at all, but I don't want her staying here around this twenty-four-seven. Besides, she has school and she's currently enrolled in Boston. I wasn't going to yank her out with only a few weeks left of the school year.

"Awesome, I'll let her know. She's a great person and a wonderful nurse so you don't need to worry. Mom will be in great hands."

That's Georgia—she might be a bit of a wild card, but she's

always taking care of us.

"I love you," I tell her.

"Aw, I love you, too. And I'm so happy you're back for however long as that is."

"Thanks. It's good to be back."

And surprisingly, it's not even a lie.

CHAPTER FOUR

Salem

Driving down to the local grocery store, I park and hesitate before going inside. The fridge at home isn't well-stocked and I want to get some things for meals, but I'm dreading this trip because I'm bound to run into someone I know, and small town love drama. Me returning to town after my divorce—that's huge news for them.

I made a list before leaving the house, so that once I get inside, I won't need to think over what I might need for cooking meals.

Regardless, I can only go so fast.

Grabbing my purse, I hop out of my SUV and scurry into the store with my head ducked low. Swiping a cart, I make my way to the produce section. If anyone's watching me, I'm sure they're amused with how fast I move. But the quicker I go, the sooner I'll be out of here, and the less chance there is of someone interrupting.

I make it all the way to the frozen section where I'm looking at the ice cream when someone says my name.

"Thelma," I smile, and it's genuine—even if she is a nosy busybody. "How are you? And you too Cynthia. It's good to see you guys. And together."

Thelma shrugs, leaning over to kiss Cynthia's cheek.

"We're too old to stay in the closet anymore. You're back in town for your mother?" I nod. "It's just awful. She's so young—well, young to someone my age, you see, and—"

"I'm actually finishing up shopping and heading back to her so—" I quickly reach inside and grab a random tub of ice cream. "I'll just be going."

"Have you seen that man of yours yet?"

I cock my head to the side. "Who?" My heart thunders. I know exactly who she's talking about.

"Don't play coy with me, girl," she snaps a finger, eyes twinkling. "You know exactly who I'm talking about."

"No, I haven't."

"Huh." She clucks her tongue. "Interesting."

I shrug. "He's moved on." It's been six years, I don't for a minute think he hasn't.

She laughs like I've told the funniest joke she's ever heard. "Oh, that's a funny one, girl. That man..." She shakes her head. "He hasn't moved on. I'm not sure you have either." She looks me up and down. "If you had, you would've come back sooner."

With that, her and Cynthia walk down the aisle away from me.

I look down at the ice cream I picked.

Peanut butter Oreo.

Gross.

I put it back and grab cookie dough.

Much better.

***

"Mom, I'm home," I call out, bringing in the first load of groceries. I tried to get it all in one trip, then quickly realized that was next to impossible. "Are you hungry? I thought I'd make chicken sandwiches for dinner?"

I set everything down, poking my head around the corner. She turns her head weakly and yawns.

"I'm not that hungry."

"What about ice cream?"

She wrinkles her nose, and I can tell the idea alone displeases her. "No."

"That's all right." I refuse to be deterred. "Is there something, anything you'd like?"

She shakes her head, her gaze drifting to the front window.

It hurts knowing she's slipping away second by second.

"If you change your mind, let me know." I won't push her on the matter right now. Maybe I'll be lucky and get something in her a little bit later.

I finish bringing everything in, exhaling a sigh of relief when I manage to do it without bumping into Thayer. I know it's not something I can avoid forever, but I'm going to try for as long as I can. That's the wimpy way out, but when it comes to him, I've never claimed to be strong.

I put the groceries away and start dinner, making some for my mom too so there's something to eat if she gets hungry.

"Should we watch a movie?" I ask, sitting down on the couch with my plate.

"I was wondering..." She starts, clearing her dry throat. I immediately hop up and hold out her water for her to sip. "Would you read a book to me? There's one I've been wanting to read, but—"

"Which one?" I look around for it.

"It's right there." She points to it on the coffee table. "I had Georgia pull it for me, but never picked it up."

Scooping up the book, I sit down and curl my legs under me. I balance my plate on the arm of the couch and open the book.

When I start to read, she smiles.

I take a mental picture of this moment, knowing it's one I'll cherish forever.

CHAPTER FIVE

Salem

"Mommy!"

Seda runs straight for me when I open the door to the brownstone.

I crouch down, catching her just as she launches herself at me. "My girl," I breathe, inhaling her scent. She smells like grass from playing outside mixed with her watermelon shampoo.

"I missed you so much, Mommy." She cups my cheeks in her soft hands. "Is Grandma okay?"

"She's all right." I put my hand over one of hers. "But she doesn't have much time left with us."

"When can I visit? I miss her. I made a drawing for her. I'll show you." Then she's running off, presumably to locate the drawing.

I stand up, just in time to see Caleb walk out of the kitchen and lean against the archway. "She's talked about your mom non-stop."

I blow out a breath I didn't even know I was holding. "I've tried to explain to her, but I don't think she fully grasps what's happening."

"She's five," he reasons, tossing a rag over his shoulder. "Are you hungry? I'm getting ready to put leftovers away."

"Starving." Seda comes running back to me with a piece of

printer paper.

"Look, Mommy." She holds it up. "See that's grandma in her bed," she points at the stick figure with yellow hair, "and that's my brother. He's an angel and he's waiting for her."

I grind my teeth together, so I don't burst into tears. Caleb and I have made an effort to talk about Thayer and Forrest with her. She knows that Caleb is her dad, but that she has another one too who was sad when her brother passed and wasn't capable of being in her life because of it. It's a whole complicated situation and trying to explain it to her in a way she understands is hard at times.

I put her in swim safety lessons as a baby too. I wanted to make sure she knew every tool she could use in case anything happened.

Reaching for her, I pull her into a hug and rest my chin on top of her head. "Yeah, baby girl. He is."

Her little arms wrap around my neck—well, they're not so little anymore, but I think I'll always see her that way. "He'll make sure she's okay, so you don't have to cry, Mommy." She holds my cheeks, looking into my eyes with ones the color of Thayer's. Warm and chocolatey. "Crying isn't bad," she repeats back to me what I tell her all the time, "but I don't like it when you're sad."

I kiss her cheek. "I'm not sad, baby. Just so proud of you." Standing, I hold on tight to her drawing. "Mommy's hungry. Do you want to sit with me while I eat?"

"I want to draw some more before I go to bed."

I laugh when she runs off. Clearly, I missed her more than she did me.

Caleb's already plating some of the dinner he made and popping it into the microwave.

"I could've done that." I grab a soda from the fridge.

"I know." He braces his hands on the counters, his muscles flexing. "How's your mom doing?" His voice is low so Seda can't overhear.

I shake my head, sliding onto the barstool. "Not good, which is expected, but she's talking and still getting around somewhat on her own—mostly because she's stubborn and tries to refuse help every chance she gets."

Caleb chuckles, pulling the plate out of the microwave and setting it in front of me with a fork. "Sounds like Allison."

"I promise once all of this is over, I'll be out of your hair." I can't help but look around the kitchen, the cabinets I picked out when we remodeled, the polka dot cannisters for flour and sugar I chose for a pop of whimsy.

Caleb rolls his eyes at me, grabbing a beer. "We're still friends. We'll always be friends. And," a shadow flickers over his face, "even if that idiot comes back into the picture, I'll always be in Seda's life. You can't take her from me, and neither can he."

"Calm down," I tell him, forking a piece of meatloaf. "We've talked about this. I would never do that to you. Seda loves you—you might not be her father by DNA's standards, but you are her dad by all the ways that count. I understand more than anyone that DNA doesn't make a father."

Caleb's head lowers and he looks at me from beneath his lashes. "Thank you."

The one and only thing we argued over during the divorce was Seda. Caleb was terrified that I'd take her from him and he'd never see her again. I could never be that cruel. Caleb stepped up to the plate, for me, for her, when Thayer was too lost in his grief for me to reach. I wouldn't only be punishing

Caleb if I took her away, I'd be hurting her.

"I'm sorry," he adds, running his fingers through his blond hair. "I guess with you back there, it has me feeling uneasy."

"Hey," I say softly, reaching across the counter to place my hand on his. "You have nothing to worry about. Not with Seda."

He clears his throat, and I can tell he's getting a bit choked up. "I'm going to watch TV."

"All right."

I finish eating in silence, then put my plate in the dishwasher. The kitchen is already spotless, so I go to the playroom on the first floor where I'm sure I'll find Seda.

She's scribbling madly on a piece of paper, creating another masterpiece. "It's bath time, missy," I tell her from the doorway.

"Ugh, but Mom—"

"No buts." I shake my head, letting her know not to argue. "After you finish your drawing its bath time and then to bed."

She gets a mischievous look. "Will you read me a bedtime story?"

"One." I hold up a finger and wiggle it. "And only one. You're not sweet-talking me into more tonight." I stick my tongue out at her, and she giggles. We both know I'm weak when it comes to her. Not that I'm a pushover, but I love spending time with my girl. These moments when she's a child are so fleeting. I want to enjoy them and make special memories with her. Especially since I'm not sure I'll have more kids. That was a big factor in the divorce. Caleb wants more kids, and I won't keep him from that.

While Seda finishes her drawing, I head upstairs with my bag to the guestroom where I moved my things months ago. Caleb tried to get me to stay in the master, saying he was fine with the smaller room, but I reminded him I don't plan on living here like he does.

"Hi, Binx." I pet my beloved cat on the head where he snoozes on the covers. "I missed you."

He opens one green eye, glaring at me. I know he's pissed at me for leaving. He's needy like that, but instead of wanting love and attention now that I'm back he gives me the silent treatment. Cats, man.

I unpack the clothes I washed at my mom's and repack some different items. I might as well have a little variety to spice up my life. I'm tired from the week and can't wait to get into bed, but I really do want to spend time with Seda first.

I'm walking out of the bedroom when she tops the steps. "I finished. I guess that means I'm ready for my bath." She sounds anything but.

"Go pick out what pajamas you want to wear and I'll start it."

"Okay!" That excites her.

Flicking on the bathroom light, I push the plug in the tub and start the water, making sure the temperature isn't too hot or cold.

Seda comes running into the bathroom with her bright pink princess pajamas. "These." She drops them onto the floor and quickly strips out of her clothes without any prompting on my part.

"Do you know what book you want?" I ask, wetting her hair so I can suds it up.

"The one with Princess Seda," she giggles, tilting her head back. She loves when I massage the shampoo into her scalp.

"Why am I not surprised?" I smile at her, giving her cheek a small pinch. When she was a baby my mom gifted us one of those books with your name in it and it's been her favorite since she was a toddler.

"It's my favorite, Mom," she says dramatically like I'm not already aware, throwing in an eyeroll for good measure.

She's five going on fifteen.

When her hair is clean and she's scrubbed her body thoroughly with the cloth I pass her, I scoop her out and wrap her in a towel.

"Egg game!" she cries, feet pounding on the floor as she runs into her room.

I chase after her, pajamas in my hands. She falls to the floor, covering her body with the purple towel.

"What is this?" I say, circling her body. "Is this an egg? What an unusually large egg. And purple too? Hmm." I tap my finger against my lips. She starts to wiggle her body. I gasp loudly. "Oh my God, it's moving." I grin when I spot Caleb watching us from the doorway with his own smile. "Do you see this mysterious egg? Look at it moving!"

"I'm cracking!" Seda cries, wiggling more. "*Crack*." She throws off the towel and stands up. "Look, Mommy! It's a Seda!" She shakes her wet hair like a dog.

"Would you look at that? Who would've guessed that's what was in the egg." She giggles. "Pajama time." I hold up the top and she takes it from me, putting it on. She spots Caleb and smiles. "Did you see, Daddy? I was an egg!"

He chuckles. "I saw. You're my favorite egg." His eyes find mine and I feel his heartbreak still. Even though we're on good terms, it doesn't change the fact that he didn't want the divorce and he's still in love with me.

"Mommy's going to read me a story. Will you help her? I love it when you both do the voices."

He meets my eyes, seeing if I'm okay with it. I nod.

"Sure, baby girl." He picks up her wet towel and drops it into the hamper.

Seda grabs her book and climbs into bed with Caleb and I on either side of her.

She holds the book, flipping the pages and doing her best to read along with us.

By the time it's finished, her eyes have grown heavy.

We each kiss her forehead and tuck her in for the night

Out in the hallway, Caleb looks at me like he wants to say something but decides against it.

I watch him head down the hall and back downstairs.

I'm a coward, because I don't follow him and ask him what's on his mind.

Instead, I go to bed, because it's the easier option.

CHAPTER SIX

Salem

"Mom?" I call, letting myself into the house.

Christy called me about thirty minutes ago during my drive letting me know everything was okay, but she had to head out instead of waiting for me to arrive.

When I pulled into the driveway, I steadfastly ignored the truck parked next door. It's bigger than the one Thayer used to have, but I still managed to act like I didn't see it, using my hair as a shield.

"In here, honey," she calls from the living room.

"Hey." The word leaves me in a relieved breath. Her skin tone is a little warmer today, slightly flushed and she looks less tired despite being in the bed. There's a tray across her lap and she's coloring. "Looks pretty," I comment, looking at the floral design she chose. She's filling it in with shades of purple and teal. "Seda sent these for you." I dig in my bag for the drawings.

"Oh." My mom takes them, smiling and looking over each one. "How sweet of her. Was your time with her nice?"

I nod, sitting down on the couch so I can remove my strappy sandals. "Yeah, but it always is. Even when she's driving me up a wall, I love her so much."

My mom smiles, her eyes crinkling at the corners. "Being a parent is the most amazing thing you'll ever do in your life. It's not for the faint of heart, though."

"That's for sure." I shudder, thinking of Georgia's young boys and how she told me once that the oldest caught a mouse and brought it into the house. Not even Binx does that.

"Is Caleb all right?"

Although my mom fully supported my decision on the divorce, she loves Caleb and likes to check on him.

"He's good."

"Is he dating anyone?" she inquires, continuing to color like she didn't ask me a monumental question.

"I don't know." I pick up some of her coloring books from the pile on the floor. "We don't talk about that kind of thing. He's free to date if he wants."

"Is he still in love with you?"

My shoulders lock, my body tensing. "Mom," I beg.

"It's a genuine question, Salem." She gives me that motherly look—the one with the arched brow daring me not to answer.

"Yes." I flip through the pages, looking for a page to color myself. Her eyes try to bore a hole through me, but I steadfastly ignore her.

"You did the right thing, you know." Her words take me by surprise, my head jerking up. She looks back at me with a tiny smile. "You love him, I know you do, but he loves you more. So, you did the right thing in letting him go."

I exhale a shaky breath. "I thought if I just tried harder, put in more effort, I could love him like he loved me."

"But you never could."

"No," I answer, even though it wasn't a question. "When he started talking about having kids, I just..." Rubbing my lips together, I search for the right words. "I couldn't do it anymore. He's amazing, the greatest guy, and I love him, but not in the way he deserves to be loved."

I look down at the page I stopped on, the black and white image blurred from the tears flooding my eyes. I never, ever wanted to hurt Caleb. Not back then and not now, either. But I'm not a perfect person, no one is and if they think they are then they're delusional. We all do things we're not proud of. I will never regret my time with Caleb. It's not possible. But I do regret not loving him enough. The worst part is, if I'd never met Thayer and known what soul-crushing, all-consuming love felt like, then I think Caleb and I would've been a good match.

But I did meet Thayer, and that single moment forever changed the trajectory of my life.

"Please, don't cry," she pleads, reaching for the box of tissues on the table beside her bed.

I reach for the tissue, taking it from her to dab my eyes. "I'm a horrible person, Mom. The shittiest. He loves me so much. Why can't I do the same?"

She looks at me sympathetically. "Honey," she says softly, her eyes pitying, "you have to forgive yourself. You did the right thing."

"It doesn't matter if it was right or not." I dry up more tears. "I still hurt him."

"Hurt is temporary."

"Yeah?" I laugh humorlessly, thinking about how it's been six years since Thayer broke my heart. That hurt certainly hasn't been temporary, but maybe things would've been different if I didn't have our daughter. She's the best thing in this world, but she's also a constant reminder of him.

"You're so strong."

"Mom." I shake my head. "You're the strong one."

She laughs. "How about we're *both* strong?"

"That works." I wipe the tissue beneath my nose.

Her face sobers, and she looks at me with worry. "I want you to be happy, Salem. It's what I've always wanted."

"I am happy," I argue, because it's true. Could I be happier? Yes. But I'm not unhappy.

"You're content. There's a difference."

She has a point. "I'll find what brings me joy one day."

"You will." Her smile is sad. "I just wish I'd be alive to see it."

Another crack is added to my already mangled heart.

***

I wake up at seven in the morning and throw on my running clothes for a jog. I don't have nightmares anymore—well, rarely, thanks to my return to therapy and sticking with it—but some habits are hard to kick and I do love running early. I just don't do it before five A.M. anymore.

Popping in my ear buds, I turn on my cardio playlist while I stretch on the driveway. Instead of turning to jog in front of Thayer's house in the direction I used to go, I turn and head the opposite direction. I never liked this loop as much. It's hillier, but I'm being petty not wanting to take my old route.

By the time I turn to head back, I'm drenched in sweat and my hair doesn't want to stay in a ponytail.

I turn onto the street that brings me home when I spot a jogger heading toward me from the opposite direction.

Tall, big build. Obviously, a man.

My steps falter as we both slow—me in front of my mom's house, him in front of—

I pull my ear buds out, my lips parting as I get my first look at the man I left behind.

"Thayer," I breathe his name into existence.

He cocks his head, taking me in. Surprise fills his brown eyes.

"Salem."

CHAPTER SEVEN

Salem

The man standing in front of me is so different, and yet so similar to the one I left. He's thirty-seven now, almost thirty-eight if I'm doing the math right in my head. I'm too stunned to think coherently. There's a hint of gray at his temples, subtle but it's there, and there's some of that same color sprinkled into the scruff on his cheeks. I didn't know gray hair would be a turn on for me, but with Thayer I think everything is. His brown eyes are taking me in as greedily as I do him. The lines around them are more prominent now. His eyes are brighter, clearer than the last time I saw him.

It was the end of that summer, and my hope had waned. I went over to his house one last time, begging and pleading for him to get up, to live, because that's what Forrest would want. He was drinking his life away, slipping through my fingers. And nothing I did was good enough. In the end, I called his brother and told him Thayer needed him, and I went back to New York City with Lauren. I had a baby to think about and that meant being strong even when I wanted to fall apart too.

I take in his running clothes and shoes, trying desperately to fight my rising smile.

"Hi," I say stupidly.

His eyes continue to rake over me. "Hi."

I keep expecting to feel an awkwardness settle in my chest—after all, this is Thayer and I haven't seen him in ages, but it just feels natural. Like it always did.

He doesn't look like what I expected.

After the way I last saw him, I guess I expected him to look even worse than he did then. But that was a man that was grieving, and this is one who somehow pulled himself out of that and has healed.

He looks *good*.

Healthy.

Somehow, that makes the last six years even worse.

"H-How are you? How has life been?" He asks in an uncharacteristic way for him—flustered and taken by surprise. I suppose, despite his friendship with my mom, she didn't mention me coming back to town.

I take my sweaty ponytail down, brushing my fingers hastily through the strands before putting it back in a low bun on the nape of my neck. His eyes watch my movements and I wonder if he senses how nervous I am. So many things are running through my head and it's on the tip of my tongue to blurt out, "*I had a baby and it's yours!*" But I think that situation needs to be handled with a little more grace.

"I ... it's been ... life."

Wow, so eloquent of you, Salem. Of course, life has been life. Could you sound any dumber?

"Heard you got married." He squints down at me, lifting his hand to shield his eyes from the rising sun.

It's not a question.

I hold up my left hand, showing my empty ring finger. "And divorced."

"He's an idiot."

I laugh, a full belly laugh that feels so good to let loose. "No, I'm the idiot." I look down at the ground between us, toeing my shoe against a piece of loose gravel on the sidewalk. The giddy eighteen-year-old girl inside me is screaming right now in excitement like I'm talking to my crush. But the twenty-five-year-old I am now is screaming at her to stand down, that we have to guard ourselves against this man. "I'm the one who asked for the divorce."

"Why?" His lips purse, eyes narrowed. He's surprised, but also curious, and trying to hide those feelings. I wish he wouldn't do that. He's so hard to read, and I value any insight he gives me into his thoughts.

"Because I could never love him like he loves me. Caleb is a great man. But he's not my forever. I already gave my heart away."

Oh, God! Why did I blurt out that last part! I couldn't keep my mouth shut?

Thayer's eyes flicker with curiosity, and a flash of heat. "That so?"

"Yeah." I try not to smile and fail. "Now that guy? He was an idiot."

Thayer throws his head back and laughs and laughs and laughs. It's music to my ears.

"I assume you mean me."

I don't hesitate when I say, "Yes."

He drops his head, the smallest of amused smiles on his lips. "I deserve that."

Now that the surprise is wearing off, panic is setting in. This is *Thayer*. The man I gave my heart, my soul, my everything to. I was a broken mess when I left him.

My marriage to Caleb might be over but *he* helped put me

back together.

Clearing his throat he says, "It's ... uh ... good seeing you."

"Yeah, you too."

Awkwardness sets in and we stand in front of each other, waiting for the other to do or say something first.

I'm the one to break the silence.

"I need to check on my mom."

"Right." He nods, backing a step away, closer to his side of the property line. "She invited me over for dinner tonight. I already said yes—I didn't know you were going to be here. She didn't say—anyway, I'll call her later and cancel."

Rolling my eyes, I inhale through my nose and out through my mouth. "I'm an adult, Thayer. Don't treat me like broken china. Just because you shattered my heart, doesn't mean I'm still damaged. You're welcome to come for dinner."

I'm glad I sound stronger than I feel.

"Oh." He looks at me surprised—did he really expect me to just crumble and cry at his feet seeing him again? "If you're okay with it, then."

"I'm fine." I don't give him a chance to respond, turning on my heel. Before I reach the door, I stop and whip around. He's still standing at the corner of the driveway. "Don't be later than five."

He wets his lips with a smooth slide of his tongue, hiding a growing smile. "Do you want me to bring anything?"

"Just yourself."

"I can do that."

I dip my head, reaching for the doorknob.

"Good."

I let myself in and lean against the closed door.

What the hell? I went from not seeing the man for years to

finally laying eyes on him again and now we're having dinner tonight—all thanks to my mom.

It's just weird.

CHAPTER EIGHT

Thayer

I close the front door behind me, standing in the foyer shell-shocked.

Salem's back in town.

She's back.

She's divorced.

And I have no fucking idea how long she's going to be here.

Now, I'm supposed to have dinner with her and her mom. I can't help thinking Allie planned this on purpose. She's known about Salem and me since Forrest's birthday that year. I guess now that Salem's divorced, she's playing matchmaker.

Rubbing a hand over my jaw, I head into the kitchen and grab a bottle of water. I gulp down half of it in just a few swallows.

I'm having trouble wrapping my head around the fact that Salem's here.

Moving on from her should've been easy in theory—I was with her less time than I was with my ex-wife. But it didn't work that way. I never expected it to, either, not with how intense my feelings were for her.

I moved on though—not in the physical sense, but mentally. I accepted that she had married and her life would carry on as it should, while I'd still be here.

That's not the course things have taken, and that means, maybe, just fucking maybe, I have a second chance to get our love story right.

CHAPTER NINE

Salem

I set the table for three and then lay out the dishes I made across the counter so Thayer and I can serve ourselves buffet style—I'll make a plate up for my mom so she's not on her feet too long—and that way the table won't be too cluttered.

"It smells good."

My mom's voice comes from the doorway, my head jerks up quickly in response.

"Mom, you're supposed to ask for help before you get up."

She waves a dismissive hand. "I'm not dead yet." This is her only argument.

My shoulders collapse. "And I'd like to keep it that way for as long as possible."

"I had to pee," she argues.

"Since you're already up, go ahead and have a seat. I'll fix your plate." There's no point in arguing with her. Unless she absolutely has no energy to do something, there's no getting her to cooperate.

"I'm not very hungry."

I narrow my eyes on her as she pulls out the chair where there's only one place setting, meaning I'll be forced to sit beside Thayer or move the placemat and everything, which would look weird if I did.

"I'm going to put a little of everything on your plate. At least try to take one bite of each." She looks grossed out at the thought, but nods. "Why did you invite Thayer over for dinner if you don't even want to eat dinner?"

"I was being neighborly, Salem. He's a nice man."

My shoulders stiffen and I turn away, washing my hands in the sink. "Do you like him?"

She snorts a laugh. "I'm dying, Salem. I don't have time to like anyone in the way you're implying. But I do like him as a person."

"Hmm," I hum.

There's a knock on the side door at 4:59 and I turn the lock, letting him in. I can't help myself when my eyes rake over him. His hair is freshly washed, still damp from a shower. I greedily take in the light stubble on his jaw, up close and personal this time. His brown eyes are warm chocolate that I want to melt in. He even smells of cologne, like he put in a little extra effort tonight.

No! Stop it! You can't let this man make you all weak in the knees again! He's done enough damage.

But I can't help it.

I'm looking at him with new eyes, older eyes. I'm no longer that freshly pregnant nineteen-year-old who was scared out of her mind. Looking back, I know I made the decision I thought I had to. Was it the best choice? In hindsight, probably not, but life is a series of choices and at the time you don't always know whether it's good or bad. You just do what you can with the information you have.

Back then, I was terrified to be a mom, but there was never a question in my mind about keeping the baby.

But Thayer was spiraling after losing Forrest.

Understandable, yes, but I couldn't pull him out of that—not on my own. *He* had to do it, and I knew it. But I had to make sure my baby was going to be safe and taken care of, so I did that the best way I could, and that meant giving Thayer space.

I thought ... I thought he'd find me.

Call me.

Text me.

Send a fucking carrier pigeon for God's sake, but he never did, and I felt used and thrown away.

"Is something on my face?"

"Oh!" I jump away, knocking my hip into the corner of the counter. "Ow!"

"Careful." He grips my wrist, steadying me. Electricity shoots up my arm at his touch.

"I'm okay." I pull gently from his grasp, not wanting to betray my true feelings.

He lets me go and holds up a bottle of wine I didn't know he was holding. "I wasn't sure what we were having, but I didn't want to come with nothing."

"Oh, how sweet." My mom smiles. "Thank you, Thayer. Isn't that nice, Salem?"

"So nice," I mimic woodenly, turning away. "Let me grab glasses," I mutter, distracted.

If I didn't know better, I would swear my mom is trying to play matchmaker with Mr. Broody. I wonder what she'd say if she knew he broke my heart or that he's Seda's father. I wonder, since they're friends, if he knows I have a child. I'm guessing not or I think he would've brought it up when he mentioned my marriage.

I add wine glasses to the table while Thayer chats with my mom. I make her a plate and set it in front of her.

"You can get your own plate," I tell Thayer.

"Salem!" My mom scolds.

My cheeks flush. "I just meant he can pick and choose what he wants."

Turning my back on them, I grab my plate and start piling food onto it. I don't pay attention to what I'm doing and it's only when Thayer says, "I don't think chicken goes on top of mashed potatoes," his long finger pointing at the gravy I made and should have been spooning on instead, that I jolt back to reality.

I close my eyes, mortified. It has to be obvious to him, that even after all this time I'm still affected by him. Still hopelessly enamored for God knows why.

He broke your heart!

He broke it, and yet, that stupid organ races in my chest at an accelerated rate for him.

I hate him.

I hate myself.

I hate *this.*

That he's here, in my mom's kitchen. That she's dying. That Seda is in Boston.

I just—

"Here, let me help you." He takes my plate from me, raking the roasted chicken off my potatoes and fixing my plate.

"Maybe I wanted my chicken on my potatoes," I grumble.

He arches a brow. "Do you?"

"Well, no."

He doesn't wait for me to say anything further. He finishes my plate, carrying it to the table. He places it on the spot in front of my mom. Pulling out the chair, he turns to me with a tilt of his head. "Are you going to sit down?"

"Um, yeah."

I really hate that he has me so disoriented. It's like I can't tell up from down or left from right.

Sitting down, he scoots my chair in, and I let out a tiny squeak of surprise at the gesture.

Does he not see how weird all of this is?

My mom looks down at her plate, but I don't miss the flash of a smile.

"What are you smiling about?"

"Nothing."

"Liar," I grumble.

She mock-gasps, and it turns into a cough, which instantly has me on alert. Luckily, it stops before I become too worried.

"You can't call a dying woman a liar."

"Why not?" I'm aware Thayer can overhear our entire conversation, but I don't care. "If the shoe fits..."

She cracks a smile. Thayer pulls out the chair at my side, his arm brushing against mine as he sits down. My treacherous body shivers—visibly so.

"Are you okay?"

I press my lips into a flat smile. "Splendid. It's just a bit chilly."

He gives me a funny look because it's anything but cold in the house. My mom is cold almost all the time these days and doesn't want the AC on.

"Dinner smells amazing. Did you make it?"

I turn to him, raising a brow. "Obviously. *Ow*. You kicked me."

My mom blinks back innocently. "I did no such thing."

Thayer's eyes flicker back and forth between us in amusement. "I really appreciate you inviting me over, Allison."

"I've told you—" she coughs and instantly my hand holding my fork lowers, "—call me Allie."

"Allie," he repeats. "Right, sorry."

"Are you all right?" I ask her.

I know Georgia mentioned with our mom's immune system being non-existent at the moment that she'd be more susceptible to illnesses.

"I'm fine. My throat's just a tad ticklish tonight."

I eye her skeptically. Even Thayer looks worried.

It hits me, in moments like this, that she's dying.

That no matter what I do, or how hard she continues to fight, this is her final battle and there is no happy outcome.

It's one thing to know something, it's another to witness it.

"Do you want to go lay down?"

She pushes the food around her plate. "I'm fine."

"Mom, if you'd feel better laying down—"

She looks between the two of us across from her. "Maybe that would be a good idea."

I stand up to help, but Thayer urges me back down. "I'll help her," he says in a hushed tone.

Before I can protest, he's moving around the table and helping my mom up and into the family room.

I stay seated, staring at my plate so she can't see the tears pooling in my eyes.

Thayer returns, his chair squeaking as it slides back on the linoleum floor.

"You don't have to stay," I mutter, not looking at him.

"I'm hungry," is his gruff reply. "I'm not about to walk away from a home-cooked meal. I'm too tired and lazy to cook most days and end up ordering takeout."

My head whips in his direction, appraising the lean body

beneath his clothes. "Doesn't look like you eat unhealthy."

His brow arches, lips twitching when he fights a smile. "Checking me out?"

"Don't flatter yourself."

He chuckles, taking a bite of mashed potatoes. "You made these from scratch."

It's not a question, but I answer anyway. "Yes." I force myself to eat a bite, then another.

"Would you happen to know anything about cupcakes showing up at my door a few days ago?" He asks it in a way like he already knows the answer, so there's no point in lying.

"I made them with my mom and she asked me to drop some off. That's all."

A.K.A.: Don't read into it.

He nods, rubbing his lips together. "Salem, I—"

"Not right now." My words are biting, cutting, but I can't do this right now. Not with my dying mother in the next room. She's my focus right now. Not Thayer. He can't be.

"We need to talk."

We need to talk about way more than he thinks we do.

I mentally start building a wall around my heart. It's the only way I can operate around Thayer. I can't—won't—let him get to me so easily. Not this time.

"Do you remember?" I snap at him, my tone icy. "Do you remember the last time I saw you? What you said to me?"

His forehead wrinkles and he looks confused. "I—I'm not sure."

"You told me you hated me." He pales, horror stricken. "That was the least of what was said, if I'm being honest. And listen, you were drunk and grieving, but I survived a different kind of abuse before and I wasn't going to let you hurt me with words."

"Salem—" His Adam's apple bobs. "I didn't ... fuck, I can't believe I said that to you." He shakes his head.

"I know we need to talk," I continue like he didn't say anything at all. "But I can't do it right now. Not after just seeing you for the first time in so long." Pushing my plate away, I stand without looking at him. "I'm not so hungry anymore. Lock up behind you."

I walk out of the kitchen, past my sleeping mom, and upstairs. I lock my bedroom door behind me and hastily close the blinds. Doing everything I can to block out the hateful words he lobbed my way that night.

You're the reason he's dead.

I was distracted thinking about you and he's gone. You did this. It's your fault.

I hate you. Get out.

I wish I'd never met you.

That last one was a massive blow to my heart. The others hurt, God did they hurt, but I knew they were the words of a broken father.

Curling up on my bed, I fall asleep.

In the morning, all the leftovers are put away and the kitchen is spotless.

There's a note left on the counter.

I'm sorry.—T

CHAPTER TEN

Thayer

When I crack my eyes open in the morning, my first thought is, *I told her I hated her?*

What a fucking bastard I am.

Salem has every right to hate me. I know I lost myself to my grief after Forrest's passing. It was something no parent should ever have to live through. There are days where the grief comes back full force and cripples me. On those days I end up calling my guys and telling them I won't be in to work, and I sit in the treehouse or visit his grave.

If only I hadn't been such a lazy fuck and gotten it built for him.

Maybe then ... *maybe then.*

"Fuck," I groan aloud, crossing my arm over my eyes.

I try not to let myself go down that path with my thoughts, but sometimes it's hard not to.

Shoving my sorry ass out of bed, I hop in the shower.

My body yearns with the need for a release. It becomes impossible for me to ignore my aching cock. Seeing Salem again has awakened desires in me I long thought dormant. Gripping the base, I stroke up and down, rolling my wrist around the tip.

I don't mean to, but I can't help it when I picture Salem in my mind.

It's always her. Even when it shouldn't have been. Even when I broke us.

My release comes fast and hard. When it's over, I lean against the shower wall.

I finish washing up and get dressed for work. Tugging the Holmes Landscaping shirt down over my torso, I reach for my cap and sunglasses.

The very same pair of sunglasses Salem bought me.

They're loose and beat up. I need a new pair, but I refuse to part with these. I guess I'm a sentimental fool like that.

Lacing up my boots, I head downstairs and scarf down a bowl of cereal. It's not the healthiest breakfast—especially with my choice of sugary cereal in the form of Fruity Pebbles—but it'll have to do. I don't have the time for anything else this morning.

Normally, I'd head out to my greenhouse before leaving, but thanks to the extra time in my shower I can't afford to spare time for that either.

Quickly rinsing my bowl, I swipe my keys from the counter and head out to my truck.

Before I can back out of the driveway, a phone call comes through the speakers. Laith's name flashes across the large display.

I don't really feel like talking to my brother right now, but I have a forty-five minute drive to the site so I might as well get this over with.

Pushing the button on my steering wheel to answer his call, I greet him with a simple, "Hey."

"Are you sober?" He laughs after he asks it.

It's his standard greeting.

I roll my eyes. He knows I've stayed away from alcohol for

years. I don't have a drinking problem, but I did rely too much on it after Forrest died. It became a drug that could numb my feelings and put me to sleep.

Now, I choose to stay away because it's not worth feeling like shit to drink it.

"I'm always sober."

"Can't blame me for checking."

"Why are you calling?"

"Because I can."

"I'm on my way to work, so if it's something important get a move on with it."

He chuckles. "Have some patience, Thayer. I can't call and check on my big bro?"

"Sorry, I'm running late this morning and it has me on edge."

What really has me on edge is how I can't get Salem off my mind.

"Somehow I don't believe that's what's on your mind."

I groan, pinching the bridge of my nose when I roll to a stop at a red light. "Salem's back."

It's all I have to say. After she was the one to call Laith all those years ago and he came to the rescue, I had to fill him in on what was going on with her.

The fucker laughs and laughs and laughs. "Oh, you're fucked."

"Why?" I bite out through clenched teeth.

"Don't play stupid, bro. You've been hung up on her all these years. She's still married?"

"No," I sigh.

"No? Well, that's good then. Why do you sound pissed?"

I'm quiet for a moment. "What if I fuck up again?"

"Easy, don't fuck it up."

"I don't want to, but I have a feeling we have a lot of baggage to wade through."

This time he's the one who's quiet. Then he asks, "Is she worth it?"

"She's worth everything."

"Then I say, don't let this chance pass you by. You deserve to be happy—more than anyone I know."

My brother's support surprises me, but I guess it shouldn't. He's always had my back.

"Thanks. I gotta go."

"Sure. Talk to you soon."

He ends the call, and I spend the rest of my drive wondering if it's possible to right my wrongs and finally get the girl.

CHAPTER ELEVEN

Salem

"I miss you," I tell the sweet face on my phone screen as I lock up my mom's shop behind me. It's been permanently closed for a few months now, once my mom got too weak and tired to work, but there are still things to move and clear out before we figure out what to do with it. Selling the store makes the most sense—Georgia's a nurse, she's not going to open a store, and I'm ... well, I don't know what I'm doing. Stupidly, though, I hate the idea of getting rid of it. It was the first thing our mom ever really did for herself.

"Miss you, too, Mommy." She smiles into the phone. "Daddy says we can have pizza for dinner!"

"Mmm, that sounds yummy." I unlock my car and set a box of my old candles in the back. I doubt they even have much smell to them at this point, but I didn't want to leave them there. Silly, I know. I stopped making candles when I left town and felt this ache when I saw the box.

I'm not ready to go home yet, so I walk across the street. Georgia picked Mom up and took her to her house for dinner. I was invited but bowed out to come to the store instead. Since I don't have to hurry back to the house yet, I think a walk around our quaint downtown area will be nice.

"What are you going to have for dinner?"

"I don't know yet."

"I wish you could have pizza with us."

"I know, baby."

"When can I come visit Grandma?"

I press my lips together. "I don't know." Maybe I can finagle a way to bring my mom to her. I can't have her coming here, risk Thayer seeing her, before I say something.

Though, with her blond hair, it's hard to tell that Caleb *isn't* her father. At least from a distance. But I know. I see bits of Thayer in her every day. From the shape of her lips, to the curve of her cheeks, down to the look on her face she gets when she's thinking about something.

But especially in her eyes.

The same warm, intelligent brown as his.

"Daddy says the pizza is here!" She jumps up, running with the phone in her hand. "I love you, Mommy!"

"Love you, too." She ends the call, my screen returning to normal.

I walk down the street, taking in shops old and new. One beckons to me, and I open the door, inhaling the scent of lavender and eucalyptus.

"Hang on, I'll be right there!" A cheery voice calls.

I pick up a homemade bar of soap, giving it a sniff.

The sound of swooshing fabric has me looking up just as a tall woman, probably in her late thirties or early forties, rounds the corner of the table. Her hair is a wild mass of dark curls, and she's wearing fitted bell bottom jeans with a plain white t-shirt. Bracelets adorn her wrists, jangling as she moves.

"Hi." She looks me over. "I haven't seen you here before."

Gotta love small towns—if people don't recognize you, they're quick to call you out on it.

"I lived here as a teenager. I'm back taking care of my mom. She owns A Checkered Past Antiques."

"Oh." Her smile falters a bit. "Allison is such a lovely woman. It's such a shame about the cancer."

"Yeah." I lower my head, picking up a glass jar of bath salts with lavender in it. "Your shop is lovely."

"Oh, thank you!" Her energy returns, lighting up with excitement. "It's been a dream come true owning my own shop."

"What would you recommend I get?" I motion to the table in front which seems to be a variety of all sorts of bath products.

"If you enjoy bubble baths, definitely this and this." She grabs two items and holds them out to me, one is the salts but this one says it's orange scented. The other is a bar of some sort. "This one is shampoo." She points to the weirdly shaped soap. "It looks strange, I know, but it does wonders for your hair."

Looking at how beautiful and full her hair is, I have to believe her.

"All right. I'll take both then."

"Great!" She smiles and takes them over to the register. "Feel free to look around some more if you want. I didn't mean to ambush you."

"It's okay." I pick up a jar of lotion in the same orange scent. "I'll take this too." I place it by the register and she rings me up. I slide my card onto the counter while she wraps everything in brown paper, placing it in a bag. She swipes my card and puts the receipt in the bag.

"I hope you'll be back. I'm Jen by the way."

"It's nice to meet you." I take the bag from her. "I'm Salem."

"Wow, that's a different name. Unique. I like it."

"Thanks. I'm sure I'll be back in."

Letting myself out, I walk around a little longer before

going into the local Italian eatery. The town is so small that there's no such thing as waiting for a table.

The hostess sits me at a table in the corner. It's small, only room for two, with a small candle lit on the table.

She sets the menu on the table and I offer a mumbled, "Thanks."

Going out to eat by myself was something I started making myself do during the divorce. I'd always had my mom, or sister, Lauren, Caleb, and even Thayer to do things with and I knew it was important for me to get comfortable doing certain things on my own. So, I'd take myself out to eat, or go to the movies, anything that I'd always felt self-conscious about doing alone.

And I've come to enjoy it—these pockets of time that are only for me.

I place my order and the waitress returns a few minutes later with a glass of wine and bread with dipping oil. My stomach rumbles at the smell of the bread. Tearing off a chunk, I dunk it in the oil and take a bite.

"Is this seat taken?"

I cough, choking on the bread.

Thayer looks down at me with drawn brows, clearly worried he might have to give me the Heimlich.

"What are you doing here?" I reach for the water glass the waitress dropped off when she first came by for my order. A couple of sips seems to help clear my throat.

Thayer looks down at me, his hand on the chair across from me—still waiting for a yes or no. That's Thayer. He won't push me or do anything I'm not comfortable with. If I say no, he'll leave or at least go to another table, and won't make me feel sorry for it.

His mouth twitches almost imperceptibly, but I'm honed

in on the gesture, always searching for his smiles. "One usually eats in a restaurant."

"I meant at my table." My fingers shake the tiniest bit when I lower them from the water glass. I hate that it's been so long since I've seen him and the man still has the ability to put me in knots. Tucking my hand under the table, I lace my fingers together.

He shrugs, still holding onto the chair like it's some sort of lifeline. There's a ring around his pinky. He never used to wear one before and I can't help but be curious why he does now. "I saw you and I thought maybe we could eat together."

"We had dinner the other night."

"With your mother." He points out, straightening. "It's okay. I'll grab mine to-go."

He turns to walk away. Lowering my head to stare at the red and white checkered tablecloth I can't help but feel like such a complete bitch.

"Thayer." I sigh, shoulders drooping. He freezes, not turning fully around but giving me the side of his handsome face. "Sit down."

He turns, facing me. "Are you sure?"

I nod. "Please."

He pulls the chair out and sits. The plain gray tee he wears shouldn't look so nice, but it hugs his chest in all the right places.

This feels so much more awkward than the other night at my house. Then, my mom was there as a buffer. Now, it's only us.

"Oh, I didn't know someone was joining you. What can I get you, Thayer?"

Of course the waitress knows him—that's how it is in small towns. I've been gone long enough that there are enough people who don't recognize me.

"The usual," he says easily, dismissing her. He doesn't take his eyes off me the entire time. "What are you thinking?"

"You come here a lot."

"They have good food." He leans forward, lowering his voice. "Besides, I told you I usually eat out."

I take a deep breath, my chest shaking when I exhale. I hate that he makes me so nervous. I'm an adult now. A full-grown woman. Thayer Holmes has no right having this hold on me.

Clearing my throat, I grab the stem of the wine glass and take a sip. "How's life been?"

He chuckles. "That's a loaded question."

"How so?"

"It's been six years, Salem," he says like I don't know how long it's been since I saw him. "A lot happens in that time. Good. Bad. Happy days. Sad ones. That's what makes it loaded. I don't even know where to start."

"At least you seem sober." I wince as soon as I make the comment.

He clears his throat. "I'm sorry you ever had to see me like that."

"I don't want you to constantly be apologizing for the past." I look away from him, watching an elderly couple get seated a few tables over. "I can't imagine what kind of shape I'd be in if that were—" I bite my tongue. "If I had to lose a child," I correct myself.

"I went to therapy. I still go once a month." He ducks his head, trying to get me to look at him. I relent, meeting that brown-eyed gaze I fell so hard for as a teen. "You inspired me to do that."

"Me?" I nearly choke on my tongue. "How?"

"You told me that you went to therapy for..." He clears his throat. "Well, you know." I appreciate that he doesn't say it out loud. "I knew if you could survive your trauma and go to therapy for help then I could as well. My brother helped too. He moved in and lived with me for over a year."

"Really?" I'm shocked. I might've been the one to call Laith, but I certainly didn't expect him to go to that extent.

"He ... I think he was scared of what I was turning into and didn't want to leave me on my own until he was certain I was in a better place. He told me you were the one to call him."

I roll my tongue in my mouth. "You wouldn't let me help you—and someone had to."

"I know." He leans across the table. "It kills me that I pushed you away. That I hurt you the way I did."

"Then why did you?" The question rolls off my tongue. It's something I've wondered about over the years. It seemed so unlike Thayer.

The waitress appears with a tray containing our food and a glass of water for Thayer. "Do you need anything else?"

"No, we're good," I tell her. "Thank you." I arch a brow at Thayer. "So?" I prompt. I swirl a bite of linguine around the fork.

"I was a broken man, grieving for my child. I had no idea how long I was going to be in that dark place and you were this beautiful, caring woman and I didn't want to drag you down with me." He rubs a hand over his stubbled jaw, his eyes haunted from days gone by. "I thought I was doing the right thing, Salem. I know now it was the completely wrong one, but you were nineteen and I wanted to set you free. You would've waited for me, however long it took for me to pull myself out of that dark place. I know you would've been there and I just ...didn't want you to do that. You deserved more than me."

I say it calmly, but there are tears in my eyes. "You had no right to decide that on your own."

"I know." He sounds choked up, his eyes watery as well.

"You broke my heart."

His eyes close. "I know."

"You made me hate you."

His Adam's apple bobs. Again, those two words. "I know."

We eat our meal in silence after that.

CHAPTER TWELVE

Thayer

"You're not paying," she argues when I pull out my wallet at the end of the meal.

"Yes, I am." I keep my tone calm and even.

"I can pay for my own," she grumbles, reaching for her purse.

I try to hide my smile. "I never said you couldn't."

I hand enough cash to cover the meal and tip the waitress when she passes by. Salem blinks at me open-mouthed.

"Thayer," she groans my name, her nose wrinkling with irritation.

I don't know what it says about me that blood rushes straight to my dick at her tone. Even her annoyance is sexy.

"It's too late now." I shrug easily, sliding the chair back. "You can pay me back in some other way."

Her cheeks flush red. "I'm not sleeping with you."

Arching a brow, I look down at her where she still sits. "Did I say anything about sex?"

She grows redder. "Well, no. But—" She sputters, trying to dig herself out of this hole.

I jerk my head toward the exit. "Let me walk you to your car."

Her tongue rolls around her mouth and I expect her to

protest, but she surprises me by replying with a simple, "Okay."

She gets up from the table and my hand goes to her waist. It's automatic—like my body can't help but touch hers. She eyes my arm with narrowed, uncertain eyes. She's guarding her heart from me, I feel it, and I can't say I blame her.

Letting my hand drop, I hold open the door for her and follow her out onto the street. The sun has gone down, stars shining brightly in the night sky. It's one of my favorite things about living in such a small town. You always see the stars.

"My car's down this way in front of my mom's store."

I walk beside her, my hands in my pockets so I don't touch her. Being around her again makes it all too easy to fall into who I was with her before.

"Thank you," she says after a minute, "for buying dinner."

I can't hide my amusement, and she rolls her eyes playfully at my grin. "You're welcome."

I spot her car and disappointment floods me that our evening is over. When I saw her in the restaurant I couldn't help but approach her table. I can't resist her. Even after all this time.

She looks up at me briefly, a soft flush coloring her cheeks. I wish I knew what she was thinking, but I don't ask. I don't have the right to know, not anymore.

Stopping by her car, I wait for her to say something. She's quiet, but she doesn't make a move to get in the car either.

Blowing out a breath, she unlocks her car. I expect her to get inside and not say another word to me, but she surprises me.

"Seeing you again ... it's different than I expected."

"A good or bad different?" I wet my lips nervously, waiting for her response.

She shrugs, opening the door. "I'm still figuring that out."

I stay on the sidewalk, watching as she starts up her SUV.

She waves before she drives away.

My truck is in the direction we came from so I head back that way.

Driving around for a while, letting my thoughts wander—mostly to Salem because I'm a sad fucker when it comes to that woman—I pull into my driveway an hour later.

Shutting my truck off, I don't go right inside my house. Opening the fence gate, I head out back to my greenhouse. Easing the door open, I step into the place that has been my safe harbor and my greatest torment.

The entire interior of the greenhouse is filled with intricately petaled, pale pink peonies.

Originally, I meant to use my personal greenhouse to grow a variety of plants.

But after that year when Laith moved out, and the reality of my actions began to set in when I learned Salem was getting married, I started growing them and I just couldn't stop.

They became my last connection to her.

I've treasured growing them, nurturing them.

Grabbing the small shears, I start cutting.

It's the first time I've ever cut any of them—except for spent blooms that needed to be removed—and lay the stems out on the table.

I swore I would never cut any.

Not unless they were for her.

I honestly didn't think this day would come, so I smile to myself as I put together the bundle of flowers.

CHAPTER THIRTEEN

Salem

"What are you doing?" My mom asks from the doorway of the kitchen, her voice groggy and her eyes still half asleep.

"Mom," I admonish for the millionth time, "you're supposed to let me help you."

I scurry around the island to help her into one of the kitchen chairs. I understand her need for independence but dammit if it isn't going to be the death of me.

"You didn't answer my question."

It doesn't matter how old you get, mothers will always be mothers.

"I found some of my old candles at your shop. I was just taking them out of the box." I point to the few already on the counter.

"Oh, I had those pulled for someone."

I laugh, not sure I've heard her right. "What? For who?"

"That doesn't matter." She waves a dismissive hand. "Take them back to the store."

"Why?"

"Because they're already paid for."

"Oh, right." I shake my head, loading the candles back into the box. "Sorry, I didn't know. I was surprised you still had any left."

She shrugs. "I held back some. That was the last of it."

"Huh." I put my hands on my hips, wondering why someone would pay and have her hold old candles. "Are you ready for some breakfast?"

"Maybe some scrambled eggs." She looks a bit queasy talking about food. I can't imagine what it must be like to be in her position—little to no appetite but knowing you need to get something in your system.

"I'll whip those right up."

She gives a forced smile, but I know she appreciates I'm here and helping. "I was thinking." She clears her throat. "I'd like to do something with you today."

I pull a carton of eggs from the refrigerator. "Are you up for that?" She was out at Georgia's for a few hours yesterday evening. I don't want her to overdo herself. "I'd like to get out for a while. It's a nice day."

"What do you have in mind?"

She toys with the tie on her robe. "I thought we could visit Seda and Caleb."

I gape at her—not because of her asking to visit, that's understandable, but—"Mom, are you sure you're up for that kind of trip?"

It's a few hours there and back and she's ... well, she's not in the best shape to put it lightly.

"It might be easier if we stayed the night," she acquiesces, with a nod, her slender fingers still rubbing against the material of her robe. She smiles sheepishly. I know she feels guilty because of the situation with Caleb, but I can't deny her request to see her granddaughter.

"Let me run it by Georgia and see what she thinks about you making the trip and I'll ask Caleb too."

"All right."

I finish her eggs and add a piece of toast just in case she ends up wanting some to nibble on some before I step outside to make the calls.

It's warm outside with a slight breeze, the birds chirping merrily. I missed this place. This house. The town. Even the people in it.

"Wha—" I gasp when my foot hits something it shouldn't.

My eyes shoot to the last step, a startled gasp passing through my lips.

A bouquet of fresh pink peonies wrapped in Kraft paper lies there waiting.

I know without looking at the note attached that they're for me from Thayer. Bending down I pick them up. Each one is perfect, not one discolored petal or imperfection to find. I look around, like I expect him to be lurking somewhere, but I don't see him. I hold the flowers close, not sure how to feel about the gesture. I'm not mad, but I am confused.

Six years.

I moved on.

Started a new life.

I *never* heard from him again.

He didn't reach out, but now he acts as if he wants to pick up where we left off—well, maybe not exactly there, but—

Shaking my head, I set the flowers back down and walk away from them.

I don't have time to think about Thayer, to contemplate how and why he does things.

Do you want things to pick back up?

I pinch the bridge of my nose.

Yes.

No.

I don't know.

And not knowing is the scariest part of all.

After all this time, I think I expected to see him again and for the attraction to have lessened but that's not what happened at all. If anything, the pull is only stronger and that terrifies me. I can't allow myself to be broken by him again.

Once was enough and the only reason I survived was because I was growing our child.

For her, I was stronger.

For her, I didn't give up.

Inhaling a deep breath, I shove all thoughts of Thayer out of my brain and focus on the task at hand—calling my sister and Caleb.

I'm not on the phone long with either and pick up the flowers again, carrying them inside with me.

"Everything's a go." I set the flowers on the cabinet, searching for a vase in the cabinet above the stove. "We'll head out in about an hour."

"Where are the flowers from?" Her tone is suspicious.

"No idea," I reply, sounding equally as mystified.

"Was there a card?" I conveniently slide the note away, planning to read it later.

"Nope. It must be from your secret admirer."

She rolls her eyes. "Ah, yes, I get a lot of those. That makes total sense."

"Smartass," I snicker, filling the vase with water.

She laughs. "Don't sass me."

"Can't help it." I unwrap the flowers gently, putting them in the water one at a time.

"Those are your favorite flower," she remarks. "How

interesting."

"I know. What are the odds?"

She shakes her head, fighting a smile. I narrow my eyes on her, but she's not looking my way. I can't help but wonder if she knows something about Thayer. I don't see how, but—

"You better get my stuff packed up if we're going to leave in an hour."

I set the vase in the center of the table. "When did you get so bossy, Mom?"

She grins at me, her lashes non-existent. "When you're dying, you don't have the time to be any other way."

I swallow past the sudden lump in my throat. Clearing it, I say, "Right. I'll pack your bag and we'll head out."

"Salem?" She calls after me before I can leave the kitchen.

"Yeah?" I pause, turning to look back at her.

"I know..." She wets her dry lips with a swipe of her tongue. "I know I didn't let myself love again, after your dad, but promise me you won't close your heart off forever? If there's anything we all deserve in this world it's to love and be loved."

My mouth twitches as I hold back tears. "I promise."

I'm not sure how easy of a promise it'll be to keep, but I'll try, if only for her sake.

CHAPTER FOURTEEN

Salem

We pull up outside the brownstone, the car barely in park when the door opens. I expect it to be Seda, but instead it's Caleb. He walks down the steps, through the front gate, heading straight for my mom's door on the passenger side.

"Allie," he says, smiling at her. "It's so good to see you."

She pats his cheek. "It's always nice to see you too."

"Do you need some help?"

"I'll never turn down help from such a fine gentleman," she jokes.

He chuckles, helping her with the seatbelt and out onto the street. Since he has her under his care, I hop out and grab her bag. I didn't bother packing a bag for myself since I have everything I need here.

Caleb helps her inside with me following behind.

"Where's Seda?" I ask.

He chuckles, looking back at me over his shoulder. "Believe it or not, passed out napping. She went to the trampoline park with Maddy," he mentions one of her good friends, "and came back exhausted."

"Sweet girl," my mom croons. "I can't wait to see her."

Caleb looks back at me, worry in his eyes. Worry for me and worry for her. He knows that losing my mom is going to be hard on me. It doesn't matter how far you know in advance, losing a parent isn't easy. She's been my rock and my sounding board. She's gotten me through some of the hardest times of my life. And now when I wish I could repay the favor more than anything, I can't, because nothing can overcome death.

Caleb settles her on the couch in the family room.

"Can I get you anything to drink?" he asks her.

"Maybe just some water."

He smiles and passes her a blanket. "Make yourself comfortable and I'll be back with your water."

Caleb leaves and I help her lay down. Wrapping the blanket around her, I prop her legs up with a pillow beneath. "Are you tired?"

"A little," she admits reluctantly.

"Just rest." I kiss her forehead and back away.

In the kitchen, I lean my hip against the counter watching Caleb fill up the cup with ice and then water.

"How's she doing? For real—no sugarcoating things."

I sigh, running my fingers through my hair. "She has good days and bad days. I feel so helpless, Caleb. It's like watching the sand in an hourglass and I know at some point the sand is going to run out. And when it happens, I'm going to lose my mom. And I just," I pause, catching my breath, feeling the tears burn my eyes. "I don't know how to live life without her."

"Come here." He flicks his fingers, pulling me into the safe embrace of his arms.

I lay my head on his chest, his fingers gently combing through my hair. I can't stop it when the tears come, soaking into the cotton of his t-shirt.

"It's okay," he croons, continuing with the gentle strokes of his fingers through my hair. "Just cry. I've got you." And I know he does. He always has. Caleb is my rock, my safe place. "You're strong," he reminds me, "but even strong people need to cry now and then." His arms are tight against me, holding me together.

"Why are you so good to me?" I only cry harder at the question. Caleb should hate me. He should be pushing me away instead of pulling me into his arms. But he's so good. He's not the kind of person that will shove you away just because you broke his heart. I know that there's someone out there for him. It's not that I'm bad for him, but I'm not good enough for him. And that thought makes me cry a little harder. I'm not deserving of him. Even though I might have asked for the divorce. Even though I'm the one walking away from him. I still love him and a part of me always will.

"Because," his voice rumbles against my ear where the side of my head is pressed firmly to his chest, "you're a better person than you think you are."

"Caleb—" I pull away from his chest slightly, angling my head back to look up at him.

He playfully covers my mouth. "Don't say whatever it is you're about to say."

When he lets his hand drop, I ask, "Why don't you hate me?"

He cocks his head to the side, eyes narrowed. "Why do you hate yourself?"

His question is like a bullet to the heart, one I've never stopped to contemplate.

"I—"

Lowering his head, he whispers, "I forgive you, Salem. It's you who has to forgive yourself."

Picking up the glass of water, he retreats from the kitchen.

I cover my face with my hands, knowing he's right.

There are so many things I haven't forgiven myself for. I drag those things along behind me everywhere I go like deadweight I can't seem to shake. Because of his question, I realize I'm the only one holding those things over my head. Not him, he never did, and if Caleb can forgive me, surely, I can find a way to forgive myself.

Taking a deep breath, I steady myself and brace my shoulders.

***

My mom settles into the guest bed, her eyes heavy from exhaustion.

After she woke up from her nap, and Seda too, she played with her granddaughter until dinner time. Caleb ended up picking up food from one of our favorite restaurants since neither of us felt like cooking. I wasn't surprised when my mom picked at her food, hardly any of it making it into her mouth. Her body is giving up on her—frankly, I think it gave up on her a long time ago, and it's been her sheer tenacity and will to live that has kept her going.

"This was nice," she yawns, her eyelids growing heavy. "Thank you for bringing me. I love that little girl so much."

I brush my hand over her forehead like I'm comforting a child. "She loves you too."

"You're a great mom. I didn't do a lot of things right in my life—"

"Mom—"

"Let me finish." Her breath is rough, her hand shaky when she reaches up to touch my cheek. "But you girls ... you turned

74

out amazing, despite my mistakes."

I close my eyes, feeling tears leak through my lashes.

"I'm sorry," she whispers, her fingers feather light on my cheek.

Clearing my throat, I say, "I am too." Lowering her hand, she yawns. "Go to sleep, Mom. I love you." I kiss her forehead just like I do Seda's when I tuck her into bed, flicking the light off beside the bed.

Easing the door shut behind me, I creep down the stairs and fix up the couch to sleep on. We only have the one guestroom, and I wasn't about to make my mom sleep on the couch all night. The nap was bad enough.

I brush my teeth in the bathroom downstairs and change into my pajamas. Padding into kitchen I'm surprised to find Caleb there, sitting at the kitchen table with a bowl of fruit.

"I thought you went to bed."

He shakes his head, picking up a piece of watermelon. "Nah, I have a lot on my mind."

"Work?" I probe, opening the fridge to swipe a can of Diet Coke.

He nods. "This case is taking a lot out of me."

"I'm sorry." He's not allowed to talk about cases with me or else I'd ask him if he wants to talk about it. Instead, I say, "Do you want me to stay up with you?"

He shakes his head. His blond hair is cut shorter on the side, slightly longer on top. He normally keeps it neatly slicked back but since he's fresh out of the shower it's damp and wavier than normal. "I'm okay. Get some rest. I'm sure you need it."

"Thank you for letting my mom come visit."

He rolls his eyes, looking genuinely pissed. "I'm not going to tell your mom she can't visit—besides, this place is still half yours, too."

"Caleb—"

"Look," he stands up from the table, putting the Tupperware lid back on the container, "I know you're way more eager to be done with me than I am you—but you don't have to remind me all the time, okay?" There's genuine hurt in his voice that stings my heart like an open wound.

"That's not what I meant." I shake my head, hair falling forward to shield my face. "You're just ... you're so good, Caleb. You're not the bad guy. I know that, and that makes this so much worse, because I am, and I never want you to think I'm taking advantage of your kindness."

He sighs, swiping a bottle of water from the fridge. "Did you ever stop to think that you're not the villain either? Sometimes relationships aren't built to last and there is no bad guy. It's just two people who weren't meant to be."

"No." I shake my head. "I didn't."

"I don't blame you for the divorce, Salem. I know you love me even now, but sometimes that's not enough and I get it. Am I hurt? Yeah, of course I am. I pictured it all with you—a house, cars, pets, kids," he waves his hand around at the house over our heads, "but this isn't the end of those things for me. I still have that little girl upstairs asleep in her princess room." He smiles, probably thinking about the day we spent together turning it into her dream space. "And one day, when the timing is right, I'll meet someone else." He shrugs, twisting the cap on the water bottle back and forth. "Life goes on. I'm not broken."

"I just want you to be happy."

"I know. And I want the same for you—but you can't put my happiness on a timeline just so you feel better."

His words smack me across the face. I didn't realize that

was what I was doing, but he's completely right.

He slips from the kitchen, and I listen to the soft sound of his feet on the stairs before I go to the family room and lay down on the couch.

Sleep never comes.

CHAPTER FIFTEEN

Salem

When I pull into my mom's driveway, Thayer is in his unloading groceries. He raises his hand, shielding his eyes from the sun. Putting my SUV in park, I silently curse when I see Thayer in my rearview mirror. He walks up to my side and taps the window. Putting the window down, I can't help my sarcasm when I blurt, "Solicitors aren't welcome here."

It's obvious he wasn't expecting that. His lips twitch, trying not to laugh, but he finally gives in. Putting his hands up in front of his chest, "No soliciting here. I wanted to see if you needed some help."

My mom leans around my body. "How sweet. We'd love some."

I have to bite my tongue to not growl out, "*Mom.*"

Thayer crosses his arms, leaning into my car. He's *right there*. I can smell his familiar scent. It reminds me of the outdoors, woodsy and rugged. All man. He smiles at me. He knows what he's doing, pushing himself into my space and he's going to keep doing it. Our roles are entirely reversed from six years ago and I'm not sure I like it. I must've been so annoying. He should've told me to take a hike.

"Why don't you give me the keys and I'll get the door unlocked for you?"

"Huh." I blink, stunned.

"The keys." He grins slowly. "To the house."

My mom reaches over, turning off the ignition. She holds the keys out to him. "Thank you, Thayer. That's so thoughtful of you."

He takes the keys, retreating from the inside of my car and taking his intoxicating scent with him.

It's really unfair that it has been this long, and he still has a way of making me drunk off his presence. He could bottle that power up and sell it like a lethal weapon. It might only work against womankind, but let's be real, the men are useless without us.

While Thayer unlocks the door, I get out of the car, taking a deep breath to help clear my head. It gets unreasonably foggy around him.

I make my way around the car to get my mom, but he's already getting her door and offering his hand.

It shouldn't make me mad that he's helping.

But it does.

He broke me—shattered my heart, and now he's acting like the past didn't happen.

Since he's helping her inside, I grab her bag and follow them, all the while keeping my grumbling to myself.

He helps her into one of the kitchen chairs, saying something to her I can't hear as he does.

I'm annoyed—that he's here. That he's helping. That he's in my space. And most importantly that he still makes me feel things. This is why I was scared to come back here. I worried my feelings for him were still just as strong. Turns out, I was right to be afraid.

Yanking open the refrigerator more forceful than necessary,

I swipe a Diet Coke and turn around, popping the top on the can. Thayer's eyes flicker from the can to my eyes.

"Water's better for you."

"I've been told a time or two."

"You really should drink more water, Salem." Now my mom's joining in on the let's slander Salem for her love of soda.

"Right now, this what I want. I could have worse vices, you know? I could be a homicidal maniac."

Thayer's chuckle is amused. "I thought most people used the drug addict analogy."

"I'm not most people."

He ducks his head, unable to hide his growing smile. "No, you're certainly not."

"I'm feeling really tired," my mom announces. I quickly set my drink down and rush to her side, but I can't get to her with Thayer's big body blocking me. "Do you want to lay down?" I ask from behind Thayer, trying to peer over his big shoulders but it's impossible unless I stand on my tiptoes and use his arm for support and I'm not touching him.

"That might be a good idea."

"I've got her." Thayer dismisses me, helping my mother up. She moves on her own two feet holding onto his side, but I know he'll scoop her up in a second if she shows signs of needing it.

She settles in the hospital bed, her eyes heavy. "Why don't you two go do something? I'm going to be napping anyway."

"Why would we—" I start, but Thayer swoops in and cuts me off.

"That sounds like a great idea, Allie. You sleep and we'll be back soon. Call us if you need anything."

Steam practically shoots out of my ears.

"You can't just—" He puts a hand on my lower waist,

guiding me away from my mom back to the kitchen. "I'm not going anywhere with you," I snap.

"Why not?" He argues back, a stupid little smirk on his lips. I hate more than anything that this *amuses* him. "We still have plenty to talk about."

I square my shoulders. "I know that, but I don't want to talk about it right now."

"I have a feeling you won't want to talk about it ever. Why don't we just go for a drive?"

"My mom—"

"Get out of here and leave me alone! I need my beauty sleep!" she yells in a croaky voice, overhearing us.

I glower at the man who towers above me. "Fine," I bite out. "Lead the way."

He saunters out first, and I almost slam the door shut and lock it behind him.

Almost.

The only thing that stops me is my mom's demand for us to leave. I know her time is limited, but I can't imagine how I'd feel in her position with people always hovering. She should be allowed to have some time to herself. Even if it'll worry me sick.

"I want to be back here in thirty minutes." I point a finger forcefully at the driveway to drive home my point.

"All right." He walks backwards, hands in the pockets of his cargo shorts. "Then walk faster. We have twenty-nine minutes and—" he looks at the watch on his wrist "—forty-eight seconds left."

I don't think I've ever met anyone more infuriating.

"Were you always this annoying and I was too dumb to see it?"

A flash of pain pierces his face, but he quickly schools his expression back into place. I can't help but feel bad for letting that comment slip. I find it particularly difficult to bite my tongue around him.

He unlocks his truck, the scent of brand-new leather hitting my nose. He lets me climb inside but doesn't shut the door right away. "Do you hate me, Salem?" He's not asking it in a joking way. He's serious, and worried to.

I duck my head, my blonde hair falling forward to shield my face. "No," I admit softly. "I could never hate you, Thayer."

He was my first *true* love—maybe my only one.

He's the father of my child.

I don't have it in me to hate him.

But that doesn't mean any of this is easy.

"Good. That means there's a chance." His eyes are relieved. He closes the door and moves around the front of his truck.

I let his one comment go, not wanting to touch that. "Where are we going?"

He cranks the engine, turning the AC all the way up.

"Like I said, for a drive."

"All right." I look out the window at my mom's house. The hydrangea bushes in the front are lush and full. I can't help but wonder if the man at my side has anything to do with that. But I won't dare ask.

We drive away and it isn't long until we're out of the town limits, cruising the roads.

"I thought you wanted to talk," I prompt stupidly.

A tiny grin graces his lips. "And I thought you didn't."

"I'm locked in a car with you, I might as well speak."

He rubs at his jaw. "Tell me something, anything about the past six years."

It's on the tip of my tongue to ask him why he cares, but

I bite back the words. I'm being defensive and it's stupid. I'm a grown woman now and I swore to myself I'd leave the past in the past, so I need to do a better job of actually practicing that. It's just that seeing him, being around him, leaves me feeling conflicted. I hate being thrown off balance.

"Well," I clear my throat, "there's not a whole lot to tell."

You know, except for the kid bomb I need to drop on you at some point.

I don't want to keep Seda a secret from him. That was never the plan. I've imagined a million different ways of telling him and none of them seem right. I don't think there is a right way to tell him. I just have to do it.

"Give me something. Anything." He sounds almost desperate to know about my life without him.

"I lived with Lauren in Brooklyn for a while, got a job waitressing. Came back to Boston and lived in an apartment with Caleb when we got engaged. We ended up moving to California for him to finish school and start practicing law. Then he got a job offer back in Boston that was too good to pass up. That's about it." I shrug, my eyes glued out the window, ignoring his gaze on me.

"Did you ever go to college?"

"No."

"What about jobs?"

I was a stay-at-home mom.

"Just some random things from time to time. Nothing really stuck."

"You just ... huh." He scratches his jaw, contemplating.

"You really thought you were holding me back?"

"I guess even after your passioned speech, it made me feel better to think I'd cut you loose so you could do something with your life."

A flash of anger erupts in my veins. "Just because I didn't go to college or have a steady job doesn't mean I haven't done anything with my life."

"Sorry," he sounds sincere, "I didn't mean for it to sound like that."

I sigh. "No, I'm sorry. I seem to be a tad defensive when it comes to you."

He smiles over at me, his fingers flexing against the steering wheel. "A tad?"

"Okay, a lot. I'll work on it."

"I like your anger."

I look at him like he's lost his ever-loving mind. "You like my anger?" I volley. "Are you insane?"

His eyes meet mine for a brief moment before they're back on the road. "If you're angry at me, it means you still care."

He has a point there. I look down at my legs, bare since I wore a pair of high-waisted shorts. "I don't want to be angry at you," I admit in a whisper.

"Then why are you?" I notice the way the muscle in his jaw twitches, waiting for my response.

"Because it's easier than admitting the truth."

The God-awful disgusting truth.

"And what's the truth?"

"Don't make me say it," I beg with a shake of my head. I don't want to say it out loud. That makes it all the more real and makes me an even shittier person than I already am.

"I think I need to hear you say it."

I bite my lip, holding back tears. My voice is barely above a whisper when I say, "I never stopped caring about you. I moved on, but my heart didn't."

He pulls the truck abruptly off to the side of the road. Gravel and dirt kick up behind us as he slams the vehicle into park. He turns slowly in his seat to look at me.

"Thayer—" I start to question, but he doesn't give me a chance to finish my thought. He cups my cheek in one hand, his mouth descending on mine in less than a heartbeat.

There's a second there where my brain wants to fight back.

He hurt you! It cries out, wanting me to push him away, but I can't. My body doesn't get the memo. It sinks into him, sighing in relief at the feel of his mouth on mine. I think I'd convinced myself that our connection wasn't as strong as I believed, but it was—it *is*. There are all kinds of different loves in the world, but the kind I share with Thayer can't be broken by time, or distance, or anything else. We could be on separate continents, and it would still exist in this form.

His name is a whisper on my lips when he deepens the kiss.

A part of my brain is convinced this is a dream.

There's no way this can be real.

But then I take inventory—the scratch of his scruff against my face, the fabric of his shirt scrunched in my hands, the rough feel of his hands on my face—and I know that this is very real.

He pulls away, just slightly, our breaths still mingling together. "You come back here, to this town, and it's like you never even left."

I close my eyes, exhaling shakily. "But I did."

His tongue slips out, moistening his lips. "But you did," he echoes. I wait for him to pull away, to put a pin in this. I didn't come back here thinking we'd have a second chance. Instead, he shocks me when he says, "Date me."

"What?" I stutter, convinced I couldn't have possibly heard

him right.

"Date me," he repeats, scanning my face. "We ... I," he corrects, "never did things right with you before. Let me change that. Go on a date with me."

My eyes narrow stubbornly. "Are you asking me or telling me?"

He grins, shaking his head. I stupidly love the way his hair falls over his forehead. I itch to brush it back, but clasp my hands together instead.

"Will you go on a date with me, Salem? A real date?"

I hesitate, my heart skipping a beat. But there's only one answer I can give Thayer.

"Yes."

CHAPTER SIXTEEN

Thayer

Salem climbs out of my truck with a quiet goodbye, walking back over to her mom's house. My phone is still lit up with her contact information where I put in her new number.

I can still taste her mouth on mine. Smiling, I rub my fingers over my lips.

I'm not sure what overcame me when I pulled my truck off the road and kissed her, but I don't regret it. I've been starved for the taste of her for too long.

And she said yes to dating me.

That gives me hope—that even through her hurt, she might find her way back to me. As for what kind of date I want to take her on, I have no idea. I don't want to just take her to a restaurant—there's nothing wrong with that, but I want to put more effort into it, show her that I'm thinking of her and want to do something special.

Locking my truck behind me, I get out and head inside to get Winnie out of her crate in the laundry room. My good girl yawns and stretches before showering me in kisses. I let her out into the backyard to go pee. As soon as she does, she scurries back in, grabs her treat from me, and dives into her cushion.

Shaking my head, I open the fridge and grab a bottle of water, guzzling it down.

It's obvious Salem still has feelings for me, even if those feelings might only be attraction. I'm hoping with her giving me this chance to take her out on a date, do things right this time around, there's a chance for us.

Passing by Winnie, I give her head a scratch and swipe up the remote. Turning the TV on, I flip through the channels, settling on the sports channel. It's a golf tournament—not really my thing, but I'm not planning on paying too much attention anyway.

Pulling out the chair at my puzzle table, I sit down and pick up a piece.

I'm not sure what it is that first drew me to puzzles. I liked to do them even as a kid. It's a dorky hobby, but who gives a fuck. I only do shit I enjoy.

Winnie waddles into the living room with a bone in her mouth, plopping at my feet.

Despite the sound of the TV in the background, it's eerily quiet in the house. It's something I haven't been able to get over in the last six years. I might not have had Forrest all the time after the divorce, but the quiet was different when he was alive.

I miss his endless chatter, the million and one questions he would ask me, the sound of his feet running through the house.

Sometimes it feels like I've been stabbed between the ribs, the pain feels so real, knowing I won't hear or see him ever again. He's forever stuck in my memory as that little seven-year-old boy. He'd be thirteen now, at the start of his teenage years. I'm never going to help him learn to drive a car, or watch him graduate, or see what he decides to do with his life beyond that.

It feels like some cruel cosmic joke.

The worst is when I dream about him and wake up and have to realize all over again that he's gone.

After he passed, Krista begged and begged for us to have another child. She didn't even care if we got back together. She just wanted another baby. She thought that would make things better for her, but I knew it wouldn't and rebuked all her advances. She's not who I wanted, and I didn't want to bring a child into this world with someone I no longer loved.

Last I heard, she's married again, but I have no idea beyond that and don't care. Our lives are separate now.

For too long, it's only been me.

Well, me and Winnie—can't forget her.

I think of Salem, next door, close but so far away.

I told her I wanted to date her and I meant it. I knew all those years ago she was the woman for me—now I have to prove that I'm the man for her.

CHAPTER SEVENTEEN

Salem

Georgia stops by to spend some time with our mom, so I use the reprieve to my advantage and go for a run. It's later in the day than I normally go, and the heat is killer, but I know it'll do me good to get a workout in.

I don't really know or understand where I'm going until my legs carry me to the cemetery. I search out his grave and stop in front of it with a wildflower clasped in my hand that I plucked along my way just because I thought it was pretty. Maybe my subconscious knew I'd end up here before I did.

I lay the flower across his name and sink to my knees.

Tracing my fingers over his name, I cry, my tears splashing on the clean marble marker. Someone takes care of his grave, it's more well-kept than the others around him and I wonder if it's Krista or Thayer who does it.

"You would be thirteen now." My chest shakes as I cry. "A teenager. A little man." I tilt my head back toward the sky.

I've thought of Forrest every day since he passed. I see him in his sister. In her smile and laugh, in her zany personality, and her love for dinosaurs. Forrest is gone, but there are still pieces of him earth side.

It's not fair that such a young life was cut short.

He deserved more.

Accidents happen, it's true, but it doesn't make it any easier to deal with.

Death is just so fucking final and no matter how hard we try, we don't really know what waits for us beyond.

When I signed Seda up for swim lessons I learned exactly how common water accidents are and how silent drowning is. It's *terrifying*. And yet every time I've taken Seda to a public pool or we went to the beach, I see parents glued to their phones, oblivious to the horror that could so easily snatch their beloved child from them. Ignorance isn't always bliss. Sometimes ignorance is dangerous.

"You have a sister," I tell him, wiping my damp cheeks. "I think you'd love her so much. Even though you're older than her, I know you'd be kind to her, let her tagalong with you. I named her after you, you know? Seda," I whisper her name into existence, tracing my finger over his again. "It means spirit of the forest." I hang my head.

Forrest's death was hard enough to cope with before I found out I was pregnant. And once I held my baby in my arms, I couldn't imagine the pain of laying a child to rest forever.

"You're a good kid, Forrest. The best." I know I'm talking like he's still here, but it's easier to pretend that he is when I'm talking to him like this. "I miss you." I press my fingers to my lips, kissing them before I press them to the stone.

Standing back up, I dust grass off my shorts.

I don't much feel like running back now, so I decide to walk instead.

Making a pitstop into the coffee shop, nearly colliding with someone when the door opens at the same time I reach for it.

"Oh, I'm so sorry!" The woman carefully balances her iced drink. "Hi," she smiles, "it's you again. Salem, right?"

"It's nice to see you, Jen."

The apothecary store owner beams. There's an airy warmness to her that can't help but draw you in. "I hope you're enjoying the salts and everything."

"Very much. I need to stop back in."

"Come in any time." She starts to walk away, saying over her shoulder, "I hope you have a good day."

"You, too."

Inside the coffee shop, I place my order and grab a table while I wait. The place looks exactly the same as when I lived here before. I don't think they've changed a thing, not even the art on the walls. It feels like no time at all has passed since I left town and yet so much has changed in other ways.

When my name is called, I grab my iced coffee and head back onto the street, circling back to the house.

It's been a few days since Thayer asked me on a date and I haven't heard from him at all, despite the fact I gave him my new number. It makes me nervous that he's changed his mind, not to mention I'm still trying to figure out the best way to drop the kid bomb on him. I'm not sure there is a best way, and I don't know that he'll understand my reasoning for not telling him or if he'll believe me that I tried.

Letting myself in the side door, I walk in to find my sister crying.

"Georgia?" I set down my coffee, going to her side where she paces by the counter. "What's wrong?"

"I'm sorry." She fans her face, emotional and trying to contain it. "She's sleeping," she adds in a whisper. "I just..." Her hands go to her round belly. "I got to thinking about how she might not live long enough to meet the baby and how this baby won't know her and I just ... it's not fair and I'm angry."

I pull my older sister into my arms, letting her cry and get this off her chest. I can't imagine dealing with the emotions of this on top of being pregnant.

"Cry as long as you need." I hold her even tighter.

"How are you keeping it together so well?"

"Trust me, I'm not. I have my moments too."

"Life's so unfair and she's been failed so many times." She pulls away from me, grabbing a paper towel to dab at her eyes. "Ugh," she groans, motioning to her smeared mascara. "I'm a mess." Sniffling, she leans against the counter for support. "I just don't know how to live life without her. She's our mom. What am I going to do when I can't pick up the phone and call her? Ask her for advice or what ingredient I'm forgetting in the cupcakes I'm making?"

I hold her arms gently in my hands, making sure to look her in the eyes. "You'll feel sad. You might cry a little bit. And then you'll call me, and we can cry together. And I'll always tell you what ingredient you're missing."

She says no more, just yanks me back into a hug, the swell of her belly in our way. "Please, move back here. I don't want you to leave again."

Rubbing my hand against her back, I bite my lip. "I'm thinking about it."

"What?" She jerks back in surprise. "Are you serious?"

I nod. "Now that I've been back here ... I feel different about staying. But nothing is decided," I warn her, not wanting to get her hopes up.

"Well," she smiles despite the tears still lingering in her eyes, "you have to do whatever feels right, but I hope you stay."

CHAPTER EIGHTEEN

Thayer

Parking my truck, I grab my thermos of hot chocolate, my lunch cooler, and head into the cemetery. It's too hot out to enjoy the hot chocolate, but it's sort of become my tradition when I come here.

I navigate my way through the gravestones. I'm pretty sure I could get to my son's grave blindfolded by this point. I come by once a week, sometimes more if I find myself really needing to talk to him.

I used to think that people who came to cemeteries to speak with their loved ones were crazy. It's all just a bunch of grass and stone—it's a place where Forrest was never alive—but I still like coming here. It's peaceful and I feel closer to him.

My eyes narrow when I approach his marker. There's a single purple flower laid above his name. Cocking my head to the side, I look around in search of whoever left it. Not that it's much mystery. Krista doesn't find the same comfort here that I do, so she doesn't visit. Which means Salem most likely left this. Recently too since the wind hasn't blown it away.

I don't know what makes me do it, but I pluck the flower off and put it in my lunch box. The urge to keep it is stupid, but I can't help it. It's tangible proof of her heart, of how even after all this time she still cares about my son, and maybe me too.

She wouldn't have kissed you back like that if she didn't still have feelings for you.

Getting comfortable on the grass, I unwrap my sloppily made peanut butter and jelly.

"How are you doing, kid?" I chomp into my sandwich. "I wish I could hear your voice—that you could tell me what it's like wherever you are. I want to know you're okay and taken care of. That's one of the hardest parts, you know?" I wipe my mouth with the back of my hand. "When you're a parent you just want to know your kid is being treated right and safe, but I have no way of knowing that now with you." Grabbing my thermos, I pour a little into the lid. "Here you go, kid. Enjoy." I tip the canteen back and take my own sip.

"I've played that day over and over in my head so many times, trying to figure out every little thing I could've changed that would've resulted in a different outcome, but I still don't know if it would've made any difference. Even if you weren't mad at me, you might still have ended up in that pool." Sighing, I take a deep breath. "I don't know what's worse—thinking I could've changed something and you'd still be alive, or thinking this was some cruel twist of fate and I couldn't do anything about it anyway."

I'm rambling now, it's usually what happens to me when I'm here. I word vomit my thoughts at him, and Forrest, of course, says nothing.

"I miss you. So much. You are the best seven years of my thirty-seven years of existence on this planet. You made me a dad. I thought for a while that I stopped being one when you died, but I realize now you don't stop being a parent just because your child is gone. No matter what, I'll always be your dad, Forrest, and when I meet you on the other side I can't wait to feel your arms around me again."

While I finish my lunch, I fill him in on mundane things in my life—like what's going on at work, the latest movie I watched that reminded me of him—all of the silly day to day things he misses out on.

I have to get back to work, so I pack my trash away, and place my hand over his name.

"I love you, kid."

Standing up, I brush the dirt and grass from my shorts.

I have to get back to work, because no matter what, life keeps going.

CHAPTER NINETEEN

Salem

The next night after helping my mom bathe—she sits on a shower chair and I take care of the rest—and in to bed, I slip out the side door for some fresh air, discovering another bouquet of peonies.

I pick them up, inspecting the petals. Each one is so delicate and perfect.

There's no note this time. When I finally read the one he included before, it said;

For my sunshine.

—T

Setting them back down, I walk to the end of the driveway and peek at Thayer's house. The sun is beginning to set, and I see him sitting on the front porch swing that I helped him put up a lifetime ago.

Hesitating for a moment or two, I finally make my way up his front walk onto the porch.

He saw me approaching and his eyes study me as I stand in front of him. He pushes his feet, the swing swaying lightly.

"Hi," I say softly, hesitant to approach.

The tiniest of smiles dances across his lips. "Hi. Do you

want to join me?"

I nod and he scoots over so there's enough room on his left side for me to sit with him.

The blue and white stripped cushion is soft beneath my butt. I have to fight my body's natural desire to want to curl into him. It's like my body has forgotten all the time that has passed and that he's not mine to touch freely anymore.

He arches a brow, noticing the way I incline away from him. "I'm not contagious. You can touch me."

I ignore his comment. "You don't have to bring me flowers. But thank you. They're beautiful."

"I'm glad you like them. They're all for you anyway."

My brows narrow in confusion, not quite sure what he means by that comment. If he got me flowers and left them, then of course they are for me, but I feel like there's a deeper meaning I'm not catching onto.

"I have to ask you something."

"Okay?" He sounds unsure.

"Why didn't you call me?"

A heavy sigh rattles his chest. He looks away from me, at the setting sun that paints the sky in a watercolor of pinks, purples, and oranges.

"For a while, I convinced myself that I'd accomplished what I wanted. I pushed you away to live a life without me and it would be weak to break the promise I made to myself to give you a chance to grow on your own." He rubs his jaw, looking pained. "By the time I realized what an idiot I'd been, it was too late."

My voice is barely above a whisper when I prompt, "What do you mean?"

"Your mom had been gone a few days, so when she came

back, I asked her if everything was okay." He pauses, rubbing his brow like it still pains him to remember this. He continues to look away from me, like it's too much to meet my eyes. "She said she had been gone for a wedding. I don't know what made me ask whose wedding, but I did, and she said it was yours." His voice grows weak with emotion. "I had just made the decision to find you—I tried calling and texting, but I think you'd changed your number at that point. I was too late." He finally looks at me, and I see years of pain, regret, and even love in his brown eyes. "It's what I deserved."

"How did we let everything get so messed up?"

He runs his fingers through his hair, blowing out a breath. "Hubris gets all of us at some point. I tried to convince you, and myself, that you were better off without me and hurt both of us in the end." He stares down at his hands, flexing his fingers. "I knew you were it for me, though, that I'd never love another person the way I love you. So, it's just been me, here," he waves a hand at his house, "alone. I decided that was my punishment—to have tasted something real and to be denied it for the rest of my existence because I pushed it away."

I stay fixated on the fact that he used love in the present tense. "Do you still love me then?"

"I don't want to scare you."

Shaking my head back and forth rapidly, I plead, "I just want you to be honest."

We've both spent too much time not saying what we really mean and I'm tired of it. So much can be wasted by keeping things to yourself.

"I never stopped loving you, Salem. Not once. Not for a minute, not even for a second."

Tears burn my eyes. I moved on thinking he truly didn't

want anything to do with me and all this time...

"Why are we like this?" I ask the heavens more than him.

"Not everything is clear cut in life, Salem. Sometimes things blur and we fuck things up. We're all human."

"I still loved you, but I married someone else. I thought you were over me and that I had to move on, so I did—and this whole time ... this whole fucking time." I stand up, facing him. "Do you not see how fucked up this whole thing is?"

"Believe me, I know."

I cover my face with my hands. "We're quite the pair," I mutter.

"You had every right to move on," he says softly, carefully. "I didn't leave you with any hope that we'd get back together. I know you loved Caleb ... It makes sense that you went back to him."

"He deserved better."

I loved Caleb, still love him in a certain way, but that doesn't change the facts. He wasn't Thayer. He never could be. Some loves are only once in a lifetime. I know he made his choices, just like I did, but it doesn't mean I don't regret feeling like I dragged him along. I never meant to, but I'm not sure that makes it any better.

"Sit down," he pleads, pointing to the spot beside him I got up from. "You're getting worked up."

"Of course, I am!" I throw my hands in the air. "I'm a shitty person. I ruined his life."

"It doesn't make you a shitty person to move on with your life. I know you, Salem, and you wouldn't have married him if you didn't have genuine feelings for the guy so stop punishing yourself. I loved Krista and even though we didn't make it, I don't think for a minute I ruined her life, or she did mine.

We weren't meant to last but that doesn't mean there wasn't something valuable in what we had. Stop punishing yourself."

Stop punishing yourself.

His words strike deep, like they were meant to, and he's right—my time with Caleb might not have been meant to last forever, but that doesn't mean it was cheap. I did love him. We had a good life together.

"I've hated myself so much," I finally admit out loud.

He reaches for my hand and takes it, tugging me forward. "You have to stop."

"I don't know how."

"It's not always easy to forgive yourself—there is no step-by-step process. Just remember no one is perfect." He lightly touches my cheek with his other hand. "At the end of the day, we're all human, and not a single one of us is better than another."

I know he's right, but it's easier said than done.

"Sit down," he says again, softer this time. "Life's too short to constantly be stuck on the past or obsessing over what ifs. We have this." He waves to the world around us. "We have now."

I know he's right, but that doesn't make it any easier.

Settling beside him, I rest my head on his shoulder, and we watch the last of the sun disappear together.

CHAPTER TWENTY

Salem

Staring at the text from Thayer, something sinks in my stomach.

"Is something wrong?" My mom notices my expression change from normal to worried.

"Oh, yeah, I'm okay. Nothing's wrong." I put my phone back in my pocket and return to folding laundry.

"You can't bullshit your mother, Salem. Out with it."

Those mom senses really are too good sometimes. "It's nothing, really."

"I'll pry it out of you eventually." She coughs, her throat dry. "You might as well tell me."

I know she isn't going to let it go. "I got asked out on a date. He just texted a day and time to see if it was okay."

"So, why did you look so ill? Is he not a good guy?"

"It's not that." I add a shirt to my stack.

"Then what is it? You're not giving me a lot to go on here. I'm dying. Time is of the essence."

I pick up a pair of cutoff shorts. "I wish you'd stop saying that."

"Why? It's true. Tell me about this guy, please. I need the distraction."

I've decided maybe her constant need to remind me that she's dying is her own coping mechanism. It doesn't make much sense to me, but I guess whatever makes her feel better.

Lowering my head, I whisper, "It's Thayer."

"Thayer? Next door Thayer?"

Shockingly, she doesn't sound that surprised. More excited than anything else.

"The one and only," I reply, moving the shorts to the growing pile.

"He's a good man, but what's the problem?"

I look up at the ceiling, fighting the burn of tears in my eyes. "It's too soon," I say, which is partially true.

The other reality is, that there's a stone sinking in my gut because I can't, not in good conscience, go on a date with Thayer before I tell him about Seda. I'm tired of this hanging over me. I have to put the truth out there, but I don't know how.

I don't say any of that to my mom, though. She doesn't know about my past with Thayer, and I'm not ready to divulge that. I'm aware I might never get the chance to tell her, but again, there's no way I can tell her the truth before I tell Thayer.

"It's never too soon to open your heart to love again. I made that mistake, thinking I couldn't, now look at me." She shrugs her bony shoulders. "I'm going to die, never knowing true love, never knowing a *good* man. I had you girls, my store, and other dreams realized, but sometimes I do wish I'd allowed myself to open my heart to someone."

"I'll think about it." My phone sits like a heavy weight in my pocket.

I know I technically already agreed to this date, but now that he's put a day and time on it, it's so much more real.

But I have to tell him.

I just don't know how.

***

Rain pounds against my bedroom windows, trees blowing relentlessly. I wish I could say it's the summer storm keeping me awake, but it's not. My thoughts keep going around and around. There's no silencing my mind.

Throwing the covers back, I toss a jacket on and shove my feet into an old pair of flip-flops. Slipping down the stairs and quietly past my mom, I let myself out the door. As soon as I step from beneath the cover of the porch, I'm pelted with rain. By the time I make it next door I'm drenched.

Are you really going to do this?

Yes.

I pound my fist against the door. I don't stop either. I just keep knocking and knocking until it swings open, revealing the man on the other side.

My eyes eat him up and I allow myself this moment because after I say what I have to, he might hate me. I wouldn't blame him for it either.

He stands before me with sleep tousled hair, his chest on display for my eager gaze. There's that smattering of chest hair I loved so much that grows thicker beneath his navel, disappearing into his sweatpants that it looks like he haphazardly pulled on. He takes me in as well, looking confused. I'm sure I'd be equally confused if he showed up at my door looking like a drowned rat.

"Why are you—"

"Can I come in?" My voice is soft, cracking on the end.

"Yeah." He steps back, opening the door wider. "Are you all right? You didn't answer my text earlier."

He closes the door behind me, but we don't move away

from it. It feels weird, standing in this foyer again. It looks exactly the same, like no time at all has passed. Six years is so short but so long all at the same time.

"I'm fine, but I ... uh..." I start get choked up. I don't want to get overly emotional telling him this. Fortifying myself, I look into his eyes and say the words that have been long overdue. "I can't go out on a date with you, not in good conscience, without telling you this first."

He cocks his head to the side, eyes narrowed and skeptical. "Tell me what?"

I clench my hands together, my fingernails digging into the skin of my palms.

Spit it out, Salem.

"I have a daughter."

There. It's out there now. I can't take it back.

He gives me a funny look. "You were worried I'd be mad you had a kid? Do you think so little of me?"

"No." I exhale a weighted breath. "It's not that."

"Then what is it?" He crosses his arms over his chest, leaning against the wall behind us.

I'm thankful for that bit of extra space between us. It allows me a second to breathe air that isn't intoxicated with his presence.

I'm realizing there's no good way to say this. No right words. Nothing to make it easier or better.

"Do you remember—that last time we had sex? You'd been drinking and—"

His eyes narrow further until I can't even see the brown anymore. "Yes."

I wet my lips, nerves sending a bead of sweat down my spine despite my wet clothes. "I got pregnant."

"You got pregnant?" he repeats, slowly, carefully, making sure he's grasping what I'm saying. "With my child?"

"Yes." I'm surprised the word comes out so sharp and clear when I feel so jittery on the inside.

He looks away, a surprised sound leaving him. It's almost a laugh, but not quite. "Pregnant?" His eyes drop to my stomach like he expects it to find it rounded and full. It's not, but it is squishier than it used to be with stretch marks on my stomach and hips. "Why didn't you tell me?"

I cover my face with my hands, letting my arms drop back to my sides. "A million different reasons and none of them are good enough. I was terrified. You were drinking yourself into oblivion and deep into grieving and I just ... I guess I thought if I couldn't manage to pull you out of this, then how would a baby? And I didn't want you to fake it for our baby's sake either." Swallowing thickly, I add, "You said you didn't love me anymore, didn't want me, and that scared me too because what if I told you and you thought I was trapping you." I'm rambling at this point, but that's how my thoughts were back then—all over the place. I was a terrified nineteen-year-old, practically a kid myself. "I stayed as long as I could—until I realized I wasn't the person who could help you."

"That's when you called Laith," he fills in the blanks. "Did he know you were pregnant?"

"No. Just Lauren at that point."

He tugs on his hair, shaking his head lightly. "Wow. This is a lot to process."

"I'm sorry. I should've told you a long time ago. I wrote you a letter one time and then chickened out and didn't send it. You'd already rejected me, and I was so scared of what it'd feel like if you rejected her too."

He rears back, almost knocking his head into the wall. "You thought I'd do that?"

"Thayer," I say his name slowly, "you turned into an entirely different person when Forrest died."

His head lowers, and he nods like he knows I'm right. "I'm so fucking sorry."

Now I'm the one stumbling back. "You're apologizing to me? Why?"

Warm brown eyes meet mine. "Because, I was an asshole to you back then. I *wanted* to push you away, and ultimately, I did, and fuck if it doesn't piss me off at myself that it was when you needed me most."

"You needed to grieve."

He clears his throat. "We both really fucked things up, didn't we?" I don't answer him so he goes on, "You said she's a ... I have a daughter?" A tiny smile fights for space on his lips.

"You have a daughter and she's perfect." Clearing my throat, I add, "I know I didn't tell you about her, but I didn't keep you a secret from her. She knows about you and Forrest too. She talks about her brother a lot."

"What's ... uh ... what's her name?" He's getting choked up talking about her, and even though this is going way better than I anticipated, somehow this makes me feel worse. I deserve his anger, for him to yell and scream, to cuss me out.

"Seda," I reply, not being able to help myself when I smile at her name. "She's perfect and beautiful. Funny and creative. She's everything."

He rubs his jaw, brown eyes pooling with tears. "Can I see a picture?"

"Yeah." I push my wet hair out of my eyes, shivering. "I have a million on my phone."

He notices me shaking with cold. "Fuck, I should've offered you a shirt."

"It's okay. I'm fine." I shiver again.

Rolling his eyes, he mutters, "Liar," and heads up the stairs leaving me in the foyer.

He isn't gone long before he returns with a cotton shirt, extending it out to me.

We both seem to remember at the same moment another time I showed up at his door completely soaked from rain. Only that time I had Binx with me and I was confessing something entirely different, telling him about my past.

"Thank you." I let myself into the downstairs bathroom and shuck off my wet jacket and tank top beneath, tugging the plain shirt down over my body. My nipples stand erect thanks to being in my cold, wet clothes so long. There's nothing I can do about it, so I just have to hope the looseness of his shirt helps camouflage it.

Stepping out of the bathroom with my wet clothes in hand, I set them by the door and find him in the living room sitting on the couch waiting for me.

A bottle of water sits in front of him with a Diet Coke beside it.

Pointing at the soda before I take a seat, I say, "You don't drink that stuff."

"No." He eyes the can, then me. "But you do."

"You just keep Diet Coke on hand in case I show up?"

He looks away, like he doesn't want me to see him vulnerable in this moment. "Ever since you came back."

Why—why does that one gesture want to send me into a fit of tears?

Picking up the soda, I take a sip and settle beside him.

Unlocking my phone, I bring up all my albums of Seda. Deciding to start at the beginning, I show him a few photos from when I was pregnant with her. His smile is sad, but wistful. He's handling this extremely well, but that doesn't erase all the guilt eating away at me.

I never wanted things to end up like this.

I certainly didn't expect to get pregnant. But when I did, there was a moment when I imagined us together. The three of us. A family.

I show him a few of the sonograms I had saved into my phone before I move onto newborn pictures. I have all her photos organized in my phone in different albums by year, so I let him take it and flick through them. He zooms in from time to time, studying her little face as it grows and changes. Laughing when her bald head gains one tuft of blonde hair that I insisted on putting a bow in. I watch her grow up through the photos alongside him, but I know it's so different from actually watching her turn from a baby to a toddler and into a child.

"She's perfect." He smiles lovingly at a photo of her on her first day of kindergarten this past August. "She looks like you."

"Like you, too." I don't know how it happened, but I've ended up with my head resting on his shoulder. "She's the perfect mix of both of us."

"Seda," he says her name softly, carefully, rolling it over in his mouth to test the sound. "That's an unusual name. Is it a family name of yours?"

I shake my head slightly since I'm still resting against his bare arm. "No. I wanted to honor Forrest. I wasn't really sure at first how I was going to go about it, but one day when I was searching for names Seda came up, and I loved how it sounded. Then when I read what it meant it felt like maybe Forrest was giving me a nudge in the right direction."

"What does it mean?" He's still looking at the last photo he stopped on. She's on her princess bike with a hot pink helmet. Caleb is running behind her since she was nervous with no training wheels.

"It means spirit of the forest."

Goosebumps pop up on his arms. "Whoa. Wow." He shakes his head, rubbing a hand over his mouth. "That's ... wow."

"I know it's unique, but I knew then that it was supposed to be her name."

"You said she knows about me, about Forrest?"

"She doesn't know you specifically, but she's aware that while Caleb's raised her and he's her dad, that she has another dad too because she's doubly special." He smiles at that. "Only Caleb and Lauren know you're her biological father. To everyone else I decided it was best if I just said it was a one-night-stand."

"That ashamed of me, huh?" He says it in a joking tone, but I can see in his eyes that he believes that might be a little bit of the reason why.

"It just seemed easier. I was still heartbroken and convinced you never wanted to see me again. I guess just being young and stupid I decided on that course. If I could do it over again—"

"Life doesn't have do overs," he says gently. His big palm comes over my knee and he gives it a squeeze. "We all make choices in moments that we might come to regret. There's no point wasting time in the here and now dwelling on it. Life's too short, too precious, for that. Forrest taught me that." He touches his fingers gently to the side of my face. A soft sigh escapes my parted lips at the caress. "It doesn't mean it doesn't hurt, knowing you didn't tell me. It's fucking painful. But I can't change either of the decisions we made. That's why I choose to go from here. From this moment." He holds my gaze, my heart beating rapidly in my chest. "You know, after you got married, I didn't think we'd have another chance, but we *do*. In all the time we've been apart, what I feel for you has never lessened, and that ... it was honestly fucking terrifying at times—realizing I was never going to get over you and have to figure out how to live life without you. Now that you're back here, now that I know we have a child together, I'm not throwing this second chance away. I'd be a fool to do such a thing when I've begged the universe to give me another chance with you." He clears his throat, eyes clouded with barely withheld emotion. "I lost Forrest in a way that there's no getting him back, but I lost you too in the process, but you're something I can fight to get back." He grabs a piece of my hair, gently tucking it behind my ear and letting his fingers skim my cheek. "If you want me back. You can tell me to get lost any time, Salem, and I will. I know it's been a long time and you might not feel the same way—"

I press a hand over his mouth, silencing him. "When you asked me to date you, I said yes because I want that."

I feel him smile against my hand. "Good." His voice is muffled by my hand, so I let it drop. He looks back at my phone, but the screen has gone black. I quickly unlock it and pass it back to him. "When can I meet her?"

"Whenever you want. I just have to arrange it with Caleb."

"I want to meet her soon. But I don't want to scare her. I know you said she knows she has another dad, but that doesn't mean she knows me."

"I think she'll handle it better than you're expecting. She's a smart kid."

"Can you send me some pictures?"

"I'll get them all to you." I lean against the back of the

couch, watching him look at her. "I should've tried harder."

Slowly, he looks away from the photo. "I gave you no reason to. You were protecting yourself and protecting her from what you thought I could be. And let's face it, Salem, I could've reached out to you sooner than I had wanted to. But I didn't. We've both made a lot of mistakes, and we can sit here and continue to rehash them, but it doesn't change anything. I just want to move forward."

"I want that too."

"Good." He passes my phone back to me. "Now are you ever going to reply to my text?"

"Oh, right." I quickly bring up my text messages and type out a reply. His phone buzzes in his pocket.

With a grin, he pulls it out and nods at my response. "See you tomorrow."

He leads me to the door, opening it and waiting for me to step onto the front porch. The rain has lessened, mostly a drizzle now. I pause, turning back to look at him in the doorway of his home.

A moment passes between us, a thousand words said without a single spoken aloud.

A second chance, he said before, but do we really deserve one?

Selfishly, a little voice in my head whispers, *I hope so.*

CHAPTER TWENTY-ONE

Thayer

I can't go back to sleep, not with this news dropped on me.

Salem went home about an hour ago, and I've been in the basement ever since.

My fist slams into the bag over and over again, alternating left then right.

I'm drenched in sweat, like I can exile all my thoughts and demons.

I have a daughter.

I have a child with Salem.

We ... we made a baby.

And she never fucking told me.

Over and over again I slam my fist into the bag. Tears mingle with my sweat and I wipe at the dampness on my face.

I keep picturing that little girl's face in my mind.

Her eyes are brown, just like mine.

I wish so badly I could've been there, for Salem, for my daughter.

I didn't get to see Salem grow round with our child, or give birth, or get to be there for any of Seda's milestones. It wasn't a lie when I told her I didn't want to dwell on the mistakes of our past, because it's true, I want to move on and start fresh, but I need this fucking moment to wallow.

Both of us made mistakes and horrible choices, not just her. I know I'm equally at fault for this outcome and I'm just as mad at myself for it as I am her.

I'm going to let myself feel that—the anger—and then move the fuck on.

When I've exhausted myself, I trudge upstairs to my room and take an extra-long shower. It's still early when I get out so I lay across my bed and check my phone. Salem's sent me albums of photos to download.

I look through them slowly, picking apart details and learning everything I can about my daughter. Like how she must love all colors, but especially pink. How she likes to dress up as a princess and have tea parties but also likes to run around outside in the rain, getting covered in mud. There are photos of her in a ballet tutu. I wonder if she takes lessons or she was only playing dress up.

I learn many things from the photos, but my questions grow too.

Light starts to peek through the blinds. Laith is living in Denver, so he's hours behind the east coast, but he's going to have to deal. I need to talk to him, and I've waited long enough.

"What the fuck, man?" He groans into the line.

"I need to talk to you."

"It's like..." He must look at the time. "Four in the morning."

"Salem came over last night."

"Ugh, you are not waking me up at the ass crack of dawn to give me a rundown on your booty call."

"Salem is *not* a booty call, and we haven't been together since she got back."

There's rustling and I know he must be sitting up in bed. "You mean to tell me your celibate ass hasn't been all over that, yet? Come on, bro, you'll be in a lot better shape once you get laid."

"Don't talk about Salem like that. She's not just ... she's more than that, okay?"

My brother knows all about Salem. All the gory details. He thought I was a fucking idiot for pushing the love of my life away—and he was right. I was the dumbest fucking idiot. I thought I was doing what was right. I didn't know how long I'd be grieving and I just ... didn't want her to see me like that. I ruined us. Not her.

"Right, right. I know. But it's *four-fucking-o-clock-in-the-morning.* Cut me a break. I'm not a morning person."

"I have a daughter. With Salem. We have a child."

He's silent for a minute, and then there's a whistle of air escaping his lungs. "Holy fucking shit."

"That about sums up how I feel."

"That kid has to be what? Like six?"

"Five."

"Fuck. That's crazy. No wonder you called me this early. This is a lot to process. Have you told Mom and Dad?"

"I just found out. You're the first person I called."

"Aw." I hear him slap a hand to his chest. "I feel special."

"Don't let it go to your head," I grumble, raking my fingers through my hair.

"Oh, I am," he chortles. "Admit it, I'm your favorite person."

"No."

"That's right—second favorite, behind Salem. I'll take it. But a kid, Thayer? A whole ass child? Wow. Fucking insane."

I scrub my hand over my face. "I think I'm in shock."

"Of course you fucking are. She kept that a secret from you all this time," he rambles, barely taking a breath. "It's a lot to take in."

"She knows about me—well, not me specifically, but that the guy Salem was married to isn't her biological father."

As much as it hurt me that she went back to Caleb, right now I'm actually kind of grateful for the dude. It's weird, I know, but he didn't steal her from me. He was there for her when she needed someone the most. He was young, but he did what I couldn't with my grief—he stepped up to the plate and became a husband and father.

"What does this mean for you and Salem?"

"What do you mean?"

"I mean, she kept a whole ass child a secret from you. That's kind of a big deal."

"I'm not saying it isn't, but I'm not throwing this chance with her away." Laith has never met his Salem—he doesn't get how fucking lucky I am to have a chance to do things over with her, to do it *right* this time.

"All this time and you still feel the same about her?"

"Yeah. I do."

When you know, you know.

I knew then but I wouldn't let myself believe it. I believe you should learn from your mistakes, so that's what I'm trying to do.

"So, what's your daughter's name?"

I smile before I even say it. "Seda."

"That's a weird name."

"Shut the fuck up," I growl at my younger brother. "It's a beautiful name."

"Sorry, my bad—need I remind you it's *four in the fucking morning*."

"Right, right. You're not a morning person. My bad."

"When do you get to meet her?"

I sigh, nerves rattling my stomach. "I don't know. Soon, I hope."

"You know, despite this early hour I've learned something valuable from this conversation."

"What?" I ask hesitantly. I never know what's going to come out of my brother's mouth.

"Always wear a condom before I go to pound town."

With that final statement he ends the call, presumably to go back to sleep, and I get ready for work.

CHAPTER TWENTY-TWO

Salem

I'm a jittery mess all day counting down in anticipation to my date with Thayer.

A date.

A real date.

I act like I've never been on a date at all with the way my palms keep sweating.

"Would you stop pacing?" My mom scolds with an amused smile. "You already spilled water on me earlier and now you're going to wear a hole in the carpet with all that walking back and forth." She mimes walking with her fingers. I open my mouth to reply but she silences me again, adding, "And don't you dare try to use me as an excuse not to go again. I'm living vicariously through you right now."

I've already tried three different times to back out. Not because I don't want to go, I definitely do, but the guilt eats me up over leaving my mom even though a nurse is stopping by for her weekly checks and Georgia will be here with her— apparently Georgia likes to supervise these visits.

"What if you need me?" I argue, still pacing.

She huffs, adjusting the blankets on her lap. A rom-com plays softly in the background, but she's been paying more attention to me than it. "Your sister is going to be here with me, and believe me, she's a hoverer. Besides, I do know how to work a phone to call or text. You worry so much about everyone else. Go out, Salem. Enjoy yourself. Have a nice time with a nice man."

I cease my pacing, planting my hands on my hips. "You make it sound so much easier than it is."

She laughs, but it quickly turns into a cough. I move forward like I can help her and she's quick to wave me off. Once she's recovered, she says, "That's the thing it is easy— it's overthinking and making your brain run through every possible scenario that complicates things."

She's totally right. Smoothing my hands down the blue and white floral dress I put on, I take a deep breath and do my best to silence my scattered thoughts. "Do I look okay?"

She crooks a finger, beckoning me forward. I bend down closer to her, and she grabs a piece of my hair, tucking it back behind my ear. The short pieces keep slipping free of the low bun I twisted it in.

Touching her hand gently to my cheek, her skin cool against mine, she says, "You look beautiful, Salem. You always do."

"Not as beautiful as you."

She snorts. "Stop trying to flatter me."

"It's not flattery." I kiss her cheek. "You're the most beautiful person I know, inside and out."

When I straighten, there are tears shining in her eyes she tries to hide.

The side door in the kitchen creaks open and Georgia calls out a hello. I hear the thump of her purse hitting the floor, or maybe it's the kitchen table. She waddles into the room, glowing and all smiles.

"Hey, Mom." She bends down as much as she can, wrapping her arms around mom's neck. "Little sis." She hugs me next. "How's the day been?"

"Good," I tell her, meaning it. Mom's been more alert and not in as much pain. It's all we can ask for, especially when I know it's so short lived.

"Feeling okay?" She reaches for our mom's wrist, and I know she plans to check her pulse, but mom quickly tucks her arm against her chest.

"Georgia, that's what the nurse is for. Why don't you take a seat?"

Georgia pouts her lips but does as she's asked. "Do you want anything to drink or a snack or something?" I ask, wanting to busy myself with something.

"I can get it myself—" She starts to stand, but I wave her back down.

"You're pregnant, working, and chasing after two kids already. Sit while you can."

She laughs, shaking her head but she can't help but smile. She loves those boys with her whole heart. She's truly a good mom. "Fine, grab me a water then and some crackers."

In the kitchen, I give myself a chance to take a few deeps breaths to calm my racing heart. Despite the fact that I know Thayer so well, and my confession is out in the open, my nerves are at an all-time high. This feels so different. Official in a way we never were before. It's out in the world, knowledge for everyone, that we're going on a date. Not some sneaky secret.

I fix Georgia a glass of water and grab a pack of crackers from the tiny pantry. She takes both from me with a smile.

"How excited are you for your date?"

"She's worn a path in the rug if that tells you anything," my mom interjects before I can say anything.

"It's been a long time since I've been on a date," I defend.

There's a mirror above the small table near the stairs, that I use to check my reflection yet again, trying to slick back stray hairs. Maybe it would've been a better idea to keep my hair down, but I had wanted to do something different.

The doorbell rings and a legitimate scream flies past my lips, making both my mom and sister laugh.

"Oh, yeah, she's nervous," Georgia cackles. "Oh, no." She looks down at her lap. "I think I peed a little."

I stick my tongue out at her playfully before opening the door.

Thayer stands there looking ridiculously good—if he had any idea just how much I'm attracted to him he'd laugh. Or run the other way.

He's clearly put more effort into his hair than usual, it's brushed back and not as unruly. His facial hair is trimmed and neat. I was worried I might have overdressed—even though my dress is far from fancy—but I feel better seeing him in a nice pair of jeans and a pale blue button-down shirt with the sleeves rolled up.

"These are for you." He holds out yet another bouquet of pink peonies. I wonder where he's getting them all. I can't imagine our local florist has much.

"Peonies are going to take over the house," I warn him with a smile, taking them and cradling them in my arms. "Lucky for you, I don't mind."

He chuckles, shoving his now empty hands in his pockets.

"Here, I'll take those." I didn't even notice my sister get up from the couch. She holds her hands out for the bouquet and I pass it over. "You two kids have fun now." She smacks me on the butt before waddling toward the kitchen.

Thayer holds out a hand for me to take before poking his head in the door. "I'll bring her back soon, Allie."

She smiles, her eyes crinkling at the corners. "Just take care of her for me."

His gaze moves down to me, his smile growing. "I will."

Shutting the door behind me, I let him hold my hand on the way to his truck that he's moved into our driveway.

"I would've walked over. You're literally right next door."

"Nope." He shakes his head forcefully. "This is a date. That means it starts with me picking you up from your house, not mine." He opens the passenger door of his truck, offering a hand to help me up.

Once I'm safely inside he closes the door, walking around the front of the truck to climb in the driver's side. He cranks the engine, grinning at me before he puts it in reverse.

"What?" I ask, wondering why he's staring at me like that.

"I'm making a memory right now."

My heart tugs at his statement. "I am too," I whisper.

He leans over, cupping the back of my neck. "I refuse to let you be the one who got away."

"What does that mean?" My eyes zero in on his lips, thinking of the kiss we shared in his truck only a week ago.

"I don't want you to be someone I think about for the rest of my life, wondering what if? What if I'd tried harder? What if I had just told you how I felt?" He lowers his forehead to press gently against mine, our breaths sharing the same space. "I want you to be *the one*. That's it. No second guessing. No wondering. Just a sure thing."

"I—"

"Don't say anything," he pleads, pulling away. "I want to

do this right. Get to know who you are now, date you for real, and I want to take my time."

"Take your time with what?"

He wets his lips, looking at me like he's afraid I might disappear. "Making you fall back in love with me."

I don't say anything to that as he backs out of the driveway, but I can't help thinking that I'm not sure I ever fell out of love with him.

CHAPTER TWENTY-THREE

Salem

I'm surprised when Thayer turns into the parking lot of the local park. I'm not sure what exactly I was expecting but it wasn't this.

"What are we doing here?" I turn around, looking for any sign of why he would've chosen this spot for our first date. But it looks the same as it always did. Lots of open fields, a wooden playground for the children, and a walking trail along the perimeter.

"We're having a picnic."

"A picnic?" I brighten, never having thought of that.

"Originally, I planned for us to eat on a blanket in the grass, but the storm last night kind of ruined that. But there's the gazebo so I figure that can work."

Somehow, I had forgotten about the storm, but that explains why it's mostly empty at the park today with no one wanting to risk the muddy mess of grass.

Thayer reaches to open his door, quickly looking back at me. "You wait there."

"Wha—"

He doesn't let me finish before he's out and closing his door. He comes around the truck and opens my door, holding out his hand.

"I'm doing things right with you."

My heart does a somersault.

I accept his help without protest. When my feet land on the ground, his hands go to my hips. He doesn't say anything, and I don't either. But I wonder if he's thinking the same thing I am—that I never thought we'd end up here. When I got back together with Caleb, I made myself say goodbye to this part of my life, to *him*. I mourned the loss of what we could've been.

But now, here we are with this second chance, and even though this, *him*—has the capability to obliterate me all over again—I can't turn away. Some things are worth the risk if you're brave enough to take the leap.

Thayer opens the back door and pulls out a packed basket—a literal basket like you see in movies when the couple goes on a picnic—and a blanket he drapes over top of it. Closing and locking up the truck, he offers his hand to me, and we trek across the muddy grass toward the gazebo. I'm thankful I wore a pair of Converse sneakers instead of the sandals I had planned on. I'll have to wash these later, but it's worth it.

The gazebo is white with vines of flowers crawling up the sides. It matches the one in the middle of town but is larger in size.

Letting go of my hand, he sits the basket down and spreads the blanket out.

"Is this okay?" He looks a bit unsure of himself which is unusual for Thayer. Normally nothing ruffles his feathers.

"It's great." I hold onto the side of the gazebo and take my shoes off, not wanting to get mud all over the blanket. Thayer does the same, then opens the top of the basket, pulling out covered dishes of food.

"What did you make?" I gather my skirt up, tucking it under me as I sit down.

He uncovers a bowl and passes it to me. "Pasta!" I cry in delight. "Is that lobster in it?"

He laughs softly, ducking his head as he rummages through the basket. "Yes."

"Wow, you really went all out. I feel special."

"You are." He says it so simply, like it's a fact I should already know.

He sets out bread and dipping oil on top of a cutting board along with a knife. He passes me a fork before uncovering his own bowl.

"This is amazing." I look at the spread of food. "You thought of everything. You could've just taken me to a restaurant, you know?"

He swirls pasta around his fork. "And what's special about that? We've already eaten at a restaurant together." Lowering his head, he adds in a deeper voice, "After everything, you deserve something different than that."

I don't much feel like rehashing the past now, so I don't remark on that. Besides, we've established that I was hurt by his silence after everything. We're adults. We both know we could've made different choices.

"Truly, this is ... well, honestly, it's perfect."

It's simple, sweet. The thought that went into him planning this for us means everything.

"Do you think you would've come back here, to Hawthorne Mills, if it wasn't for your mom?"

I wrinkle my nose, contemplating his question. "Eventually." Picking up a piece of bread, I dip it in the oil to busy myself while I sort through my thoughts. "I think I would've had to. As much as I've avoided this place, it's always called to me."

"You stayed away because of me."

He makes it a statement, but I answer anyway. "Yes and no. Because of everything, this place became somewhere I dreaded to be. And I think, even after I got married, I was afraid of what it would feel like to see you with another woman."

He clears his throat, his cheeks pinkening. "About that..."

"Yes?" I prompt curiously.

"I haven't been with anyone."

"For a while?"

"A long while." He looks out of the gazebo at the trees, mumbling, "Not since you."

"Since me?" I blurt loudly, taken by complete surprise. "Thayer," I laugh, more from shock than any genuine humor, "That's ... you have to be joking. I mean, don't you remember that night after my sister's wedding? Caleb brought me home and you were there with a woman. Granted, she left," I ramble, talking animatedly with my hands, "but I saw you."

He lowers his head, but not before I miss the shame swimming in his eyes. "I was in a bad place. A really fucking bad place and I was being an asshole because I was hoping you'd see. I wanted to push you away. I didn't want you wasting your love on me when I felt like all the good in me had left. I wouldn't have gone through with it. I never planned to." He rubs his jaw, the muscle clenching at the memories. "I'm not saying I haven't gone on any dates in all this time—mostly in a vain hope that maybe I'd feel some sort of spark—but I haven't had sex with anyone."

I blink.

Blink again.

Surely, I haven't heard him right.

There's no way.

He gently pushes my jaw back up. "Don't want you catching flies like that."

"You haven't had sex in six years?"

Stunned. I'm completely speechless. There's no way. This has to be a joke, right?

"No."

"I ... whoa ... *wow*." I'm having a hard time wrapping my head around this and then I start laughing, because this means— "The last time you had sex you got me pregnant. You really went all out, didn't you?"

Even he has to snicker at that. Sobering, he clears his throat. "Were you alone when you found out?"

Shaking my head, I stretch my legs out fully and adjust my dress around my legs. "I was with Lauren."

His eyes drop to the blanket. "Good. I'm glad you had someone. You had to be scared."

"Terrified." I laugh, and I'm glad I can find the humor in the situation now. I was so worried about becoming a mom so young, especially pregnant by a man who was going through such a tragedy. "I never missed my birth control, but Seda didn't get the memo. That girl is a force of nature."

He smiles, sadness in his eyes. "I can't wait to meet her."

"I don't know what I'd do without her."

"And Caleb ... he's been good to you? Good to her?" He looks away from me as soon as the words leave his mouth. He never liked Caleb much before, so I can't imagine how he feels now, but he's handling it, all of this, better than I could've ever expected.

"The best."

His eyes shoot back to mine, brows furrowed. "I remember what you said before, but I have to ask again, why did you get divorced?"

I rub the blanket between my thumb and index finger, seeking a small amount of comfort in the gesture to get me through this. "I didn't lie to you then—when I gave my heart away to you, I never fully got it back, and I realized that I would never be able to love Caleb the way he loved me. It was infinitely unfair to him, and I couldn't do that. I was already planning to file when he told me he was ready for us to have a baby. He wanted Seda to be a big sister and I just—" I close my eyes, treacherous tears leaking from the corner. I feel his fingers collect my tears in a gentle caress, but I don't dare open them. When his touch disappears, I continue on. "Caleb is a better person than I am, and I couldn't..." I shake my head. "He deserves to find the love I had once, because he won't have that with me. I think if I had never met you, we could've had a beautiful life together, but the fact of the matter is, I did meet you and that changes everything." He flinches like I've slapped him. "Oh, Thayer." Now I'm the one reaching out to touch him. I place my hand on his cheek and he puts his over mine.

"I've really ruined your life, haven't I?" He says it with a hint of humor, but I know he's aching at the thought of it.

I shake my head. "No, Thayer, that's not what I meant at all." Stroking my thumb over his cheek, I go on. "You taught a broken, abused girl what love is *supposed* to feel like. Before that, I had no idea what to base it on. Falling for you was the most confusing, all-consuming thing I've ever done. I don't regret it. I never have."

He exhales a breath and it's like he loses a hundred pounds with it. "I've worried a lot, over the years about how you felt toward me—if you ended up feeling like I took advantage of you or something. Especially with your history." He shakes his head sadly. "I didn't want to have been a cause of more trauma in your life."

"Trust me, Thayer—" I'm not sure I'll get used to being able to say his name again. "You're one of the best things to ever happen to me. No regrets." Dipping a piece of bread in oil, I venture to ask, "After Laith came ... what happened? You were in a bad place. It worried me. Leaving you was the hardest thing I've ever done."

He sets his food aside and lays down on his side, propping his head in his hand. A curl falls over his forehead, my fingers twitching with the desire to push it back, but I keep my hands to myself. I want to take things slow. Thayer and I ... it's so *easy,* so right with him, and that makes it feel difficult to go at a speed that's necessary.

"Mostly he yelled at me—which I needed. Told me I was a waste of space and a shame to my son's memory." He takes a deep breath, the pain of that loss always hard to bear. "It worked. I started grief counseling and learned to channel my emotions in healthier ways."

"Like what?" I ask, curiously.

His cheeks turn the barest hint of pink. "Crafts ... and stuff."

"Crafts?" I repeat, trying not to smile. "Care to elaborate for me?"

The pink in his cheeks deepens until he's full-blown blushing. "Well, my therapist had me try out some different things until something stuck."

"You're really going to make me pull this out of you, aren't you?" He says something in a rush of words that is impossible to decipher. "Huh?"

Slowing down, he says, "Sewing, okay? I started sewing

dog bows for Winnie and that morphed into dog clothes."

I stare at him, stunned.

Did this lumberjack looking man just tell me he sews clothing for his dog? I can't possibly have heard him right.

"She said I had to find something that wasn't already something I enjoyed, so that knocked out a lot of things like carpentry, plants, puzzles," he starts ticking things off on his fingers, "camping—"

"You like camping?"

I hate that I'm practically panting at the visual of Thayer in the outdoors. A shirtless Thayer chopping wood? Sign. Me. Up.

I suddenly have a desire to go camping.

"I love it," he says with a grin, his eyes lighting up. "I go a lot. You should come with me sometime?"

"Are there bathrooms?"

His smile grows bigger. "There are trees."

I sigh dramatically on purpose, fighting a smile. "I guess that could work."

"You'd seriously go camping with me?" Now, he chooses to look doubtful.

"Sure, why not?" I set my plate aside and lay down on my side, mimicking his pose.

"Huh. I guess I thought that wouldn't be something you'd enjoy."

"You don't know until you try."

"You never went camping as a kid?"

I snort at that. "No, definitely not."

"I'll take you sometime. I know it's hard right now with your mom, but I promise someday we'll go."

"I'd like that."

And it's crazy, but I really would.

The sun starts to set in the distance, and I'm surprised by how much time has passed. Thayer must be too, because he sits up and starts gathering our plates up.

"I better get you home before it gets any later."

I help him pack everything away, and we make the trek back through the muddy grass to his truck.

"I want to see those bows and outfits of Winnie's sometime."

He shakes his head. "Never gonna live it down, am I?"

"No," I laugh lightly, "definitely not."

In the truck he holds my hand, our fingers wrapped firmly together. I keep looking at them, his skin, a golden-tan against my paler tone, and I can't help thinking to myself how I never want to let go again.

Thayer drops me off in my driveway, giving me a peck on my cheek. A part of me is disappointed after the kiss we shared previously, but I realize he's trying to take things slow with us.

Letting myself into the house, I find my mom asleep already and Georgia sitting in the chair crocheting a pair of baby booties.

Never thought I'd see the day that my sister was doing such a thing, but here we are. It makes me smile, seeing her so happy and content with her family. She deserves all the happiness in the world.

She makes a shushing motion with her finger when she sees me in the doorway, as if I hadn't already noticed mom's sleeping form.

"How'd it go?" She mouths the words.

"Amazing," I mouth back.

She smiles, tucking the booties back into her bag. She stands up, pressing a hand to her lower back. She points to the kitchen, and I follow her.

"It's not even that late and I'm ready to crash." She yawns, covering her mouth with her hand. "But I expect a full report on this date later, you hear me?"

"Yes." I stick my tongue out playfully. "How was Mom?"

"The usual." She shrugs, biting her lip. "I don't think she has much time left." Her eyes dart helplessly to the living room. "I know she's fighting to hang on as long as she can, but ... I think it's coming soon. Doing what I do, you start to sense it after a while."

I close my eyes and nod. "I hate this."

"Me too."

I open my arms and my sister returns the gesture. We hold on tight, united in our pain and grief. It's so difficult mourning someone who isn't even gone yet—it feels like a betrayal in a way, even though she knows it's coming too.

"I've gotta go." She pulls away, dabbing beneath her eyes with a finger. "I'll talk to you tomorrow. Probably stop by too. I want to spend as much time with her as I can."

I open the door and see my sister out to her car.

Standing on the driveway, I watch her pull away. Before turning to go back inside, I hear the clinking sound of a dog collar and spot Thayer with Winnie across the street.

A big pink bow is around her neck.

Like he can feel the weight of my eyes, he looks over at me and lifts a hand in a wave.

I smile, and it feels good despite the heaviness in my heart.

CHAPTER TWENTY-FOUR

Salem

The next morning, I'm sitting on the front porch with my mom after eating breakfast, knowing I have to drop a bomb on her. Despite the already warm day, there's a blanket draped over her lap. She rubs the material between her fingers like she's trying to memorize the sensation. Across the street, she watches some kids playing in the front yard with their golden retriever. I wonder what she's thinking, but I don't want to ask.

"Mom," I say softly, getting her attention. I wrap my fingers tighter around my cup of orange juice, trying to brace myself for what I'm about to tell her. "There's something I have to tell you."

Her eyes slowly move to where I sit in the rocking chair beside hers. "What is it?" She looks curious, alert.

"You know Seda isn't Caleb's biological child, but I never told you who her father is."

"And you've waited until I'm on my deathbed to tell me?" She's amused, not a hint of anger, but I still feel bad.

"It never seemed like the right time," I admit. "It's stupid, I know, but I don't think I knew how to handle a lot of this. Getting pregnant wasn't a part of my plan, and then I got back with Caleb. We were married, and it all just..."

"Life passes in a blink." She covers my hand with hers,

her skin cool to the touch despite the warmth of the outdoors. "Time is strange, the way it feels like not much has passed but then you realize it's actually been an entire lifetime."

"Yeah." I tuck a piece of hair behind my ear with my free hand.

"Why do you want to tell me now?"

"Because it should've never been a secret." I duck my head with shame. "I was scared, and angry, and I just ... I didn't handle things the way I should have."

"You were young, Salem. We all do stupid stuff, even when we're older. What matters is that you *learn* from it."

I swallow past the lump in my throat. "I fell in love with someone older than me," I start the story. "He didn't take advantage of me, I promise you that, but it was intense. I had never felt anything like it before. I didn't *know* I could feel things the way he made me feel them. I thought I knew love, but he showed me everything I thought I knew was wrong." I take a deep breath. This is harder than I thought it would be. "I fell hard and fast. I thought I'd get over him, but I never have." I wipe away a tear that tracks down my cheek. I make myself say it, put it out into the universe and make it real. "Thayer is her father."

She stares at me for a long moment, never breaking my gaze.

Nothing at all could possibly prepare me for the words that come out of her mouth.

"I know."

"You know?" I flounder to understand how she could possibly know. "How?"

She shakes her head. "Well, I couldn't be certain he was Seda's father, but I did notice resemblance and as far as your relationship with him ... honey, I'm your mother. I know you thought you were being sneaky, but you really weren't. I figured it out pretty quickly."

"And you never said anything because?"

"Because you were happy. After everything, why would I try to take that away from you? I'm not saying I *liked* it, but I understood it."

"And you ... all these years you've been friends with him since I left, why?"

"Because he needed a friend." She shrugs like it's so simple. "And he knew that I knew, so I think he felt safe talking to me."

My jaw drops at that. Here I thought I was the one who was going to be dropping bombs on my mom and it's reversed. "When did he know?"

"Forrest's birthday that year."

I sit back in the rocker, stunned. "Wow. I wasn't expecting this."

"I never told him about Seda or that I suspected she was his. It wasn't my secret to tell."

"I told him. He knows now. He wants to meet her." I run my fingers through my hair, trying to gather my breath. "I really made a clusterfuck of things, didn't I?"

She doesn't say anything for a moment, so long in fact that I think maybe she's not going to say anything at all. But then she says, "We all make messes, Salem. It's how we deal with them that matters."

I lower my head. "I'm trying to make things right."

"You'll get there, my girl." She rubs my hand, trying to soothe me. She's the one dying, but she's comforting me, because even now she can't stop being a mother. "I believe in you." She grows quiet after a while and I think she might doze off, so it surprises me when she speaks again. "I know we don't talk about what your father did, but trauma like that lingers. For you, for me, for Georgia. It affects your mind and choices you make. I don't think it's something therapy can fully erase. That means, sometimes, you're not going to handle things the way a normal person would. Trauma is deep-rooted and sometimes we don't even realize how it's influencing us."

"I never thought about it like that."

"Just don't let it affect you too much. I see the way that man looks at you and you look at him. A love like that ... it doesn't come around again. You deserve to be happy. Let yourself have that—because that's another effect of trauma."

"What is?"

She looks down sadly, and I think she might be thinking of herself. "Self-sabotage. Thinking you don't deserve certain things because you're dirty, tainted."

"Mom." My heart breaks for the woman at my side, who dealt with a bastard like my father and now sits at the end of her life much too soon.

She sniffles, her eyes watery. "Don't worry about me, baby girl. But when I'm gone, promise me you'll remember the things I say."

"I promise." My voice is soft, barely audible. It's like my voice has fled me. I hate talking about this, the inevitably of her death. But it's here. Staring all of us in the face.

You have to be strong, I tell myself.

I'm tired of it, though, always being the one who has to keep myself together.

Eventually, we all have to break.

CHAPTER TWENTY-FIVE

Salem

My nerves are at an all-time high when Caleb's Mercedes pulls into the driveway. I've had a whole week to prepare for this moment, even made a drive back to Boston to explain in person to Seda that she was finally going to meet her father.

"And my brother too?" She had asked me, and I promised to take her to his grave so she could say hello.

"My hands are sweating," I whisper to my mom at my side on the front porch.

"Mine would be too."

"Mommy!" Seda rolls down her window and waves.

I smile despite my nerves. That girl can quiet every ridiculous thought in my head. I talked to Lauren on FaceTime for over two hours last night while she tried to calm me down through intermittent fits of laughter. I warned her if she didn't stop laughing at me, I wouldn't be her maid of honor for her wedding in a few months. She only laughed harder since we both knew it was an empty threat.

Seda unbuckles her seatbelt, launching herself out of the car and into my arms before I can reach her.

"There's my girl." I wrap her tight in my arms, inhaling the scent of her kid shampoo.

"Daddy said this is where you grew up. He said you both

used to sit on the roof."

"We did." I tweak her nose playfully. "But don't think I'm going to let you sit on it."

She giggles, spinning in a circle. "Daddy! Show me the roof!"

Caleb comes around the side of the car, tucking his phone in the pocket of his pants. He gives me a small smile, ruffling Seda's hair. "She wanted to hear all about us when we were teenagers the whole drive," he explains. "It's right there, sweetie." He points out the spot on the roof to her and she smiles.

"That's so cool. I wish I could do that."

"And give me a heart attack?" I counter. "I don't think so."

Behind me in her chair on the porch my mom laughs. "Payback," she says loud enough for me to hear.

Caleb scoops Seda into his arms, her eyes round and big as she continues to look around. "Whoa, Mommy! Look! That house has a treehouse!" She points out the structure in Thayer's backyard. "That's so cool. Do you think I could play in it?"

Caleb's eyes meet mine, but he says nothing.

"I'm sure we can ask." I brush my fingers through her blonde hair.

I've waited for this day for a long time, for her to meet Thayer, for him to meet her. I always knew it was inevitable and as much as it terrified me, I looked forward to it too. And now that day has come.

"Do you need to use the potty?" Caleb asks her, setting her back on her feet.

"No, Daddy." She rolls her eyes with a huff. "I peed before we left and I don't have to do number two either, so don't ask."

My mom cackles. "I hope you two are ready for the teen years with her."

Caleb salutes her jokingly. "Thanks for the vote of confidence, Allison."

Seda starts up the front porch to my mom, hugging her tightly. "Hi, Grandma. I missed you. Did you make cupcakes?"

We all laugh, because of course Seda has sweets on the brain. "Your mom and I might've made some." She winks at her granddaughter. "Why don't we go get one?" She starts to get up, struggling a bit. I move to help her, but she waves me off. She heads inside with Seda, Caleb and I watching them go.

"She doesn't look good," he says mournfully beside me. "She already looks way worse than when you guys visited."

"I know."

He can hear the raw pain in my voice and quickly wraps his arms around me, rubbing his hands up and down my back. "I'm sorry, Salem." He rests his chin on top of my head. "I wish I could make this better."

"I have to enjoy what time I have left." It's a shitty fact, and the worst part is every day my mom is in more pain. I'm not sure there's any joy in her final days for her at all.

"I'm going to head over to my parents. I don't want to be in the way for this."

"You're not in the way." I step back from his embrace. "I'm not going to send you away either. If you want to be here you can stay."

He shakes his head. Clearing his throat, he says, "I think it'll be better for me if I'm not."

"All right." I won't push him to do anything he's not comfortable with. As long as he knows I'm not pushing him away from Seda, that's all that matters.

"Hey."

We both turn at the sound of Thayer's deep voice. He stands

at the end of the driveway. His hands are in his pockets, eyes watching us curiously. But he doesn't look jealous or irritated seeing me standing so close to Caleb.

"She's inside," I tell him. "Caleb's getting ready to leave."

"I'm glad I caught you then." He walks closer, stopping in front of my ex-husband.

Caleb gives me a curious look and I shrug, because I truly don't know what's going on.

Thayer holds out a hand to Caleb. My ex eyes it warily, like a snake he's not quite sure is poisonous or not. He looks back at me, gauging my reaction. With a sigh, he takes the offered hand, and I think we're both more than a little shocked when he pulls Caleb into a hug.

"Thank you," Thayer says, an overwhelming amount of emotion in those two words. "Thank you for taking care of them."

"I didn't do it for you," Caleb responds, not in offense but more as a statement—a reminder that he did it for us.

"I know, but that doesn't mean I'm not grateful."

Caleb nods, clearing his throat. I think he might be a little choked up. "All right ... okay ... you're ... welcome, I guess." I press my lips together, so I don't laugh. It's kind of cute how flustered he is. "I'm going to head out."

He points at his car and says goodbye. Thayer and I stand on the driveway side by side watching him back out.

"Fancy car," he remarks, watching the Mercedes disappear down the street. "Yours, too." He points at my Range Rover.

"It sure beats my old clunker, but I did love that thing."

He looks at the spot where it used to be parked in front of the house on the street, like if he stares hard enough, he can bring it back.

"I sold it," I ramble, feeling the desire to fill the silence for once with him. "I didn't need it in Brooklyn, and it made sense to have the extra money since I was..."

"Since you were pregnant," he fills in the blanks for me.

"Are you ready to meet her?"

He looks at me through thick lashes, nervous excitement in his brown-eyed gaze. "Yeah." A tiny smile graces his lips. "Yeah, I am."

"Come on then." I hold my hand out to him. He takes it, holding on so tight it's like I'm a buoy and he's been adrift at sea, desperate to find something to keep him afloat.

Up the porch steps we go, the screen door creaking when I open it.

"Mommy!" Seda comes running from the kitchen, cupcake in hand and frosting all over her face. "This one is my favorite! Grandma said it's cookie dough!"

Thayer's hand goes limp in mine.

He's seen photos. He knows what she looks like. But there's a vast difference in looking at an image and staring at the living, breathing person in front of you.

When I was pregnant with her, I used to think about what would happen if I was able to reunite with Thayer before I gave birth. How he might look at her when she entered the world.

He wears the exact expression I dreamed of now—one of wonder and surprise, like someone who has just discovered one of the world's greatest secrets.

I can almost hear his thoughts—how she looks like us, how she's this beautiful little light in the world. She's precious. The world is infinite in the eyes of our child. She's the reminder that there's always good somewhere in life.

Thayer looks at me, his eyes filled with awe. I can tell he

doesn't know what to say to her.

But Seda doesn't need prompting. Tilting her head to the side, her small pink tongue licking the icing from around her mouth, she blurts, "Are you my dad? My mommy said I was going to meet my dad today. Did you give me DVD? No ... that's not right, what did you call it, Mommy?"

"DNA," I correct. I move behind her, pulling her soft blonde hair behind her shoulders and facing Thayer. "And, yes, baby. This is him."

Thayer clears his throat, crouching down on one knee so he's more her height. "Hi." He offers his hand to her to shake if she wants.

She stares at his outstretched hand. I don't urge her to take it. That's her decision to make. Slowly, carefully, she shakes his hand and lets hers drop quickly back to her side.

"Mommy said when she had me you were in a bad place and weren't ready to be my dad."

Thayer looks up at me briefly and back to her. "That's right. You know about your brother?" When she nods, he goes on. "I was in a bad place after he died. It's not easy for parents to lose their child."

She reaches out, placing her small hand gently on his cheek. "It's okay. I'll help you."

He smiles, putting his hand over top of hers. His big hand completely swallows the small one beneath it. "I'm sure you will."

Seda's eyes flicker up to meet mine before she refocuses on Thayer. "Mommy says I'm so special I got two daddies to love me. Is that true? Do you love me?"

Thayer visibly swallows. "Yeah." I can hear how choked up he is in the way his voice breaks. "It's true. I love you."

The love of a parent is so beautiful in that way—how you can look at your child and see *everything*. It makes me wonder how people like my father ever exist. It feels like it goes against the laws of nature.

He reaches out with his other hand, giving her plenty of time to step away or say no to his touch when he puts his hand on her cheek the same way she has hers on his.

My heart beats rapidly and I fight back tears.

Turning away from the sight, I step outside to catch my breath. I don't want Seda to see me break down and think she's done something wrong, because it's the complete opposite. She's so kind and open-hearted. She's able to trust and understand so much and I love that about her. I love that she'll never be tainted by the darkness my own childhood endured.

Sitting down on the porch steps, I glance over my shoulder when I hear the door open. Thayer steps out and settles beside me.

"Why did you come out here? You didn't have to follow me."

He drapes his arms over his knees. "I know."

"Then why did you?"

"I was worried about you."

"About me?" I laugh incredulously. "Why?"

"You tell me." He nudges my arm with his. "What's on your mind?"

"Just mad at myself," I mumble, watching a bumble bee buzz near some marigolds around the walkway.

"Mad at yourself?" His face twists in confusion. "Why?"

"Because I kept her from you. It wasn't right. Not for her and not to you, either."

Thayer sighs, leaning back on his elbows and stretching

his legs out on the stairs. "I've lost out on six years with our daughter." I wince at that. It's a punch to the gut, but it's a truth and those are always the hardest to hear. "That fucking sucks, Salem, and yeah, it's shitty that you kept her from me—but we all have our reasons for the things we do. I can't go back in time and change your mind, so things work out differently. This is the reality we're dealing with and I'm not going to waste my time being mad about the past. You're back, Salem—and that's a chance I swore to myself I wouldn't throw away. And that kid in there? She's a miracle as far as I'm concerned. Let's not linger on the could-have-beens, okay? I want to move forward—do you want that?"

"So much."

"All right, then." He holds his hand out to me. "Let's shake on it. The past belongs to the past and the future is ours for the taking."

I slip my hand in his with a wobbly smile. "Ours."

With his hand still on mine, he helps me up and we head back inside to our daughter.

CHAPTER TWENTY-SIX

Thayer

"This is the best spaghetti I've ever had, Mommy." Seda chews on a meatball on the end of her fork.

"I'm happy you like it, sweetie." Salem eyes the takeout containers in the trash from the dinner I had delivered to her house. My lips twitch with the threat of a smile. I can almost hear her mind spinning from here, wondering why our daughter prefers restaurant spaghetti over something she'd make from scratch.

"Seda," I say, getting her attention. "What's your favorite color?"

She wrinkles her nose. "Rainbow, but mommy says that's a thing not a color, so pink then."

My heart beats a little faster. Just like I had guessed. It makes me feel good that even from some photos I was able to guess something about her.

"What about your favorite food?"

She sticks her tongue out in thought, but it takes her no time to decide. "Strawberry ice cream. Ooh, Grandma, do you have strawberry ice cream?"

Before her grandma can reply, Salem says, "You already had a cupcake, remember?"

"That was before dinner. It doesn't count."

My shoulders shake with laughter. Leaning into Salem, my lips brush her ear. "She really is my kid."

Her eyes sparkle. "Definitely."

As we eat, I continue to ask Seda questions to get to know her. I can't help but smile when she starts turning questions around on me.

"You have a treehouse." She pushes her empty plate away. "Can I play in it?"

Salem looks at me, worried about how I might react to this question. It doesn't upset me. If anything, it makes me happy. I think Forrest would like knowing his little sister is as excited about it as he was. "Sure. Yeah. Let's clean the dishes and you can come over and check it out."

"Really?" Her eyes light up.

"I want you to see it," I insist. Beneath the table, Salem's hand finds my knee, giving it a light squeeze.

Seda can't clean things quick enough then. She jumps up, helping to clear the table and even tries to do the dishes but Salem helps her when water starts immediately sloshing on the floor. She does let her load the dishwasher on her own.

When the door closes on the dishwasher she starts jumping up and down. "Treehouse now?" Her eyes bounce between Salem and me. I helped get Allie settled in her bed while they cleaned up.

I look at my daughter, never wanting to take my eyes off her. "We can go now."

"Sweet." She grins up at me, grabbing my hand. I look down in surprise at her small one wrapped around my larger one.

Seda is so open and loving. She doesn't hesitate with her affection. I expected her to be shy, maybe even to be intimidated by me. But she's not. Kids are so much more resilient and accepting than we give them credit for.

Salem turns away, but not before I see the tears in her eyes. I hope they're good tears.

The three of us walk next door to my house and into the backyard. Seda looks around, taking in all the details. Her eyes grow round with excitement at the pool. "I love swimming!"

Salem senses the fear sliding through my veins.

"She's had extensive lessons since she was a baby and understands water safety. It was important to me."

Taking Salem's hand I give it a small squeeze, silently acknowledging my thanks. She smiles back, but it's a bit wobbly, and I know she's thinking about Forrest. That day left a scar on more people than just Krista and me.

Seda runs ahead of us to the treehouse. Her blonde hair is wavy, hanging halfway down her back. I see myself in her, but mostly she's a mini Salem. Looking at the woman beside me, my heart warms. She's been through more in her life than most people endure in a lifetime. She's strong and fierce—a fighter through and through. As much as I wish I could've been there for her when she was pregnant, been the man she needed, I think she was right in knowing that I wasn't capable of it. Not truly, anyway. I imagine I could've pretended for a while, but I was so checked out from myself, from *life*, for a long while after Forrest's passing. I hate that someone else had to step up to the plate that should've been mine, but I'm also so fucking glad she wasn't alone.

"Can I climb up?" Seda grabs onto the ladder that's secured to the treehouse and cemented into the ground.

"Go for it." I let her climb up on her own, but hover behind her in case she slips.

I'll be there to catch her—from now on that's where I'll belong, at my daughter's side guiding her through life.

She reaches the top and gasps. "Mom! There are bean bag chairs in here!"

Salem laughs, her hands in the back pockets of her shorts. The sun is almost completely set. Behind her fireflies start to glow sporadically.

"She loves bean bag chairs."

I arch a brow. "That so?"

"Yeah." She shakes her head, smiling at a memory. "She begged for one for her bedroom. I kept saying no, but I ended up giving in. She has a reading nook and so I put it there."

Seda pokes her head out of the entrance. "Are you guys coming up?"

"It's big enough," I tell Salem, in case she wants to go up.

"All right." She starts her climb, and I don't mean to, but I can't look away from her ass. It's perfect and round. I want to grab it and pull her back down, kiss her long and slow and make love to her. My body aches with the need. It's been too fucking long—six years too long—but I want to take things slow with her.

Once Salem is inside, I climb up.

With the three of us, it's crowded, but there's enough space for me to rest my back against the wall and spread my legs out.

Salem looks around taking it all in. It took a while to get it built since I took my time with every detail, but I'm proud of how it turned out. "This is really nice."

"Thanks."

"Forrest would love it."

"Forrest?" Seda asks curiously. "Is this his treehouse? Can I say hi?"

Salem brushes her fingers through Seda's blonde hair. "Forrest is your brother."

"Oh. So, he's ... gone?"

Salem nods sadly. "Yeah, baby, he's gone."

Seda turns her intelligent brown eyes to me. "Can I see a picture of my brother? Mommy didn't have any."

"Sure." I sit up, pulling my phone from my pocket and flip through my photos. "Here he is."

Seda studies the picture. "Do you think he would've liked me?" She addresses me, not Salem.

"I know he would have. He always wanted a sibling and a dog."

Her eyes light up. "Do you have a dog? We have a cat. He's kind of old though and sleeps a lot. His name is Binx."

My eyes find Salem's. She still has Binx. She gives a half-smile and shrugs.

"I have a dog. Her name is Winnie."

"That's cute. Can I meet her?"

"Sure."

Salem watches our interaction with a smile, tears shimmering in her eyes. I'm sure this is as emotional for her as it is for me.

"Can we go now?"

"If you want."

"I do."

She starts to move to climb out, but I shake my head. "Let me go first."

That way if she has any trouble I can help.

"Okay." She waits for me to crawl—yeah, I have to fucking crawl—to the opening and climb out. As soon as my feet touch the ground she's already on the second rung. She handles it like a champ, never needing my help. "Come on, Mommy. We're waiting for you."

Salem starts down the ladder, her foot catching on the second to last step.

"Oh," she cries, losing her balance.

I'm right there though, wrapping her in my arms and helping her down before she falls. She turns in my arms, her hands on my chest. Her big eyes look up at me, and I see the desire in them—I'm sure she can see the same in mine.

I've wanted this woman ever since she brought me cupcakes and rambled her way into my heart. When I look at her like this, it feels like no time at all has passed, like we were never separated. I think that's how you know a person is yours—when not time, nor distance, can lessen the love between you.

"Are you okay?" I ask, brushing a stray hair back from her forehead.

"Y-Yeah," she stutters, breathless.

The urge to kiss her is almost too much to bear. I think I'd give in if it weren't for Seda.

"Hurry up, you guys. I want to meet the doggy."

I set Salem fully on her feet. "Our daughter beckons," she says, her eyes never wavering from mine.

"I love the sound of that."

She wrinkles her nose in confusion. "Of her beckoning us?"

I shake my head. "Our daughter."

CHAPTER TWENTY-SEVEN

Salem

I wake up with a mouthful of Seda's hair.

"Ew," I gag, trying to get away from the wild tangle of hair in front of my face.

I put her in Georgia's room for the night, but at some point she climbed into bed with me and I let her. Soon, times like these where she comes to me for comfort will be long gone. I want to cherish them while I have them.

Rolling over, I pick up my phone from the nightstand and peer at the screen. There's a text from Thayer and Caleb. I open Caleb's first.

> **Caleb:** I'll pick Seda up at noon if that's okay.

I type back a reply.

> **Me:** That's fine.

I open Thayer's message next.

> **Thayer:** I thought I could pick you two up for breakfast and visit Forrest's grave. You mentioned last night that

she wanted to go by. If it's a bad idea,
it's fine.

Stifling a yawn, I look over my shoulder at her sleeping form.

Me: That's a great idea. I just woke
up. I have to get Sleeping Beauty up
too.

Thayer: Take your time.

Me: Caleb is going to pick her up
around 12.

His reply takes a little longer this time.

Thayer: Okay.

Setting my phone back down, I ease from the bed and go to the bathroom. I pee and brush my teeth, then quietly go downstairs to check on my mom. After I've helped her into the bathroom and dressed for the day, I go back up and wake up Seda.

"I want to sleep," she grumbles, holding on tighter to the pillow.

"We're going to go get breakfast and visit your brother's grave."

Her eyes pop open at that. "Really?"

"You said you wanted to go. Is that still true?"

She nods soberly. "I'm going to shower, so don't fall back asleep," I warn, tapping her nose.

She giggles, wiggling around. "I won't."

"Get dressed and go talk to grandma if you want."

"Okay!" She grins, kicking off the covers. She runs from my room to Georgia's where her overnight bag is.

Taking a quick shower, I hop out and wrap myself in a towel. I apply a bit of mascara to my lashes and gloss on my lips. I don't have time for anything else since I need to get dressed and check on Seda and my mom.

Pulling on shorts and a red tank top, I slip my feet into a pair of white sneakers. My hair is wet from my shower, so I decide to leave it down to air dry until we leave. Then I'll pull it back into a bun.

Downstairs I find Seda sitting beside my mom's hospital bed. They're both coloring and talking quietly. I can't help myself when I take my phone out and snap a photo to catch the sweet moment.

"Mommy!" Seda cries when she sees me. "Are we ready to go? I'm hungry. I want pancakes with chocolate chips and syrup and—"

I chuckle at her enthusiasm. "Take a breath, girl."

She pauses, inhaling a deep breath. "Grandma, are you going with us?"

My mom shakes her head. "No, sweetie. Not this time."

"Aw, that's too bad. But it's okay, I'll bring you back something."

My mom pats her hand gently. "You do that, sweetie."

"Can we keep coloring when I get back?"

"Sure, if you want."

"Your dad is picking you up at noon to go back to Boston," I tell her, padding into the kitchen. I open a yogurt for my mom, setting her pills in a bowl. It's mostly pain pills at this point, just trying to keep her feeling the best she can.

"Aw, man. I like it here," she says when I come back into the room.

"You'll be back. Don't worry."

My mom takes the pills with the yogurt, and I silently encourage her to eat the rest of it.

I can tell she doesn't want to, but she obliges.

When the yogurt cup is empty, I throw it away and send a text to Thayer that we're ready.

"We'll be back soon, Mom. Behave yourself. Georgia will be here in about fifteen minutes."

She sighs. "You two don't trust me by myself, do you?"

I laugh, kissing the top of her head. "No, we don't."

She studies the page she was coloring. "Have a good breakfast."

"I love you, Mom."

"I love you, too."

Seda wraps her arms as best as she can around her grandma. "Love you, grandma!"

"I love you, peanut." My mom kisses her cheek.

Taking Seda's hand, we step outside onto the front porch. I lock the door since Georgia will come in from the side.

"Mommy?"

"Yeah, baby?" I drop my keys in my purse.

"Why does grandma have to die? Why did my brother have to die?"

Having this conversation with a five-year-old is hard. I don't want to lie to her, but I have to explain it in a way she'll understand.

Crouching down, I grasp her arms gently in my hands. "Life is beautiful." I brush her hair back from her forehead. "It's running through fields of flowers, catching butterflies in the summer and snowflakes on your tongue in the winter. Death is just another part of life. It's inevitable for each of us. The great equalizer." She listens intently, taking in every word I say. "Death doesn't have to be seen as this scary thing. It's a beautiful reminder that each of our breaths, each heartbeat," I point to her chest, and she places her hand over her thrumming heart, "is a gift to cherish."

She stands before me, and I know she's thinking over what I said. "So, I should be happy for grandma?"

"You should be understanding—death is scary, especially for the people left behind. We feel the sadness and pain of loss."

"And grandma?"

"I'm sure she doesn't want to die, but she won't be in pain anymore."

"So," she twists her lips back and forth, "death is nicer than life then, right?"

"What do you mean, sweetie?"

"Well, I get a boo-boo and feel it. I cry and I get sad. But death takes that away so it can't be so bad."

I smile at her. "That's a great way of looking at things."

Stepping off the porch, I hold her hand and walk next door to Thayer's. He's coming out of his house. His hair is damp from a shower, curling around his ears. He's dressed in a pair of khaki cargo shorts and a green shirt. Butterflies take flight in my stomach just looking at him.

"Are you ladies ready for breakfast?" He pushes the button on his keyfob to unlock his truck.

"Yes! Yes!" Seda jumps up and down. "I want pancakes with chocolate chips and syrup and whipped cream and—" I place my hand gently on her hand to stop her bouncing around. She giggles, smiling up at me. "Sorry."

Thayer is grinning at the whole thing, his eyes lit up as he watches us. "Pancakes, got it."

"Oh, shoot," I smack my forehead, "let me grab her car seat." I turn to walk next door, but Thayer stops me.

"Already taken care of." He opens the back passenger door, revealing a booster seat almost exactly like the one in my own car. Except this one is bright pink. I picked one that matched my car's interior, but Thayer's chose one that's Seda's favorite color—well, second favorite after rainbow.

I am not going to cry over a car seat! I admonish myself.

"Oh, wow. Okay. When did you get this?"

"Last night." He says it so casually, like he didn't run out late at night and buy a whole booster seat for Seda. It's such a little thing in the scheme of things, but it means everything.

"Hurry up, you guys. I'm hungry." Seda climbs up into the back and in her seat. She buckles herself in, but just like I always do Thayer tightens the straps, making sure she's secure.

He closes the car door, arching a brow when he finds me standing there staring at him. "What? Did I do something wrong?"

"No." I shake my head slowly. "You do everything right. That's what is so annoying."

He laughs, crossing his arms over his chest. "Annoying? How so?"

"Because nobody else can measure up," I mutter, skittering around him to get in the car.

He doesn't let me go that easy. His warm hand closes around my wrist, spinning me around until I collide with his chest. "I don't do these things for that purpose. I would never try to ... to *bribe* my way into your good graces."

Shaking my head, I can't take my eyes off his hand around

my wrist. "I know that, Thayer."

He doesn't say anything, but I see it in his eyes.

He loves me. He still loves me as much as he did back then. It's never changed, but he won't say it because he won't push himself back into my life.

"We better go," I say, breaking the moment and gently pulling my arm from his. "Seda's hungry."

He nods, turning away with a mumbled, "Okay."

The two of us are quiet on the drive to the diner, but Seda entertains us telling Thayer stories about her school and her best friend Maddy. He takes in every word, memorizing every detail she gives him.

Thayer parks behind the diner. Almost immediately Seda is unbuckling herself, reaching for the door but it has kid safety locks so she can't get out.

"Open sesame," she groans, trying to force the door open. "I want pancakes in my tummy!"

Soberly, I warn Thayer, "She's a monster when she's hungry."

"It's too bad I ate my emergency Snickers."

"Chocolate chip pancakes, please!" She shakes the door handle again.

Putting her out of her misery, I get out of the truck and open her door. She climbs down, staying by my side since she knows better than to run off.

Thayer locks up the truck, the three of us heading inside the diner. This might be a small town, but this place is always busy. Several people look our way, and I know they're probably figuring out what's going on here.

It'll be all over town soon that not only did I just come back to town, but I had Thayer's love child at nineteen. This will fill the town's gossip quota for the next five years—at least.

You seat yourself, so Thayer leads us to a booth in the back. He slides in one side and I know he's expecting Seda to sit opposite him with me, but instead she chooses his side. His eyes dart from her to me with surprise.

I take my spot across from them and I know this is one of those times I'm taking a snapshot in my mind. I don't want to forget this, how perfect they look side by side.

"Can someone get me chocolate chip pancakes in this place?" Seda asks loud enough that almost the entire building hears. If they weren't already staring, they would be now.

"Seda, that's not how we ask for things we want."

"Oh, I forgot the please. Sorry."

I shake my head. She's right on forgetting that, but I was thinking more along the lines of using her inside voice.

"Well, well, well, look at you. I thought I'd never lay my eyes on the Salem Matthews again."

I smile up at Darla who was always my favorite waitress here. "Hi, how are you?"

"I'm good." She nods, her eyes bouncing around the three of us. "This one yours?" She points at Seda.

"Yeah." I grin proudly. "She's mine."

"And … Caleb's?" It's a presumptuous question, rather rude actually, but I know she doesn't mean any harm. That's how people in small towns are—your business is everyone's business.

"I assume you mean biologically?"

"Y-Yes?" She stutters it out as a question.

"Then the answer is no. Thayer," I wave my hand at him, "is her biological father. If everyone must know he wasn't aware of that until very recently. Caleb is her dad too, he's raised her, and that's that."

I keep my chin high, refusing to cower from these people.

Across from me, Seda's lips puff out with frustration. "Why do all these old people care who my daddy is? I have two daddies because I'm twice as special as all of you. *Now* can I have my chocolate chip pancakes?"

And with that statement from her, the volume in the diner picks up as people return to their food and coffee. Leave it to Seda to put people in their place.

CHAPTER TWENTY-EIGHT

Thayer

The situation at the diner wasn't the best, but Salem handled it like a champ just like she does everything.

Once all of us are full, I take my girls to the local flower shop to let Seda pick out flowers for Forrest's grave. I expect her to run around excitedly looking at all the pretty flowers, but I'm learning Seda rarely does what I expect. Instead, she quietly meanders the tiny shop, carefully peering at every flower and being careful not to touch.

"You're smiling," Salem says at my side. "What are you thinking about?"

Tilting my head her way, I tell her, "That I'm a lucky bastard. I got to have breakfast with my girls—and I fucking love the sound of that. My girls," I repeat, my smile growing when Salem blushes.

She tucks a piece of hair behind her ear. "You think I'm yours, huh?"

"Think? No, baby, I know. I knew then and I know now—you're mine in the same way I'm yours. I don't own you, but you're my perfect fit—the puzzle piece I didn't know I was missing."

Her eyes soften, lips curling into a soft shy smile. She likes what I said and I meant every word.

Up ahead, Seda points at a bunch of flowers. "These."

It's a ready-made bouquet filled with sunflowers, eucalyptus, and small purple wildflowers similar to the one I suspect Salem left on Forrest's grave.

I grab up the bunch and carry it to the checkout counter. "We'll take these."

After it's paid for, I hand them over to Seda for safe keeping.

Salem stands off to the side, watching me interact with our daughter. I can see the guilt in her eyes, the worry that she really fucked things up. I wish I could get rid of those thoughts for her. Because no matter what happened before, we're here now.

Caleb has her past, but I have her future. That's all that matters to me.

"Come on, ladies, we don't have much time."

We load back into my truck, heading the short distance to the cemetery. We were at the diner longer than I expected and since Caleb is picking Seda up at noon I want to make sure we're back on time. It irks me to know I have to hand off my kid, but I don't want to step on Caleb's toes. I know in the long run it's better to keep our relationship cordial.

At the cemetery Seda hops out of the truck and stands there stoically. "It's quiet here," she whispers.

"Cemeteries are almost always quiet. I guess that's why they call it the final resting place."

"Hmm," she hums. Salem reaches across Seda's car seat and grabs the flowers, passing them to her. "Can you hold them?" My little girl asks me. "They're too big for my little hands." She holds up her hands, wiggling her fingers.

I take the flowers from Salem, surprised when Seda fits her hand into my empty one and her other into one of her mom's.

Seda doesn't know me—not really, anyway—but she has such an open loving heart that she doesn't hesitate to show affection.

The three of us walk hand in hand through the freshly mowed grass. I spot Forrest's grave up ahead and point it out to Seda.

"That one right there. That's your brother."

She looks up at me with big brown eyes—*my eyes*. I'm not sure I'll ever get used to that.

"Do you think he would have liked me?" She's already asked this before. It must be a question weighing on her mind.

"I know he would have loved having a little sister like you."

"I wish I knew him," she says softly as we finally reach the gravestone. She lets go of our hands and takes the flowers from me with a grunt. "Here you go, Forrest." She puts the flowers beside the grave. "I picked these out just for you. They're so pretty. I hope you like them." Seda looks up at us for support, like she's questioning whether or not she's doing this right. When I nod, she goes on. "I love dinosaurs—my mommy says you loved them too. That's cool. Do you have TV where you are? You probably don't, but if you do there's this show—"

Salem and I sit down in the grass a few feet away, giving Seda space to talk to her brother. I stretch my legs out, Salem scooting close enough to me that our legs touch and she rests her head on my shoulder.

This ... it feels like a dream.

I accepted my fate, that she'd never be mine, but the universe has given us another chance and I can't help but think it's because it was always supposed to be us.

"She's pretty amazing, huh?" She whispers the question so only I can hear.

I smile, watching our little girl sit cross-legged with Forrest, chatting animatedly like he's right there beside her.

"She's perfect."

***

Caleb's shiny Mercedes sits in the driveway when we get back. I try not to let that piss me off. I need to be a mature ass adult about this.

"Daddy!" Seda cries excitedly from the backseat.

I feel a tiny sting in my chest, because that excitement isn't for me. I have to earn it, just like he did.

I park my truck on the street in front of my house. Caleb walks over, scooping up Seda when she jumps out.

"There's my girl." He spins her around.

My frustration melts a tiny bit, because I see how much he loves Seda. He loves her as if she really was his own—that's more than a lot of people are capable of.

He sets her down and turns to me, holding out his hand. "How's it going?"

I know I blindsided him yesterday thanking him for taking care of them, because let's face it, when he was a teenager heading off to college I wasn't exactly his biggest fan. But I guess we're both trying to put our best foot forward and be decent about this.

"I'm good." I shake his hand. "How was your night?"

"Good," he laughs. "My mom was happy to see me." I turn just in time to see Salem roll her eyes. "My mom doesn't like Salem," Caleb explains.

Salem huffs. "She liked me just fine when she thought we weren't that serious. But when you didn't break up with me that summer after senior year she got scared." She looks up at me, and finishes, "She's one of those boy moms that can't let go."

Caleb laughs more fully this time. "You're not wrong."

Salem goes on to add, "She definitely didn't like it when Caleb took Seda on as his own."

Caleb squeezes Seda's shoulders lightly. "Her loss, because this is the most awesome girl in all the land." He picks her up again, spinning her. Seda's giggles fill the air. When he sets her back down, he says, "I haven't seen my parents much the past few years so I'm trying to make some effort, but it isn't easy."

Salem gives him a sympathetic smile.

"I'm sorry she's the way she is."

Caleb shrugs. "Don't be, she could change. Anyway," he taps Seda on the head, "are you ready to go?"

"Yeah! Can we go to Target? There's a new princess toy I want and—"

"I'll think about it."

To me, Salem whispers, "He's going to stop. He's a sucker for whatever she wants."

"Hey," Caleb chortles, "I heard that."

"Well, it's true." Salem lets her hair down from the bun she had it in, and I must be a fucking pervert because even her hair turns me on, swaying around her shoulders.

Or maybe it's just that I really need to get laid.

Six years is a long time to be celibate, but honestly it didn't seem so bad until I saw her again. Now, I'm horny twenty-four-seven. Going to job sites with a boner is kind of awkward and hard to explain.

"I'll go get her bag so you can be on your way."

"I already got it. Georgia let me in, and I wanted to say bye to your mom anyway."

"Oh, okay." She bends down and opens her arms up to Seda. "Bye then, my little munchkin."

Seda dives into her, wrapping her arms around Salem's shoulders. "I love you, Mommy. I'm gonna miss you so much."

Salem lets her go and holds her fingers up. "How much is so much? This much?"

"No, more!" Seda giggles. "Like *this* much." She opens her arms wide.

Salem pulls her into a hug again, burying her face in Seda's neck. "I love you, baby girl."

"Love you too, Mommy. Now let me go. You're squishing me."

Salem releases her, standing back up. "You guys better go so you miss traffic."

Caleb rolls his eyes. "There's always traffic."

She laughs. "This is true."

Crouching down, I say to Seda, "Be good. I hope you can come back soon."

She nods eagerly. "I want to go in the treehouse again. That was fun."

"When you come back I promise you can play in the treehouse as much as you want."

"Awesome! Thanks, Dad!"

I don't expect a hug goodbye from her, but she wraps her little arms around my neck and squeezes me.

Fuck, I'm getting choked up.

With the goodbyes said, Caleb loads her in the car with Salem and I, watching from the sidewalk when he backs out and leaves. He gives a honk of his horn before the car disappears from view.

Salem lets out a heavy sigh. "I miss her already. It's like a limb is missing."

"I know," I murmur, thinking not only of Seda but Forrest too.

Sympathy fills her eyes, no doubt thinking about Forrest now. Her hand finds its way to mine and she gives a small squeeze.

She doesn't say anything. She doesn't have to. Sometimes saying nothing is just as meaningful as saying everything.

CHAPTER TWENTY-NINE

Salem

It's late and I'm exhausted. I want nothing more than to fall face first into my bed, but I want to see Thayer more.

The last week with my mom has been rough.

The time is coming.

She knows it.

I know it.

Georgia knows it.

I'm terrified for her to take her last breath, leaving this realm for good, but I don't want her to hurt anymore. She's in so much pain that even morphine isn't doing a great job masking it, but it does make her sleep a lot which helps.

Walking next door, I climb his porch steps to ring the doorbell. The urge to sneak over here was hard to resist, but I reminded myself I'm an adult now and there's nothing to hide. I'm single, Thayer's single—I'm twenty-five, he's thirty-seven.

The door opens. He doesn't say anything, just steps to the side to let me in.

"Hi." I rock back on my heels, suddenly feeling awkward now that I'm here.

"Hi," he says back, fighting a smile. "Do you want a glass of wine?"

I let out a soft laugh. "I'd love one."

I don't drink much, but right now it's exactly what I need.

Following him into the kitchen, I stare at the spot where we had our first kiss.

He stops in front of a cabinet. "Red or white?"

"Red."

He pours a glass, sliding it across the counter to me. Sitting on the barstool, I watch him pour his own glass and then make us a plate of crackers and cheese.

He settles beside me, his arm brushing mine in the process. A shiver runs down my spine. It's been so long since I've been touched by him in the way my body craves. Just one touch from him sends my body into flames. He notices the way I start to wiggle, his eyes narrowing. He sucks his cheeks in, I'm sure his ache is even worse than mine.

This man hasn't touched another woman for six whole years.

I wouldn't be mad if he had. I would've expected it. But the fact he didn't is one of the biggest turn-ons.

"Do you ... uh ... wanna talk?" He tries—and fails—to inconspicuously adjust his hard-on.

My mouth waters—and not because the wine is delicious, or I really like cheese.

I know he's asking about my mom, so I answer with, "Not really, but I probably should."

"You don't have to." He picks up a cracker, putting a slice of cheese on top.

"I know."

Thayer has never pushed me to do or say anything I didn't want to. I know people might look at our age difference and assume otherwise, especially with our past, but it's not true. Thayer is an alpha-male, but he understands my past and has always made sure I know who really has the control in our dynamic.

Sipping at the wine, we're quiet for a little while before I say, "I don't think she'll make it through the week."

Thayer hisses through his teeth. "Fuck." He scrubs a hand over the scruff on his cheeks and jaw. "I'm sorry, Salem. I don't really know what to say."

"We knew it was coming. It's not like it was a secret, but it feels so different now that it's here."

He surprises me when he puts his hand around the back of my neck, gently tugging me toward him. The ring on his pinky finger is cold against my skin.

"No matter what, Sunshine, I've got you."

A breath shudders through my whole body. It feels good—more than good—to hear him say that. His lips press tenderly to my forehead. My body sinks into him on a sigh. Thayer has this way about him that makes me completely melt. I feel *safe* with him.

When he releases me, I grab for his hand. "What's your ring?" As soon as the question is out of my mouth, I already know. The suns stamped onto it look up at me. "I thought I lost this," I murmur, tears burning my eyes. I trace my finger over the cool surface. "I threw it at you." I'm lost in the memory. "I went back the next morning, and it was gone."

There's a lump in my throat, because Thayer took it. He *kept* it all this time.

"I always meant to give it back."

"But I left for good," I fill in the blanks.

He nods, taking his hand from mine. He slips the ring off his pinky and grabs my left hand. I hold my breath when he slips it on my bare ring finger, bringing it up to his mouth to press a tender kiss to it.

"That stays on," he says with a low growl, "until I'm the one to take it off and replace it."

I wet my lips. "Is that so?"

"Yeah." His voice is deep and husky. I wiggle in my seat, pressing my thighs together. I'm aching to be filled. "Just to make things clear, Sunshine, so we don't have any misunderstandings—I fully plan to make you my wife."

My heart beats loudly and rapidly. "You want to marry me?" My voice is high and squeaky.

"I want more than to marry you."

"W-What does that mean?" The man has me so flustered I'm stuttering now.

"It means, I want to have more babies with you. I want to go on vacations with you. I want to cook meals in this kitchen and do stupid mundane shit like clean the fucking house together. I want your clothes with mine in the fucking laundry. I want to laugh and cry together. I want to hold you every night when you sleep. I want to kiss you goodnight and good morning. I want to make love to you slow and fuck you hard. I want to sit out on the front porch and rock on the swing. I want, not only to grow old with you, but to live life with you. I want it all."

I tackle the man.

Literally jump out of the stool I'm sitting in, where it falls with a loud bang to the floor and wrap my arms around his neck so I can kiss him. He holds me tight against him, kissing me back.

He stands up with me in his arms, my legs going around his waist.

His lips never leave mine as he sits my butt on the counter.

My hips grind against him and he puts his hands on them,

forcing me to still. I mewl in protest.

Need. I need him.

"Thayer," I plead between kisses.

His lips glide softly, delicately to my ear. "I want to take things slow," he reminds me.

Leaning back, I grip his shirt in my hand forcing him to look at me. "Fuck slow. I went six years without you. I want you. Today, tomorrow, fifty years from now, and even when we've turned to stardust." He smiles at my words. "Now, *please*, for the love of God—"

I don't have to finish my sentence. His mouth slants over mine, stealing my breath.

My hands skim beneath his shirt, feeling the heat of his stomach. His abdominals flex at my touch. I pull him closer, between my legs.

Kissing his way over to my ear, he murmurs, "You are everything to me."

Gliding a hand down my chest, between my breasts, he gently guides me to lie back. The stone is cold against my back, but I don't feel that way for long when he quickly undoes my jean shorts, sliding them down my legs to drop them on the floor.

I cry out at the first swipe of his tongue against my pussy. I slap a hand over my mouth, stifling my sounds. He senses this somehow, grabbing my arm to pull it away from my mouth. He wants to hear me. He works his tongue against me like a man who's been starved too long—which I guess in a way is true. His hand moves, and I see him palming himself over his sweatpants. I whimper at the sight. Thayer touching himself is a ridiculously big turn-on.

With his freehand he rubs my clit and between that and

the stimulation of his tongue, my orgasm spirals through me.

"*Yes, yes, yes!*" I cry out, the orgasm feeling never-ending.

When I finally come down from the high, my legs shaking, I climb off the counter and drop to my knees in front of Thayer.

I don't waste any time in freeing his cock from his sweatpants. He's big and hard and ready for me.

Biting my lip, I look up at him from beneath my lashes. "For the record, you're still the only man I've done this with."

I don't give him a chance to respond. Swiping my tongue over the bead of pre-cum and letting the slightly salty taste settle on my tongue.

His eyes are dark and hooded, his head dropping back with a soft, "*Fuck.*"

Swirling my tongue around his tip, I take him deeper, stroking his length with my hand. From the sounds he's making I must be doing an okay job. I haven't been sucking him off long when he pushes me back.

"I'm not coming in your mouth. Not tonight."

He gets on his knees, taking my face between his thumb and forefinger he pulls me into a rough kiss. He bites my bottom lip, quickly soothing the sting with a swipe of his tongue.

We rid ourselves of the last of our clothes, and then he's laying me down on the floor. He bends one of my legs, and slides into me with one hard thrust.

"Oh my God!" My nails scratch at his back searching for purchase.

His eyes are molten, taking me in beneath him. He traces his fingers lightly over the stretch marks on my stomach.

"I fucking love these." I blush at the compliment. He lays his hand over my stomach. "You grew our child in there. Your body loved her so much it always wanted to remember her." He trails his finger over the line of one and I nearly shiver. "You feel so good, baby. You've always felt like mine." He buries his head in my neck, pressing open-mouthed kisses to the sensitive skin there. I hold him tight, never wanting to let go—never wanting to forget this. The weight of his body on mine is a reminder, that this, us, is real.

"Keep going," I beg, tugging on his hair. "I'm almost there again."

He moans when my pussy squeezes around his cock. "Keeping doing that and I won't last long, Sunshine."

"Can't help it." I do it again. "You feel so good in me."

"Fuck, yes, I do." He rises above me, taking my neck in his hand and squeezing lightly. "That's because I was made for you. And—" He pumps into me harder—"you were made for me."

The sounds he's making are such a turn on. Knowing he's enjoying this, *hearing* his pleasure, is enough to send my second orgasm rattling through me.

"Fuck, baby." He squeezes my throat a little tighter. "I can't—" He grits his teeth, trying to stave off his release. "I have to—" He throws his head back, flicking his hair out his eyes. "Oh, *fuck*."

He comes long and hard, his body shaking from the force of his release. His sweat-dampened body drapes over mine, his hold on my neck slackening.

He rises up slightly, placing a tender kiss on my swollen lips.

"Wrecked," he struggles to get a breath. "You have completely, and utterly wrecked me."

We fall asleep like that, right on the floor—a tangle of limbs and promises of a tomorrow.

CHAPTER THIRTY

Salem

Georgia sleeps soundly on the couch, her hands cradled under her head, mouth hanging open. She can't be comfortable. I knew she wouldn't go home, so I told her to at least go upstairs and lay in bed. She didn't listen. She wanted to be here.

My mom inhales a struggled breath.

This last week, we've known this time was coming, and I feel it now.

I had dozed off asleep, but I woke up—sensing the time is imminent, probably within the next hour. Nudging Georgia awake, we climb awkwardly into the hospital bed on either side of her. I rest one of my feet on the floor. I want to be close to my mom, for her to know she's not alone.

Her eyes crack open the tiniest bit. "Hey, Mom," Georgia sniffles.

"M-y my girls," she says groggily, the two words so quiet they're barely audible.

"We're here." I take one of her hands, her skin paper thin. Georgia takes the other. "We're not going anywhere."

"L-Love you b-both."

"We love you too." Tears stream down my face.

"D-Don't be m-mad at the world g-girls." Her chest inflates with a breath, making her cough. "Be h-happy b-because I l-lived."

Georgia and I hold onto her tiny frail form, both of us crying, and less than twenty minutes later, the alarms on her monitors that she's been wearing the past few weeks sound, alerting us to the fact that she's really and truly gone.

"Bye, Mom," I sob brokenly. "I'll miss you every day."

"Love you," Georgia cries. "I hope you're not hurting anymore, Mom."

Our mom suffered so much in her life, a life that was much too short, and all we can do is hope that there really is a better place out there. Because if there's anyone who deserves it, it's her.

CHAPTER THIRTY-ONE

Thayer

The sound of sirens wakes me up from a dream, returning me to a nightmare. Every time I hear them now, I'm transported back to that dreadful day with Forrest. My stomach rolls as I get up from bed. Stumbling into the bathroom, I relieve myself and realize I still hear the sirens and they're *loud*.

Salem.

I yank on a pair of shorts, shoving my feet into a pair of shoes as I rush down the stairs. I don't even bother grabbing a shirt.

Rushing out the door, I see the ambulance is next door at her house.

I don't think, I just run over.

And there she is, standing on the driveway in her pajamas with her sister. They cry holding onto each other like if they let go one or both of them will completely crumble.

"Baby," I whisper, and somehow Salem hears me.

She opens her tear-streaked eyes, and I see the instant relief when she realizes it's me.

While she holds her sister, I hold her. She needs my support right now and I'm more than happy to give it. I'd give this woman anything.

Her body sinks against mine, inhaling audibly like she can

breathe for the first time.

"I've got you," I murmur, kissing the top of her head. "I've always got you."

They roll her mother's body out of the house, loading it into the back of the ambulance.

"She's gone," Georgia cries loudly. "She's really gone."

"It was time."

"She didn't get to meet the new baby."

"I know. I'm sorry. I know you wanted that."

Salem's the youngest, but here she is comforting her older sister. Salem's always been that person though—putting everyone else above herself. But she has me now. I'll be her rock, her support when she needs it. With me, she doesn't have to be the strongest person. I'll help her weather any storm.

The ambulance leaves, the street getting eerily quiet once more and very dark. Across the street, my two favorite nosy neighbors, Thelma and Cynthia, stand on their porch watching. Thelma throws her hand up in a wave before the two of them scuttle back into their house.

"I need to take Georgia home," Salem whispers up to me.

"I'll take her."

"No." She shakes her head. "I need to do this."

"Are you sure? I can drive you both."

She hesitates, struggling to let me help, but finally she nods. "Okay."

"Let me grab my keys"

I run back over to my house, swiping my truck keys. Salem sits in the back with a crying Georgia while quietly giving me directions to her sister's house. I park out front and hop out to open the door. Salem gets out with her sister, walking her up to the door and unlocking it. I stand outside by my truck, waiting.

She's in there for about fifteen minutes before she comes out. Her blond hair hangs in her eyes, her shoulders hunched with exhaustion. I want to take her in my arms and hold her. I want to make this all go away.

And I realize, with stunning clarity, that when Forrest died that's all she wanted to do for me and I wouldn't let her.

I was such a fucking asshole.

I know I was grieving. I know I was in the darkest place imaginable. But I still think I should've been more understanding that she was only trying to help me because she loved me. You don't go out of your way for people who you don't really care about.

I meet her halfway on the driveway, wrapping my arms around her. She's nearly swallowed whole in my arms, but she doesn't seem to mind. I still didn't put a shirt on when I went back for my keys, I was in too much of a hurry, and her warm tears coat my bare skin.

"Don't worry, Sunshine," I cup the back of her head, "I've got you."

Her fingers grapple against my sides like she's having trouble holding on, but I know it's not that. It's just that her hands are shaking too much.

"She's gone," she hiccups. "She's really gone. I know it's for the best. She's not in pain anymore, but I just want my mom."

"Shh," I croon, resting my chin on top of her head. "It's okay."

"Why do the people we love have to leave us?" She forces my head back, looking up at me with a tear-streaked face.

Wiping away her tears with my thumbs, I say, "I don't have an answer for that. I've searched for one for years and come up empty."

Eventually I get her in my truck and drive her home—and by home I mean to my house.

She's fallen asleep on the drive, so I ease her from the truck, into my arms. Carrying her inside and all the way up to my bedroom, I lay her beneath the sheets and cover her up. Her breaths are even, her face still red and splotchy from crying.

She's beautiful, though. She always is. Staring down at her, it feels like every beat of my heart is saying *mine*.

I get into bed beside her, wrapping my arms around her and holding her to my chest.

Kissing the skin of her neck, I murmur, "I love you."

I swear, even in her sleep, she smiles at those three words.

***

I hear her before I see her. Her feet quietly tiptoe down the stairs. Leaning against the kitchen counter, I sip at my morning cup of coffee. I smile against the rim when she pops around the corner. Her hair is messy from sleep, her shirt rumpled—but I fucking love seeing her like this, just out of bed, in my house.

"Hi," she says quietly. "You got anymore of that?" She points to the mug in my hand.

"Sure thing. Sit down."

While she sits I pour a cup, adding her specified amount of cream and sugar. Sliding the mug across to her, I ask, "Can I make you anything for breakfast?"

She frowns, wiggling her nose. I itch to reach out and run my finger along the freckles dotting the bridge of her nose. "I don't think I can eat."

"I understand."

"Do you want to talk about it?"

"No." She shakes her head. "Yes. I don't know." She takes a sip of coffee, wrapping her fingers around the warm cup. "Is it okay if I stay here? I don't think ... I'm not ready to go back to the house yet."

"You can stay here as long as you need." *Stay forever.* I don't say that though. "Want me to grab some things for you?"

She bites her lip, looking unsure. She looks up at me from beneath her lashes, her green eyes hesitant. "You don't mind?"

"Nope."

"That would be great. All of my stuff is upstairs in my old room and the bathroom." She runs her fingers through her hair, trying to straighten the messy strands. She sighs in frustration when she decides it's a futile effort. "I knew this was coming. We've known it for months, and this last week it was obvious her body couldn't fight anymore and yet ... it feels so sudden." She shakes her head. "That sounds so stupid."

"I think death, even when it's expected, still feels sudden. It's so final."

She nods woodenly. "Most everything is already taken care of as far as funeral expenses and all that, but I just—" She rests her head in her hand. "I don't want to deal with any of it. Even the small decisions, but I can't burden Georgia with all of it. She's already pregnant and with two little ones."

"I'll help you. Whatever you need, I'll help."

"I know."

"I'm going to make breakfast, then I'll go get your things. If you decide you want to eat, that's great, but right now I won't force you."

She arches a brow. "Meaning there might come a point where you do force me?"

"Coerce might be a better word. I can be very persuasive."

"Is that so?"

"Mhmm," I hum, turning away from her to open the refrigerator, searching for something to make. "I have my ways."

She gives a soft laugh. I'm glad I can manage to bring her some sort of amusement through her grief.

Pulling out the eggs and some vegetables I already have chopped I get to work on some omelets. I don't ask her how she'd like hers. I just make one, then slide it in front of her. Grabbing a fork from the drawer I set it beside the plate, take one for myself, and sit down beside her.

"It smells good. Thank you."

"You're welcome." I dig into mine, not pushing her to eat. Surprisingly, she takes a bite and a few more until half is gone. That's all she manages to get down, but it's way more than I expected so I count it as a win.

Cleaning up the dishes, I let her sit quietly. After washing my hands, I nod upstairs. "Why don't you go up and shower? I'll go get your clothes and stuff."

"That'd be great, thanks."

She slides off the barstool, slowly leaving the kitchen. I wait to leave until I hear the shower start up.

The front door is unlocked to her mom's house. In some places, that would be a scary thing. But Hawthorne Mills is a town with so low of a crime rate it almost doesn't seem real. Small towns might be filled with nosy people, but they're good for some things too.

Upstairs, I find her room easily since I know it has to be at the front of the house. I scoop up a bag, tossing random clothes inside, and then head to the bathroom. Her toothbrush and toothpaste are on the rim of the porcelain sink. I stuff those in the bag along with some hairbands. I shove the shower curtain aside, swiping her shampoo and conditioner.

If there's anything else I missed, I'll have to come back later.

When I get back to my house and upstairs, she's still in the shower. I pull out her shampoo and conditioner figuring she'd prefer that over my man smelling ones.

"Salem?"

She eases open the glass door. "Yeah?"

"I brought these for you."

"Oh, thanks." She takes them from me.

I grab her chin before she can shut the door.

"Your eyes. You've been crying again." She nods, lower lip trembling. "Baby," I murmur, cupping her cheeks in my hands.

"Will you get in here with me? No funny business." She laughs brokenly, lifting her hands innocently. "I mean it. I'll be on my best behavior."

"All right." I let her go and step back, slipping out of my sleep pants. My dick is already hard, but I mean with a naked wet Salem right in front of me what do you expect? "Ignore him." I point at my cock. "He has a mind of his own."

She giggles, the sound surprisingly genuine. "I don't want to be alone."

Taking her face in my hands, I press my forehead to hers beneath the spray of the rain shower. "As long as my heart beats, you are never alone in this world."

She swallows thickly. "I love you too, Thayer."

She heard me last night.

"No funny business," I promise, "but I really need to kiss you."

She nods eagerly, like that's exactly what she needs. I kiss her. "I love you." I kiss her again. "I love you." I kiss each of her cheeks, murmuring those three words. "I love you." I kiss her forehead and then I just hold her for a few minutes.

When I let her go, I motion for her to turn around. She doesn't protest. Grabbing her shampoo bottle I lather the soap in my hands and then gently massage it into her scalp.

Sex is intimate, there's no denying it, but these are the raw, real, intimate moments that build your foundation. When you love someone, you take care of them in whatever way they need. Once her hair is washed, I grab my body wash since I didn't see hers back at her house and pour it onto a loofah. I wash and clean her body, making it completely non-sexual because that's not what she needs right now. She just needs to be cared for.

Stepping out of the shower I wrap her in a clean towel. I wrap another around my waist.

She exhales a shaky breath. "Thank you."

"You don't have to do that—thank me for everything."

"But I want you to know what it means to me."

"Believe me," I say slowly, carefully. "I know. I see it in the way you look at me. In how you say my name. The way you smile when I say something. I know, baby. I've always known."

She waddles forward in her towel. I know what she wants without asking. Wrapping my arms around her, I hold her. She soaks in my touch like it's a lifeline. I would be lying if I didn't say I wasn't doing the same with hers.

Six years ago, this smiley blond woman wormed her way into my cold, angry heart and made it hers. I've never wanted it back. I still don't. But I do want to give her even more. When she's ready.

CHAPTER THIRTY-TWO

Salem

I step inside the funeral home—the same one Forrest's service was held at. A shiver runs down my spine. I hate it here. I didn't think I would ever set foot in this place again. I didn't want to. I guess the universe had other plans.

Thayer's hand tightens against my waist. This is hard for him, but he refuses to be anywhere but at my side. I told him repeatedly that he didn't need to come for this, but he was adamant that he was going.

I'm thankful he's here, for his support, but I would understand if he couldn't face this.

The casket sits at the end of the aisle, the seats full of people. I expected no one to show up and instead the whole town is here.

I was supposed to be here earlier, but I just couldn't do it.

So, now I'm late. My sister sits at the front with her family but stands when she sees me.

"Hey." She eyes Thayer behind me but says nothing. She looks pleased though. "I was getting worried about you."

"I'm sorry." I reach to push hair behind my ear and realize that it's all pulled back in a low bun. I let my hand fall awkwardly to my side. It's not left hanging for long. Thayer entwines our fingers, giving my hand a small squeeze. "I didn't mean to be late. I just..."

"It's okay. I get it."

"Caleb and Seda will be here soon."

There's still twenty minutes until the service is set to begin.

"If we need to wait, we will," Georgia assures me. "Do you want to see her?"

I glance for a second at the open casket. "N-No," I stutter.

I know for some people it brings them comfort seeing their loved one, but not me. That's not my mom. That's a shell. Everything that made that body my mom is gone. Her spirit has left this realm. I hope she's saying hi to Forrest and carving pumpkins with him. Maybe they're looking down at us right now while drinking cups of hot chocolate.

"All right." Georgia doesn't argue with my choice. "You guys are to sit right there. Caleb and Seda will sit with you." She points out the spot reserved for us, and I nod gratefully.

My sister knows now all about my past with Thayer, that he's Seda's biological father. She wasn't surprised. She said she never knew for sure, but she had suspected. Apparently I'm way more of an open book than I thought.

Thayer and I take a seat. I blow out a breath, grateful so many people turned out for my mom, but at the same time I'm hoping I don't have to talk to them. I can't put on a smile right now and make small talk. I think it's wrong for people to expect that of those who are grieving. This is all so hard.

Thayer squeezes my hand again, reminding me he's here.

I love this man so much. And I know, even with the horrible tragedies we've gone through, I'd live it all again and again if it meant it led me to him.

When Caleb and Seda finally arrive, she cries out a loud, "Mommy!" when she sees me, diving into my arms.

"My girl." I hold her tight. She's getting so big. Soon the days of her saying mommy and letting me hold her like this will pass, becoming nothing but a memory.

She takes a seat between me and Caleb, with Thayer on my other side.

When the service begins, it feels like I'm not even in my body. I've checked out. It's the only way I can deal with this.

And Thayer had to do this for his child. His son.

I hold Seda's hand a little tighter.

A basic speech is given by some man, I can't even remember who he is, maybe a preacher, or maybe he works at the funeral home, but then Georgia gets up to speak. I didn't even know she was going to say anything.

She clears her throat, angling the microphone to her mouth. She shuffles some index cards, nodding like she's giving a mental pep talk to herself.

"My mom was a wonderful, tough woman. She endured things no person should ever have to. As did my sister and I." She taps the cards against the podium. "When my father died, she moved us to this town to get away from it all. A fresh start. She'd always dreamed of having something of her own and so she opened her shop. A Checkered Past Antiques was her special place, her calm against the storm. The name of her shop was a reflection of herself, just like many of the things she carried to sell. All beautiful and unique in their own away, a little battered and scarred, but still worthy of love." She sniffles, wiping beneath her nose. "My mom deserved the world, but the universe is rarely fair. When she got cancer the first time it was hard enough, but the second time around? She'd done everything right, so why was it back?" Georgia sighs, shaking her head. "Even when you do everything right, it can still go incredibly wrong. My mom's time came all too soon, and even if her past was speckled in darkness, she made the most of things when she got out. She loved us, my sister and me, with every beat of her heart, right until the end. She made us cupcakes, and braided our hair. She tucked us into bed at night with kisses on our foreheads. There was ... was a monster who haunted the three of us." She wipes at tears wetting her cheeks. "She thought she failed us. Thought she wasn't good enough. But she tried. She tried so many times to protect us, to get us away, and she couldn't. She was trapped in a marriage to a monster. Many of you don't know that, but now you do. Now you know that Allison Matthews was a victim of domestic violence, of marital rape, and so much more. But that's not *who* she was. She was light. She was happiness. She was *love*. She was a store owner. A baker. A grandma. Our *mother*. She might be gone, but she lives on in every beat of our hearts and those of our children." She pauses, taking a breath to gather herself. "Thank you."

She returns to her seat, and Michael pulls her into his arms, kissing her forehead.

I know I should probably get up and say something, but I can't.

Besides, Georgia said it all anyway.

The service comes to an end, and Thayer drives Caleb, Seda, and me to the cemetery for the graveside portion of the service. I feel emotionally drained and exhausted, but I know I have to make it through this part as well. Then I can crash.

At the grave side, it's only Georgia's family, Caleb, Seda, Thayer, and me. It seems like such a small amount of people, but I know my mom would only want us here.

Seda stands with her cousins, happy to see them.

"Are you okay?" Thayer whispers in my ear, his lips

brushing my sensitive skin.

I force a smile. It's on the tip of my tongue to lie, but I don't want to lie to him anymore. "No." He wraps his arms tighter around me. His gaze drifts in the direction of Forrest's grave. "You don't have to stay." I know how hard this must be. I'm not expecting him to stay glued to my side if this is too much.

He shakes his head. "I'm not leaving you." Warm brown eyes meet mine and I instantly feel comforted. "Wherever you are is where I belong."

Luckily the graveside service is short and sweet, and we all start to head back to where we parked our cars.

Seda tugs on Caleb's hand. "My brother is over there." She points in the approximate location of Forrest's grave. To me she says, "Don't worry, Mom. He'll look after Grandma."

I pull my black skirt up slightly so I can crouch down to her level. I stroke her soft cheek. "You think so?"

"Mhmm. They're family." She looks at me, then Caleb, and lastly Thayer. "We're all family."

"Yeah, we are." Caleb scoops her up, her arms going around his neck.

It's unconventional, the three of us raising Seda, but we are a family and we're going to do the best we can.

CHAPTER THIRTY-THREE

Thayer

Caleb heads back to Boston, leaving Seda behind since she's out of school now and she wanted to stay with her mother. I could tell it bothered him leaving her, but he didn't fight it since it's what Seda wanted.

The three of us are on the couch in my living room, watching some PIXAR movie Seda loves. She rests her head on Salem's leg, her body draped in a blanket, snoozing away. But neither of us makes a move to change the movie or turn the TV off all together.

"I was thinking," I start, and Salem turns her eyes up to me. She looks exhausted, her eyes red from crying off and on today. "Do you think ... I mean, would it be okay if I turned a room upstairs into a bedroom for Seda?"

She smiles slowly, stretching slightly. I'm sure she's stiff from not being able to move with Seda sleeping on her leg, but she never complains. "I think that's a great idea."

"You do?"

"You look so worried." She pokes my cheek. "Don't be. She should have a room here."

"I don't want her to feel obligated to stay here if you're not here, but I'd like for her to have a space that's her own."

"Trust me, Seda doesn't do anything she doesn't want to

do."

"We can go furniture shopping tomorrow. I'll get whatever she wants."

Salem laughs lightly. "You're such a pushover."

Her phone vibrates on the coffee table. I lean over and grab it, handing it to her.

Her brows furrow at the screen. "Wha-?"

"What is it?" I ask.

"It's Lauren. She said she had something delivered and I need to grab it right now."

"What do you think it is?"

"I have no idea, but I better go see."

"Let me go."

"No." She shakes her head. "It's fine."

Somehow, she manages to get up without disturbing Seda. She heads quietly to the front door and opens it, looking around. I get up too, joining her. I put my hand on the back of her neck, massaging my thumb into the skin there.

"She probably meant your mom's house, love."

"Oh," she blushes, "right, of course."

Barefooted, she scurries off my front porch and runs next door. A moment later I hear a shrill, high-pitched scream. I look back at my house for one second and close the door before I take off in a run.

Is she being attacked? What's happening?

I get my answer seconds later when I run onto the driveway and find Lauren and Salem jumping up and down hugging each other.

That was a happy scream? I thought she was being murdered.

The two girls can't stop shrieking and my eardrums hurt. "Ladies," I interrupt, "do you mind if we head over to my house?"

Salem lets go of her best friend.

Lauren is tall with dark hair and tan skin. She's Salem's complete opposite, at least in looks. I can't say anything about her personality.

"Oh, look," she looks me up and down for emphasis, "it's Baby Daddy."

Salem busts out laughing while I shake my head.

"Seda's sleeping, come on," I encourage.

Salem grabs Lauren's hand, dragging her with her. "Thayer, grab Lauren's bag from her car will you?"

With a sigh, I unload the massively large suitcase from the back of the rental and wheel it behind me.

The girls' excited chatter grows softer as we approach my house since Seda is still asleep on the couch. I take Lauren's suitcase upstairs and put it in the first guestroom. It has an attached bath which I'm sure she'll prefer.

When I get back downstairs, I find both of them in the kitchen drinking wine with Salem gushing over a diamond ring on Lauren's finger. Salem hears me approach, looking over her shoulder with a smile. I'm glad Lauren came. She needs a friend during this time to help lift her spirits.

"Hi, Baby Daddy," Lauren says again. "It's nice to finally meet you."

Salem stifles her laughter. She's a little too amused at her friend's nickname for me.

I hold a hand out to Lauren. "It's nice to meet you, too."

She shakes my hand, squeezing a little tighter than necessary. "Hurt my bestie again and I have diplomatic immunity in six countries."

Salem snorts. "Don't listen to her."

Lauren releases my hand. "I mean it." She points a warning finger at me. "The minute you make her cry again—you're out." She makes a slicing motion across her throat. "I've seen *Dexter*."

"*Lauren*," Salem admonishes with a giggle. To me she says, "She's not serious."

"Like hell I am," Lauren grumbles.

Some guys might be turned off by Lauren's forward defensiveness, but I'm glad Salem has someone like her. Lauren has every right to be wary of me. I *did* break Salem's heart.

"You ladies have fun. I'm going to grab a water and carry Seda up to bed." I smack a kiss on Salem's cheek. "Don't get into too much trouble. I'm not sure I have enough bail money."

Lauren makes a yikes face and whisper hisses, "If he doesn't have money for bail you better run now."

"Lauren!" Salem playfully slaps her friend's arm.

Leaving them to their antics, I scoop Seda up off the couch and into my arms. She wiggles a bit and I still, praying she stays asleep. Luckily, she keeps snoozing. Upstairs, I lay her down in the other guestroom, carefully pulling the covers back and up over her.

I can't help but take a second to look at her.

It's unreal how perfect she is. I still have a hard time wrapping my head around the fact that this is my daughter. I have a little girl. My heart feels full for the first time in a long time.

Before Krista and I knew Forrest was a boy, I couldn't imagine myself having a daughter. I knew I'd be happy either way, but I hoped for a boy. I knew I could handle that. Being a boy dad would be easy. I'd had a brother and always done traditional guy things.

When Salem told me she'd had our child, a girl, there was

no disappointment in any way. Seda is a gift, one I didn't know I even deserved. This little girl was created from the true love Salem and I have—a tether to always tie us together and bring us back.

Smoothing her hair off her forehead, I tell her I love her and slip out of the room I fully plan to redecorate from the generic furniture I put in there for the rare occasions I have visitors.

***

I don't know how much time has passed when Salem gets into bed. She snuggles up to me, pressing her cold toes against my legs. I crack an eye open.

"That was mean," I joke.

She wiggles her toes. "I need you to warm them up." She puts her hand on my cheek. "I'm sorry about Lauren," she whispers, then hiccups. "Too much wine, me thinks." With another hiccup she adds, "She means well."

"She loves you. I like that she's protective of you."

Salem smiles. "She really is a great friend. Can you believe she's getting married? He's a billionaire too. Yeah, with a B. Billionaire. Lauren would fall in love with a rich guy. She gets to live out all her billionaire romance lover dreams now." She slaps her hand over her mouth, stifling a yawn. "I'm drunk and rambling." She giggles.

Tracing my finger over her lips, I say, "There's something I want to talk to you about."

Her eyes widen. "Oh no. Am I in trouble? I swear I'm not that drunk."

"You're not in trouble, baby. But it's not something I want

to talk about when you're drunk and sleepy."

"In the morning then?"

"In the morning," I promise.

Wrapping my arms around her, she rests her head on my chest just when I think she's asleep, her tears wet my skin.

"Sunshine," I whisper, holding her closer.

"She's gone, Thayer. She's really gone," she sobs. "I'm never going to see my mom again."

I press my lips to the top of her head and say, "I'm here. If you want to cry, scream, whatever you need to do, I've got you."

And so she just cries, because sometimes that's the only thing you can do.

CHAPTER THIRTY-FOUR

Salem

Waking up, I press a hand to my pounding temple. I drank way too much wine last night. I didn't mean to, but I stayed up late chatting with Lauren, catching up, and frankly just trying to forget about the events of the day. Since I'm not a big drinker it's caught up to me this morning.

Not to mention my eyes are practically swollen shut from crying myself to sleep.

My mom is really gone.

I can't walk next-door and see her.

I can't call her and hear her voice.

I'm never going to hear her laugh again or see her smile.

Rolling out of bed—*Thayer's* bed—I stumble into the bathroom. There's a separate space for the toilet so I relieve myself—my bladder damn near bursting—while he's in the shower.

"Toothpaste," I mutter to myself, wanting to get rid of the fuzzy feeling in my mouth.

Thayer gets out of the shower, and I shamelessly ogle him in the mirror's reflection. My mouth literally waters. I hastily spit out my toothpaste before I make a fool of myself.

Only Thayer has the ability to completely ransack my thoughts and make me forget how sad I am just by looking at him.

Thayer swipes a towel from the rack, wrapping it around his waist.

I whimper as he approaches me, squeezing my legs together. Apparently hungover me turns into horny me.

He wraps his arms around me from behind, kissing the sensitive skin of my neck. I lean back into him, inhaling the scent of his woodsy body wash.

Just being held by him instantly makes me feel better.

Rinsing out my mouth with mouthwash, I spit it back into the sink and then reach for my hairbrush.

"My drunk memory might be hazy, but I think I remember you wanting to talk about something."

He leans his hip against the sink. "I did."

"And?" I prompt, setting my hair brush down.

My mouth waters just looking at him. He really needs to go put some clothes on because Thayer still wet from the shower with only a towel is my kryptonite.

His eyes narrow on me. "Stop looking at me like that."

"L-Like what?" I lick my lips. I can't help it, I'm so insanely attracted to him, and something about my grief has me wanting to be held and loved by him.

"Like you want me to fuck you."

I lift my chin defiantly. "Maybe I do."

I don't know who moves first, but suddenly I'm in his arms, his hand cupping the back of my head. Our tongues tangle together, and he backs me into the bedroom. He lets me go, a soft cry leaving me at the loss of his body heat. He checks that the door is locked and then he's back in front of me.

"God, I fucking love you," he growls, devouring me.

Some people wait a lifetime for a love like this.

I found it at eighteen in my grumpy, plant loving, lumberjack of a neighbor. Our paths diverged for a while there, but we were always meant to end up back here.

Thayer lays me down on the bed. Sitting up, I tear off my top. He hungrily takes in my bare breasts, leaning over me to suck first one nipple and then the other into his mouth.

I undo his towel, letting it drop and quickly grip his hard cock. His breath hisses between his teeth. Grabbing my boy short underwear I slept in, he yanks them down my ankles and drops them on the floor. His fingers find my core, rubbing my clit.

"Right there," I beg, rolling my hips.

He keeps rubbing just like I asked him, while I stroke his length.

"Need to be inside you," he begs. "You're gonna make me come just like this."

I guide his cock to my pussy and he doesn't waste any time sinking inside. His head falls back with a moan. I fucking love hearing his sounds. It's the biggest turn on knowing he gets so much pleasure from my body.

My nails dig into his ass cheeks, urging him on.

It's hard, fast, and a little bit wild. But I love seeing him let go.

"Fuck, baby," he groans, gripping my hips tighter. "You're squeezing my cock so tight."

He stands at the edge of the bed, wrapping his arms around my legs to pull me impossibly closer. He lifts my hips higher and the change in position is all I need for my orgasm to rip through me. He pumps his hips harder, faster, until he spills inside me.

He collapses on top of me, holding his weight up by his

hands positioned on either side of my head.

"I love you," he whispers in my ear. "I love you so goddamn much."

I cup his scruffy cheeks in the palms of my hands, staring up into his eyes. "I love you, too."

I cherish being able to say those three words to him.

He pulls from my body, his cock still half-hard. "Stay here."

I watch him unabashedly as he pads into the bathroom. The faucet runs and he returns a minute later pressing a warm, damp cloth between my legs. I move my hips, unable to help myself. I just had him, but I already want him again. Thayer has this way of turning me into a fiend.

He bites his lip, still wiping gently at my core. His eyes flick up to mine and I'm surprised when he asks, "Do you want more kids?"

I used to wonder if I did want more. It's something that's been in the back of my mind more as of late. Especially with Seda turning six in a matter of months. When Caleb approached the topic of having a baby, I didn't freak out because I didn't want more kids, but over the fact that it felt wrong to have a child with him when I felt like he deserved more than me.

"Yes." I feel sure of the answer this time.

He sets the cloth aside. "Do you know..."

"Do I know what?" I prompt when he grows quiet.

He yanks a pair of boxer-briefs out of the dresser drawer and tugs them on. "Do you know when?"

"I'm not sure." I look away from him nervously. "Soon, I guess. Seda will be six and I know she'd love to be a big sister."

He leans over my body, cupping my face. Gently, he rubs his thumb over my bottom lip. "You can say no, I won't be mad..."

I narrow my eyes. "Okay?"

"I'd like for you to go off your birth control."

What?

"I ... like now?"

He nods. "I love being a dad, and I want to have more babies with you. I want to watch our kids grow up in this small town with its quirky traditions. I want to smell you baking cupcakes for school events. I want ... I already told you I want everything with you, and I want that future to start now." I can't help it, I start crying. "Fuck, baby," he wraps my naked body in his arms, "I didn't mean to make you cry."

"They're happy tears, I promise," I hiccup.

I didn't expect to have this kind of talk this morning, and I know it's fast, but it feels ... right. My mom would be happy, she'd want this for me. She wanted both Georgia and me to understand that life's short even if you die old and in your bed. You can't let fear hold you back. You have to *live*.

He doesn't look convinced as he brushes the wet droplets from my cheeks. "Are you sure? I know this is kind of out of left field, but I want everything with you, and fuck waiting. But I never want to push you if your timeline isn't the same as mine."

"Y-Yes. You want to have another baby with me?"

"Another and another and as many as you'll let me."

I laugh, my body shaking. "Let's get through one more first before you start planning on kid number three and beyond."

"Deal."

His smile sets my soul on fire—it's cheesy, but it's true.

"I'll stop taking my birth control today." His smile grows impossibly bigger. "Don't look so happy at the idea of knocking me up."

He chuckles. "I already did that once *with* birth control,

excuse me for being a little cocky."

I poke his side. "Get off me. I need to shower and get dressed. Seda will be up soon. Lauren will probably sleep for half the day."

He eases up and I start to stand but he scoops me around the waist, spinning me into his body. My hands land on his hard torso.

"Are you sure you want this?"

I roll my eyes. "If it wasn't, I'd tell you."

"This is all happening faster than I planned. I wanted to do things right, take it slow with you—"

I press my hand over his mouth. "This is *our* right. You can't put love on a timeline. I've waited what feels like a lifetime to call you mine. I don't want to waste a single second more."

"Fuck, I love you."

"I love you, too. Now, let me go. I smell like sex. And I have birth control to throw in the trash."

He lets me go with a swat on my ass. I smile at him over my shoulder.

"Wait," I pause in the doorway of the bathroom, "was that what you wanted to talk to me about? The baby thing?"

He opens another drawer on the dresser and pulls out a pair of cargo shorts. "It wasn't, actually."

"Oh?" I wait for him to elaborate.

He shakes his head. "Don't look so scared. We'll talk about it later."

He swipes a shirt from the closet and heads out of the bedroom, closing the door behind him and leaving me no choice but to wait for that conversation, whatever it might be.

CHAPTER THIRTY-FIVE

Thayer

I raid my pantry for the ingredients to make homemade waffles for breakfast. I figure it'll help soak up the last of the alcohol in the girls' systems.

I didn't mean to spring the baby thing on Salem, but it just kind of happened. I love her, I want to spend the rest of my life with her, and it seems like she wants the same, so what's the point in waiting?

But as sober as she seemed this morning, I still want to bring up the conversation again when I know for sure she has a clear head and ask her about moving in.

I've just finished stirring up the waffle batter when Seda pads into the room in her footy pajamas, rubbing her sleepy eyes.

"I'm hungry."

"I'm making waffles—do you want those or something else?"

Her brown eyes light up. "Waffles!"

"Do you want to help spoon it onto the waffle maker?"

"Yes, please." She nods eagerly.

I lift her onto the counter and pass her a spoon. She ladles the batter on, and I close the lid.

"When the light turns green that means it's done."

"Can I have chocolate chips in mine?"

I chuckle. I should've known she'd want chocolate chips. "Yep. Let me grab them."

It only takes me a second to swipe them from the pantry and set them on the counter with everything else.

"The light's green!" She cries excitedly, pointing at the waffle maker.

"Let me do this part," I tell her, grabbing a rubber spatula. "It's hot." I take the waffle out and set it on the waiting plate. "All right, time for more batter."

We work together, finishing all the waffles by the time Salem and Lauren come down.

Salem's freshly showered, her hair damp, and dressed for the day in her usual shorts and tank top. Lauren looks like she got run over by a car. Her hair is an untamed mess, there's drool dried in the corner of her mouth, and she's still wearing a pair of matching pajamas.

"Auntie Lauren!" Seda shrieks, climbing off the counter.

Lauren presses her fingers to her temples. "Quiet down my favorite little gremlin."

"I didn't know you were here," Seda jabbers, wrapping her arms around Lauren's legs. Poor Lauren looks like she's about to throw up. "Are you hungry? My dad made waffles. I helped."

"We'll see, kid." She ruffles Seda's hair and sits down at the table, laying her head on the surface.

Salem grabs the bottle of orange juice, pouring a glass for all of us. She carries one over to Lauren and says something about going to grab ibuprofen for her.

Lauren raises her hand, giving a thumbs up.

I plate up waffles for everyone, and Seda helps me set the table.

Salem returns, handing Lauren two pills. She gulps them down and mutters something under her breath. Salem laughs, pushing the plate closer to Lauren.

"Eat," she admonishes. "It'll make you feel better."

"When I throw it all up in your lap don't say I didn't warn you."

Salem rolls her eyes, mouthing to me, "She's being dramatic."

Breakfast goes relatively smoothly, despite the glares Lauren sends my way every other minute. I don't let it bother me. I know she's being protective of Salem, and I'm glad she has a friend that cares so much.

Once the kitchen is all cleaned up, I join Salem and Lauren out on the deck while Seda plays in the treehouse.

I pull out a chair and sit down. Lauren has a big pair of sunglasses on her face, shielding her eyes. Salem props her legs up on the deck railing, tilting her head back to absorb the sun.

"Are you still up for taking Seda furniture shopping?"

Salem nods, wiggling her toes. They're painted a blue color. "Absolutely. I think she'd like having her own space here."

"Good. I might have to run by the hardware store too."

"For what?"

"Paint—I'm sure she'll want to change the color."

Right now, it's just a beige color I put in the guestroom because I had it leftover from a project.

Lauren snorts. "Pushover."

I shrug. "If it'll make Seda happy I don't think that makes me a pushover."

"Ignore her, she's just grumpy because she can't party like she used to."

"We didn't even party. We *drank* and now my brain hates

me because it's literally pounding against my skull." Lauren points at her head to drive home her point. "I only just turned twenty-six, and my body apparently has decided I'm forty and my life is over."

"Your life isn't over at forty."

Lauren lowers her sunglasses, her lips twitching when she tries not to smile. "You'd know, Old Man."

Salem shakes her head. "I need a babysitter for you. You're more of a handful than Seda."

Lauren tips her sunglasses like they're a hat in some old timey movie. "Happy to be of service. Someone has to keep you on your toes."

"Yeah, because life hasn't already done that to me yet."

Lauren wags a finger. "Touché."

"Seda!" Salem calls out. "Come down from there. We're going to run some errands, get some things to decorate your room!"

"Really?" Seda pokes her head out of the treehouse window. "Can I get a princess bed?"

"You can get—" Salem slaps her hand over my mouth, trying not to laugh.

"You are such a pushover. You can't tell her she'll get anything she wants. She might only be five, but she'll take full advantage of that."

"I wasn't going to say that." I grin when she lets her hand go.

"Oh, you weren't?"

My smile grows bigger. "Maybe."

She shakes her head, and I tug her into my lap.

Before Salem came back into my life, I was living every day just to make it through. Now, I'm living *for* every day.

It's like I can finally breathe again.

CHAPTER THIRTY-SIX

Salem

I'm exhausted by the time we get home from shopping. I've never grown into a love of shopping and I doubt I ever will. But Seda has a brand-new furniture set on the way, along with a new bedspread, and what she's dubbed Perfect Princess Pink paint for her room's walls. It's actually called Melted Ice Cream, but try telling her that.

"I normally love shopping," Lauren says, lugging in a bag of décor items, "but your daughter is making me question it."

"She's something," I agree.

Seda let loose to shop is like trying to wrangle a wild bunny. She runs and hops all over the place—skips too—says hi to almost every stranger she sees, and dances in aisles if she likes the music the store is playing.

Basically, my child is the complete opposite of what I was. Then again, I'm not really sure what I would've been like as a child if it hadn't been tainted by a monster.

We unload all of the bags while Seda runs around the front yard singing a made-up song.

"Don't go near the street," I warn, walking up the porch steps to set bags in the foyer.

"I won't, Mom. You don't have to worry so much."

She has no idea but that's like half of being a parent, maybe even more, constantly worrying.

"Do you think you'll have kids?" I ask Lauren when she sets down a bag of throw pillows beside my bag of blankets—because Seda can't just have one blanket, she needs twelve. That she did get from me.

"Maybe when I'm thirty." Lauren wrinkles her nose, pursing her lips like she tastes something sour. "No, not even then." She glances out the open door to where Thayer is now chasing Seda around the lawn. "I like your kid, but that's it. I'm not sure I'd be a good mom."

"You'd be a great mom," I assure her, because she would be if that's what she chose. "But not everyone wants to be a parent and that's okay, too."

She shrugs. "We'll see in the future. Right now, I like it just being me and Anthony." She glances down at her ring finger. "Gotta get through the wedding first."

"I can't believe you're getting married in the Hamptons," I bump her shoulder playfully, "you boujee bitch."

She cackles. "Anthony's parents' place is there, and it's stunning. It's perfect."

The way she lights up talking about her fiancé makes me happy. She deserves that. For a while there I wasn't sure she'd ever settle down. There's nothing wrong with that, but I could tell she was searching for someone to tame her. Not that Anthony has completely tamed her wild side, but when she's with him she is a slightly calmer version of her normal self.

I have to head up to Manhattan soon for the final fitting of my Maid of Honor dress. The wedding is at the end of the summer, and in just a few weeks we're headed to Vegas for her bachelorette. With the loss of my mom, I don't know how much fun I'll be on that trip, but I wouldn't miss it.

"Speaking of the wedding, now that you're with Thayer I assume you'll be bringing him?" She asks as we head back out to my SUV for more bags.

"I mean, I guess, yeah. I hadn't even thought about it."

"I'll add him to the list." I reach for a bag when she catches my arm. "You know, I love to give you a hard time, but I'm happy for you. You and him..." Her eyes drift to where he has Seda draped over his shoulder, spinning her around. "Anyone can see it's special. I'm glad you got this second chance. Not everyone gets that. You deserve to be happy more than anyone I know."

I throw my arms around her, squeezing my best friend tight. I miss living closer to her. "Thank you."

"Ew," she playfully shoves me off, "you're giving me cooties."

I stick my tongue out at her. "You wish."

"Save them for Thayer. I'm pretty sure that man loves your cooties."

"Lauren!" I shriek, swatting her arm.

She just grabs a bag and cackles all the way into the house.

***

The next day, Lauren's heading back to Manhattan. I'm so happy she was able to come out—she said she had intended to be in early enough for the funeral, but her flight from Chicago got delayed; her fiancé has another place there where they stay sometimes depending on what he's doing with work.

I hug her tight beside the rental car—already loaded with her suitcase thanks to Thayer.

"I don't want you to go."

"I don't want to go either, but I'll see you soon for dress fittings and then it's Vegas time, baby!" She lets me go, doing a little wiggle.

Thayer arches a brow. I haven't had a chance to fill him in on the wedding and all the details, but with Lauren heading back to New York we'll have more time. Plus, we're taking Seda back to Boston today. I wanted to keep her longer, but Caleb and I are still trying to figure out this whole system. Plus, I need to start cleaning out my mom's house and it'll be easier if Seda isn't around, just because she'll get into everything. Regardless, it already feels like a piece of my heart is missing and she isn't even gone yet.

"Love you, girly," I kiss Lauren's cheek, "see you soon."

"Don't be a stranger." She winks playfully, trying to mask the tears in her eyes.

Standing on the driveway, I wave as she backs out and drives away. Thayer comes up behind me, putting his hand on my shoulder. Winnie barks in the yard, chasing after Seda. They both wear matching rainbow tutus that Thayer sewed himself—talk about swoon.

"I'm sorry she had to leave so soon." His voice is deep and husky beside my ear.

I exhale, trying not to be too upset about it. "It's okay. I'm happy she came at all."

That's what means the most, knowing my friend came to support me during this time.

"We haven't had a chance to talk about the other thing."

I turn to face him, brows wrinkling. "What thing?"

"The one I wanted to talk to you about."

"Oh." Clarity comes to me. "Right. What was it?"

"When we drop Seda off, I was thinking you could get

more of your things, Binx too, and..."

"And what?" I prompt.

He ducks his head, his shaggy hair hiding his eyes from my view. "Do you want to move in with me?" His cheeks turn bright red like he's embarrassed and nervous. I think I love seeing him flustered way too much. Thayer is normally the definition of cool, calm, and collected, but this has him feeling floundered.

"You want me to live with you?" He nods. "Like share the same bed? My hair clogging your shower, clothes on the floor, my crap taking over yours—that kind of live together?"

He nods again. "It makes sense, right? Why wait?"

He has a point. I mean, I did throw my birth control away. We had another conversation about it that night. He wanted to make sure I was clear headed and making a sound decision. I wasn't that drunk that morning. I drank way less than Lauren. It just makes me feel foggy-headed, but it made me happy that Thayer always puts me first and understands how important my consent is.

I glance next door at my teenage childhood home. I don't want to live there. It's not that it holds bad memories—my dad never lived there—but it doesn't feel like mine. It reminds me of her, and I don't think I could ever do anything to change that. The best course of action is to clean it up, fix some small things, and sell it. Georgia and I can split the money, and it'll help out both of us.

The store is a different situation. I know it's stupid to keep it, makes no logical sense, but I have way more trouble parting with it than the house.

"Yes," I say softly, then a bit louder I add, "I'll move in with you."

His smile starts small, then it grows into a full-blown grin. He doesn't say anything. Instead, he scoops me into his arms, spinning me around and around. My feet lift off the ground, and I giggle.

He sets me down, cupping my cheeks. "I swear to God, Sunshine, I'm going to make you the happiest woman on the planet." He doesn't give me a chance to respond. Slanting his mouth over mine he kisses me deeply.

Some people never find this kind of love in a lifetime. I found it at eighteen, lost it for a while, and now I'm never letting it—letting *him*—go.

CHAPTER THIRTY-SEVEN

Salem

I could tell Caleb was sad when I packed up more of my stuff and took Binx with me. I told him why and there was the briefest flash of pain in his eyes before he forced a smile and said he was happy for me. I don't like that I'm always breaking his heart, but I remind myself we're divorced now, and we were both going to move on eventually.

One day, he'll find his person, and then he'll understand.

I'm hanging up a dress in Thayer's closet when he comes in, wrapping his hands around me from behind. He smells like sweat, earth, and cigarette smoke from his day on the job site. He doesn't smoke anymore, at least that's what he says, but some of the guys he works with do.

"I missed you." He lays his head on my shoulder. His hands go to my stomach. "Do you think you're pregnant yet?"

I giggle, swaying out of his arms so I can turn to face him. "You're obsessed with knocking me up out of wedlock, aren't you?" I can't help but joke. Truth be told, I don't feel the need for him to propose. Now that we're together again I know everything will happen in the timeline it's supposed to.

He looks me over with a half-smile. "Fuck yeah. I love the thought of you round with my child." I roll my eyes. He grabs my hips, gently pulling me into his space. He towers over me, so I angle my head back to see him. "I didn't get to see you the first time. I didn't get to feel her kick or take you to doctor's appointments. I want that."

I wet my lips, feeling shame.

He cups my cheek, forcing me to look at him when I try to drop my gaze. "Don't do that. Don't hide what you're feeling from me. I want us to be honest with each other, always. That's when things get tough, when you hide things, or lie about how you feel."

I sigh, my shoulders feeling impossibly heavy. "I wish you could've been there too and I feel awful that you didn't get to be."

"You did the best thing," he reminds me for the umpteenth time. "I wasn't ... I couldn't have been the man, the father, I needed to be back then. You knew that." He rubs his thumb over my cheek. "I refuse to let you have regrets, because we have right now. I get to wake up every day with you in my arms. I get to hear Seda running in the halls when she's here. Winnie and Binx get to be best friends." I laugh at that, because surprisingly they are. My black cat and the corgi like to sleep together on the couch. "And one day, whenever it's meant to happen, I'll get to hear our crying baby down the hall."

A tear leaks out of the corner of my eye. He quickly swipes it with his pointer finger.

"Now," he grabs my hand, "come shower with me." He grins wickedly, eyes dark with desire.

I let him tug me along and when he presses my naked back against the shower tile, sinking inside me, I finally let go.

***

After a FaceTime call with Seda, we settle on the couch with a bowl of popcorn for a movie night. Thayer lays down, plopping his head in my lap.

"What are you in the mood to watch?"

"To be honest," he yawns, "I'm probably going to fall right to sleep, so whatever you want is fine."

I flick through the movies I have saved on my account, settling on a rom-com. If he's truly about to fall asleep then I'd like to watch Matthew McConaughey's Benjamin Barry get tortured by Kate Hudson's Andy Anderson in *How To Lose a Guy in 10 Days*.

Thayer doesn't protest when it starts. I rub at his scalp with one hand, popping bites of popcorn into my mouth with the other. On the other end of the couch Winnie snoozes with Binx curled up against her.

It's only fifteen minutes into the movie when I look down and find Thayer fast asleep. He works a lot of long days. He might be the owner and therefore the boss, but when it comes to his business he likes being as hands on as possible.

Not to mention he's spent the past couple of days painting the room that's now Seda's, as well as putting together her furniture.

When she comes back in a few days she'll have her very own princess room.

Thayer even went back to the store and got the bean bag chair I had previously convinced him to leave behind.

There are a total of three spare rooms upstairs, one is Seda's now, and I guess, if Thayer manages his goal of getting me pregnant, another will be turned into a nursery.

The idea of watching Thayer rock a precious newborn in his arms at night has me feeling all kinds of warm and gooey.

Then almost immediately another feeling overcomes me, one of sadness and pain when I think about Forrest's old room that Thayer did away with a long time ago. I asked him about it, and he said he left it for a while but seeing it just became too painful so he packed most things away, sold the furniture, and moved some of Forrest's more prized possessions like his favorite dinosaur and a toy car to different spots around the house. It says it makes him smile seeing those little pops of Forrest but that the whole room was just too much.

I look down at him, his face calm in his sleep.

The pain he's had to live through must be unbearable.

He told me his therapist described grief as a ball in a box. When the pain is fresh that ball is large, constantly hitting the sides of the box, but then the ball grows smaller over time and hits the box less.

Right now, for me, that ball is pretty large. It's why I'm avoiding going back over to my mom's house.

I don't want to touch her stuff. I don't want to pack it away in storage or donate it or—

I wipe away my tears with the back of my hand.

When I do that, it'll finally feel real.

Right now, I'm in this state of pretending she's still in that house baking cupcakes or watching a movie or just sitting at the kitchen table eating a bowl of cereal.

Grief is strange that way—how it tries to defy logic.

I saw her die. I went to the funeral. The grave.

I did all those things, yet my mind is still holding onto the illogical hope that she's in that house.

The movie continues to play, but I'm not paying attention anymore. When the end credits roll, I turn the TV off and gently wake Thayer. He takes one look at me and knows that the grief is consuming me. He doesn't say anything. He doesn't have to. He just wraps me in his arms, letting me grab onto him in a koala hold, and carries me upstairs to bed. He doesn't let me go even then, and I wonder if he thinks he can hold me tight enough that I don't fall apart.

CHAPTER THIRTY-EIGHT

Salem

Two weeks pass before I'm ready to start clearing out the house. Georgia insisted on helping when I let her know I was finally taking on the job, but I was more persistent in getting her to let it go since she could go into labor at any time. With this being her third, she's more likely to come before her due date and she definitely doesn't need to be doing anything strenuous despite her stubborn behavior.

"Where do you want to start?" Thayer asks, hands on his hips.

We stand on the front lawn since I haven't made the first move to step inside yet. Thayer's been keeping the lawn immaculate so at least we don't have that worry.

I open and close my mouth, no words willing to come out.

Thayer doesn't let my silence deter him.

"Maybe we should go around and mark the bigger furniture items with different colored tape. What you want to keep, donate, and trash. That might make it easier with those things."

I nod steadily, willing my tears not to fall. It's just a house. It's just things. So why is this so emotional?

"That's a good idea."

"All right." He nods to himself. "You wait here, and I'll

grab tape from my truck."

I wrinkle my nose. "You keep tape in your truck?"

"I keep lots of things in my truck."

While he gets the tape, I wander closer to the side door. It feels easier to go through there than the front door. That puts me too close to the living room and I'm not ready to tackle that.

Thayer returns, finding me fumbling with my keys by the door.

He swipes them from me, juggling three different rolls of tape in colors of yellow, blue, and green. "Which is it?"

"That one." I point to the one with the white daisy rubber holder on the end.

He slips it easily into the lock and turns it. The door squeaks loudly, in desperate need of some WD-40 on the hinges—another thing to add to the to-do list—and steps inside first.

"Are you coming?"

He doesn't ask it in a taunting way. It's more like he's trying to gauge how I feel about this and whether or not it's a good idea to start today.

But if I don't cross this threshold now and start this process, I don't think I ever will.

I do it. I put one foot forward and keep going until I'm standing in the kitchen. I flick the switch to turn the ceiling light on, bathing the room in a yellow tone.

Thayer wastes no time. I think he wants to distract me, so I don't get lost in my thoughts, and starts spewing out questions. "What about the table? Keep? Donate? Or trash? It's in pretty rough shape, but it could be sanded down and painted, so I'm thinking donate. And what color tape do you want to put with each category?"

I can't help but smile at his need to keep my mind from wandering. "I think yellow for donate, green for keep, and blue for trash."

"Okay, got it. Committing it to memory."

"We'll donate the table."

He rips off a piece of yellow tape and applies it to the table. "Chairs?"

"Also donate."

He tabs each of the chairs with tape. "You can just point and tell me what you want to do with each thing."

"Okay," I sigh, looking around the space.

"Trash." I indicate a picture across the room. It was a yard sale find shortly after my dad died. I thought the picture was so ugly—a muddy looking watercolor that reminds me of some kind of ugly wallpaper, but my mom loved it for some reason, or maybe she just loved it because it was something she could buy with her own money for the first time. "Actually, I want to keep it."

Thayer doesn't even question why I'd want to keep the ugly painting. He just switches the tape color and moves on.

It takes us a few hours just to go through the kitchen. I end up keeping all of the baking supplies. Despite not baking for years until I came back here, I want to keep them, and I even want to bake on my own again. I think it'll do me good and help me feel close to her. There are a few things I put in the keep pile for Georgia as well, things she already asked for—like the cookie jar that's shaped like a circus tent and a set of plates.

"How do you feel?" Thayer asks me, picking up the last of the donate boxes to load in his truck to drop off. We figured it would be easier to take the smaller items as we go and then when it's all finished, we'll rent a truck to pack up the home's bigger items to get rid of.

"I think we made good progress, but I'm also worried about how long this will take. We spent hours on one room."

"I don't mean about this." He looks around the room. "I mean about you. I know this isn't easy."

I pull out the kitchen chair and sit down. "Exhausted. Both emotionally and physically. But strangely ... happy." I shake my head. "That sounds so strange but it's true. So many of these items hold memories and it's like I get to relive them all over again." I pick up the wooden spoon I'm keeping. "Like this." Tears pool in my eyes. "It's just a wooden stirring spoon to you, but I remember stirring up cupcakes with my mom when I was little and sneaking licks of the batter when she wasn't looking. I think she knew anyway." I set the spoon back down. "It's nice, remembering the things I forgot."

Thayer sets the box back down, joining me at the table. "It doesn't sound strange. I felt the same way packing up Forrest's room. It was the hardest decision I've ever had to make, but I knew for my mental health I needed to change the space. As I packed up his clothes and toys, I remembered so many good things I'd forgotten because that one day put a dark cloud over my memories." He clears his throat, getting choked up. "Losing him was ... the worst fucking day of my life. But every day he was alive was also the best day and I realized then I was letting one day overshadow all the others. Remembering didn't feel so painful anymore after that." He shrugs. "So, yeah, I get it."

"Grief is weird."

He gives a soft laugh. "Yeah, it is."

"Do you ever wonder..." I pause, biting my lip—unsure if I should say it or not, but I decide to just go for it. "Do you ever wonder what would have happened if..."

"If Forrest hadn't died? If we'd told your mom?"

"Yeah." I look down at the table, not wanting to meet his eyes. "I know it's stupid, to waste time wondering when there's nothing you can do to change the outcome but..."

"I used to," he says softly. "All the time. But I stopped doing that a long time ago, because it was driving me insane. I'd like to think that if things had gone according to plan that your mom would've understood, but she also might've been pissed. I mean, she already knew, but making it official is different." He sighs warily, sinking further into the chair. "And then maybe we would've dated a few more years. And I would've gotten down on one knee, proposed, and we would've gotten married with Forrest as my best man. But there's also the chance that because of how young you were that the pressure would've been too much. Society looks much differently on the ages we are now, than what we were." He flicks a finger between us. "That might've torn us apart. We don't know."

"You're right." I look around the kitchen, the walls now bare, the drawers empty, cabinets and countertops completely wiped down. "I guess this just has me dwelling more than usual."

He reaches across the table, squeezing my hand. "Come on," he stands, still holding onto my hand and using it to tug me up with him. "Let's go drop this off and grab something to eat. I think we deserve it."

My stomach rumbles in answer. "Good idea."

CHAPTER THIRTY-NINE

Salem

We work on clearing out the house as much as possible. With Thayer working, he's not around to help during the weekdays so I do what I can that doesn't involve heavy lifting. After that first day it's gotten easier. I think I've managed to put blinders on and not think too much about it, which has helped. Plus, I know this needs to be done. We can't just leave the house sitting here. Sometimes, you have to set your grief aside and take care of what has to be done.

I'm elbow deep in dust, cleaning out a storage closet when my phone rings. I can't grab it right now, so I let it go to voicemail.

It rings again right away.

"Huh." I set down my cleaning supplies and get up off the floor, my body groaning in protest since I've been in a hunched position for too long. I knew I should've gotten up and taken a break, but I didn't bother.

I don't make it to my phone in time before it stops, but it starts up yet again just in time for me to find it under a pile of trash bags. Lovely.

Georgia's name lights up the phone.

"Hello?"

"I'm in labor," are the first words out of her mouth. "I know we didn't talk about this, but mom was with me both other times and I want you to be there this time. Are you okay with that?"

My heart warms that she wants me there, that she trusts and loves me enough to be there when she brings her third child into the world.

"Yeah, of course. Are you at the hospital?" I start gathering up my stuff and trying to leave things in some sort of order, but quickly realize that's a futile effort since everything is a mess.

"We're dropping the boys off with Michael's parents and driving straight there. Oh, fuck," she curses. "This hurts. I don't remember it hurting this bad before. Was it always like this?"

Michael answers her and I hear his reply of, "Yeah, and you just always forget," through the speaker phone.

"I'll be right behind you guys."

"Thank you." I can hear the tears in her voice. "I just don't want to be alone."

"What am I? Chopped liver?" Michael asks.

"You know what I mean," she argues, and they launch into a back and forth.

"All right, I'm going to hang up now so I can finish up and head to the hospital."

"Okay," my sister replies. "I love you."

"Love you, too."

I turn the lights off, set out the garbage, and run over to Thayer's to have a quick shower since I'm covered in dust and change my clothes.

When I get into my car to head to the hospital, I shoot him a quick text to let him know what's going on and that I won't be home.

He texts right back as I'm backing out of the driveway.

Thayer: I'll head to the hospital when
I'm done with work.

The local hospital isn't far, only twenty minutes away, so I call Michael through my car's Bluetooth speaker.

"Hey, I'm on my way. How is she?"

"Uh ... for the moment, calm. But as soon as she has another contraction, she'll be demanding that I get a vasectomy. As soon as that has passed, she'll threaten me that I better not because she wants one or two more. Honestly, Salem, if she keeps this up my balls are going to shrivel up and die."

I can't help but laugh. The poor guy. "Sounds like my sister. Let her know I'm on my way and I—"

I don't finish my sentence, because in that exact moment someone runs a red light, and the sound of screeching metal fills my ears. My head slams against the window, the airbag exploding, and then there's only blackness.

CHAPTER FORTY

Thayer

Saying goodbye to my crew, I hop in my truck to head home. I'll take a shower and grab a bite to eat before going to the hospital.

I'm halfway home when my phone rings and it's Georgia's name on the screen.

"Hello?" I answer skeptically, wondering why Salem's sister would be calling me. Maybe Salem's phone died, though, and she's wondering where I'm at.

"Thayer," Georgia says my name in a rush of relief. "Oh, ow! Son of a bitch! Fuck, I better not say that, because that makes me the ah!" She screams in my ear. "Michael, take the phone."

A moment later, her husband comes on the line. "Uh, hey, man."

"What's going on? Is something wrong with Salem's phone?"

He's silent for a moment. I know it's only seconds, but it feels like minutes.

"Salem's been in an accident."

I drop my phone. It falls somewhere on the floor between my feet. Making a very illegal U-turn, I speed back in the opposite direction toward the hospital.

My brain keeps repeating two words over and over again.

Salem.

Accident.

Salem.

Accident.

I'm fucking hyperventilating by the time I get to the hospital and park my truck, rushing inside through the emergency entrance.

The lady at the front desk is startled by my sudden appearance.

"Salem Matthews. Was she brought in?"

Fuck, they could've taken her to the city. Life-flighted her. What if it was really bad? What if she's in surgery? What if she's—

No. I won't fucking go there. I won't think that. She's not. She can't be. I would know if she were dead. I'd feel it. I have to believe that.

"Who's asking?" She sounds peeved, and I guess that's my fault for coming in here acting like a mad man.

"Her fiancé," I lie, but it does the trick.

"Security will take you there." She nods her head at the guy in a black and white uniform.

He hands me a sticker, and I quickly slap it on my shirt.

He walks as slow as fucking possible through the emergency section. I count the seconds. All two-hundred and sixty-three of them so I don't fucking murder the man and never find her in this maze of sectioned off rooms.

"Salem Matthews. Right here." He taps on a door.

I don't say thank you. I push past the man and into the room. "Salem?" I shove aside an ugly blue curtain, preparing myself for the worst.

She sits on the end of the bed in a gown. There's a gash beside her eye that looks like it'll need stitches and she cradles her arm tenderly.

Her eyes widen with shock when she sees me standing there. "Thayer? How did you get here? How did you know?"

"Your sister and Michael. I rushed right here."

The adrenaline flees my body, and I drop to my knees in front of her. I don't even feel the pain of my kneecaps hitting the hard surface of the floor, because I'm so fucking relieved she's okay. I thought ... well, I thought the worst. I didn't want to believe she was gone, but my brain couldn't help going to the worst-case scenario.

Her fingers delve into my hair, and she leans her body over mine. "Don't cry," she begs.

I didn't even realize I was, but she's right. I'm shaking with the sobs.

The fear that I might lose her just when I got her back was overwhelming.

But she's here. She's alive. Breathing. Sitting up. Not seriously injured.

My feelings are raw, though. Nothing makes you feel more helpless than someone you love being hurt and knowing you can't do anything about it.

"Shh," she croons. "I'm okay. I'm sore. And I think my arm is broken. But I'm okay."

She keeps saying it over and over—that she's okay.

I manage to pull myself up off the floor, gently taking her face in my hands. She lets me look her over, appraise her for more bumps and bruises. After I've finished a thorough inspection she arches a brow, fighting a smile.

"What's the verdict, Dr. Holmes?"

"The verdict," I brace my hands on the bed, bending so I'm eye-level with her, "is that you tried to give me a heart attack,

Ms. Matthews. I'm an old man now. You can't do that to me."

"You're not even forty yet." She rolls her eyes. It makes me want to spank her. She's in the fucking hospital after a car accident and she's rolling her eyes at me? The nerve. "And forty isn't even old so cut the shit."

"Are you okay?" I ask her. "Not just physically, but mentally."

She exhales shakily and I place my hand on her knee, trying to instill some warmth and comfort into her body.

"Shaken up," she admits. "It happened so fast, and I blacked out when I hit my head." She points to the side of her face where the cut is. There's a lump on her skull as well. "My arm is killing me though."

Her left arm is already swollen and there's a purplish bruise near the elbow.

"Have they X-rayed yet?"

"No." She shakes her head tiredly. "That's what I'm waiting for. Poor Georgia, she wanted me here to help with her labor and now this happened."

"Don't stress about it, Sunshine," I beg. I don't like seeing her like this.

"I'm just upset." Her bottom lip wobbles with the threat of tears. "It seems like it's always something and I can't catch a break. I'm just exhausted from life." She sniffles and I grab a tissue from the box by the bed, handing it to her. She smiles gratefully, wiping beneath her eyes. "I'm being dramatic. I know I'm so blessed and lucky in so many ways—"

"Don't degrade your feelings." I cup her cheek in my palm. "A car accident is traumatic for anyone. Don't feel guilty for being upset. You've been dealing with a lot already."

She nods, swiping the tissue beneath her nose. "You're

right."

"Ms. Matthews? I'm here to take you to our X-ray department."

A nurse enters the room pushing a wheelchair. I glance from it to Salem. "Why do you need a wheelchair? Are your legs—"

"It's just standard hospital procedure, sir." The nurse interrupts my line of questioning. "Nothing to worry about."

In other words, I need to calm my ass down.

Got it.

Salem gets into the wheelchair, and I'm forced to stay behind. Luckily, she isn't gone more than fifteen minutes.

"A doctor will be in shortly after the images have been reviewed."

"Thank you," Salem tells the nurse, settling onto the bed and lying down. When the nurse is gone, she says to me, "I'm so tired now."

"It's the adrenaline." I'm feeling it too, to be honest, but I don't tell her that because I don't want her to think I'm trying to lessen how she feels. "Close your eyes and go to sleep. I'll be right here. I'm not going anywhere."

"You're not?"

I take her hand in mine. "I'm going to be right here."

Despite all the beeping machines, her eyes close a few minutes later, her breaths evening out, and I know she's fallen asleep.

I'm glad she's able to doze off. The rest will do her body good.

An hour later a doctor finally comes in and I'm forced to wake her up.

He doesn't waste any time telling her that her arm is

broken, but doesn't need surgery, so they'll be fitting her into a cast and that the cut by her eye won't need stiches, but the nurse will apply butterfly bandages. Thank God it doesn't need stitches since she's already been here for roughly two hours. If she had needed them, you'd think they would've taken care of that already.

When the doctor leaves, Salem says, "I've probably missed the baby being born."

"You don't know that."

Her lips pout out. "I feel so bad that I disappointed Georgia."

"Oh, fuck," I curse. "I should've called her and let her know you were okay." I yank my phone out of jeans pocket, but I don't have any cell service. "I'll go outside and call her."

She grabs my arm, yanking me back down into the chair. "I had the nurse call her and let her know since I was on the phone with Michael at the time. I didn't want her in labor and freaking out about me."

I brush her hair back from her forehead, looking at her in awe. "Do you have any idea how remarkable you are, the way you always put everyone else first?"

She shrugs like it's no big deal.

Luckily, the wait to get a cast put on isn't long and she lights up like a little kid when she gets to pick the bandage color. She chooses a light pink, saying that Seda will love it. I don't think she realizes it but I'm pretty sure pink is her favorite color too.

It's dark out by the time she gets discharged and we head up in the main elevator to the maternity level.

"Do you think she's had the baby yet?" Salem looks up at me, eyes wide with excitement.

"I don't know. I guess we're about to find out."

The elevator opens and we step out onto the maternity floor. Salem strides up to the desk, giving her sister's name.

"Down that hall. Room 216."

Salem books it in that direction. With my long legs I'm able to keep up with her easily, but I am more than a tad amused at her enthusiasm.

She reaches the door and gives a soft knock. We wait a minute and then Michael eases the door open.

"Hi." His eyes are lit up with happiness, and I already know before he says it that the baby is here. "Do you want to meet the baby?"

Salem jumps up and down excitedly. "Yes!"

"How's your arm?" He eyes her cast.

"It's fine, now let me see the baby."

He chuckles, stepping aside. "You can come in too, man. Everyone's decent."

I follow Salem inside, watching her light up when she sees her sister lying in the bed. Tired, but glowing as she holds her sleeping newborn.

"Oh my God." Salem's hands go to her chest, her mouth turning down in a frown when she smacks her boob with the fiberglass cast. Undeterred, she goes on, "Look at him and that sweet little face."

"Her."

"Her?" Salem reels back, stunned. "What do you mean her?"

Georgia smiles from ear to ear, perhaps the happiest I've ever seen her. Michael moves to her side, his chest puffed out with pride. "Apparently the doctors got it wrong. We have a little girl. A daughter." She smiles up at her husband and he leans down to kiss her.

There's a pang in my chest. Not exactly jealousy, but I want that. I want *this* with Salem.

One day, I remind myself. *In due time.*

"Oh my God." Salem moves closer to the bed, peering down at the squished face of the newborn, her head covered with a pink and blue hat. "What's her name?" she asks softly so as not to disturb the sleeping baby.

"Victoria Allison."

"Oh." I settle my hand on her back, her eyes filling with tears when she looks up at me. Focusing back on her sister, she whispers, "It's beautiful. Perfect."

"Do you want to hold her?"

Salem's eyes widen with excitement. "Can I?"

Her sister doesn't say anything more. She lifts the baby up for her to take. Salem cradles baby Victoria carefully in her arms. I don't think she even realizes it, but she immediately starts rocking her.

"Look at you, precious one. So little. Your brothers are going to adore you." She lifts her gaze to her sister and brother-in-law. "Do the boys know yet?"

Georgia smiles, shaking her head. "No, we thought we'd surprise them tomorrow when they come to visit."

"They're going to be so excited." Salem turns to me. "They wanted a sister and were a tad disappointed it was another boy."

Georgia laughs, rolling her eyes. "Disappointed? Jackson, our oldest, fell to the ground crying when we told him."

Michael rubs her shoulder. "They're going to think we lied to them."

"We *all* got played with this one." She points at the baby. "Only a few hours old and she's already giving us a run for our money."

"How are you feeling?" Salem asks her. "How was labor?"

"Once I got my epidural it was fine and dandy."

Salem shakes her head in amusement, still rocking the baby. "Do you want to hold her?"

"Me?" I ask shocked.

"Go ahead," Georgia encourages.

Salem passes the baby to me. She looks so tiny in my arms. Like a little potato or something. Her small pink lips are parted in sleep, her eyelids a light shade of blue. One little fist is curled up by her face, having escaped the swaddle she's in.

There's a loud sniffle, drawing my attention to Salem. She sobs openly watching me hold the baby. I don't ask her what's wrong. I can see it written all over her face. She's thinking of Seda and what could have been. I want to tell her not to cry, that it's in the past, but I think she needs to feel this. I want her to let her pain go.

I hold the baby a little longer, until she starts to stir. She's probably hungry so I hand her to Georgia.

"We better be going." Salem hugs her sister, kissing her cheek. "It's late and you need to rest and love on your new baby. Let me know if you need anything. Especially now that this sweetie is a girl, not a boy." She lightly taps the baby's nose.

Georgia beams at the newborn in her arms. "I wouldn't mind a few new outfits. All I have is boy stuff, and I'd like something cute to bring her home in."

"You got it. I'll bring a few options." She hugs her sister again and then we're headed out of the hospital.

We exit through the emergency room since that's where I parked.

She sighs when she sees my truck, a frown marring her lips. "I'll have to get a new car."

"Yours was totaled?"

"The whole right side was really messed up. I doubt it's going to be worth fixing." She rubs at her forehead, and I grab her hand so she doesn't mess up the bandage. "I need to call Caleb and let him know what happened. He probably wonders why I haven't called to say goodnight to Seda."

"Call him on the way home."

"Yeah," she says sleepily, "I will."

The day has clearly caught up with her. She speaks with Caleb for a while. He's clearly worried—I can't hear what he says, just the rapid speed at which he shoots questions at her. She assures him she's all right while I swing by a drive-thru and pick up something for us to eat.

"I'm okay, I promise. Seriously. It's just some scrapes and bruises." There's a pause on her end of the conversation. "Yes, I realize a broken arm is more than a scrape, but—" Caleb's voice gets a bit louder, more animated. "No, we're not suing the other driver. Caleb, I swear I'm fine. The car isn't, but I am." She shakes her head, trying not to smile. "I know you don't care about the car, but I'm telling you I'm okay. I wouldn't be talking to you if I wasn't."

I pull up to the speaker and order a bunch of random things. Pulling around, I sit up to pull my wallet out. Salem is already waving her card at me, and I push her hand gently away.

She sticks her tongue out at me, but slips her card away.

"Mhmm, I'll call you in the morning. All right. Bye." She ends the call. "Caleb worries too much."

"He cares about you."

"You actually don't sound jealous saying that. I'm surprised."

I shrug, handing cash over at the window. "I'm not. Not

anymore at least."

She grins, her eyes crinkling at the corners. "So, you admit it? You were jealous of him at one time?"

I grunt, taking my change and driving up to the next window. They hand over the bag of food and I pull out of the lot.

"Use your words, caveman," she bosses.

"Stupidly so, yes. At the time I didn't even realize that's what it was. I rationalized that I was only looking out for you. Someone had to."

She shakes her head, her lips twisted in amusement. "Lumberjack caveman," she mutters softly.

"What was that?" I try not to smile, rubbing my hand over my mouth to hide any hint of one.

"You're such a lumberjack. The beard. The plaid shirts. The muscles. And you act like a hulking caveman sometimes. So, you're a lumberjack caveman."

"Well," I turn onto the street and pull into my driveway a moment later, "that's a new one."

"Hey, if the shoe fits wear it."

I'm not even touching that one.

Grabbing the bags of food, we head inside to immediately be greeted by Winnie and Binx. I let Winnie out back and set out the food on the counter.

"I didn't think I was hungry, but this actually smells really good." She picks up a fry, biting off the end.

After I let Winnie inside, we sit down to eat and head upstairs to bed.

I pull her into my arms, burying my head into the crook of her neck. I inhale her scent, thinking about how I could've lost her today. But I didn't.

I hold her that much closer.

CHAPTER FORTY-ONE

Salem

"Your cast is going to be a unique accessory to your bridesmaid dress," Lauren says with amusement, signing her name to the hard pink arm cast.

"I know," I sigh, frowning at my reflection in the mirror of the dress shop. The light pink of the cast seems to stick out like a blinding light against the sage color of the bridesmaid dress. "I'm sorry. It totally clashes."

She rolls her eyes. "I don't care about the cast. I care about you."

"I know, but I feel bad." I frown at my reflection in the massive floor length mirror. The cast is thick and bulky, sticking out like a sore thumb.

"Stop." She waves her hands through the air, flapping them in my face. "Nuh-uh. We're not doing this. None of this feeling bad shit. No moping. I mean it."

"Okay." I paste a smile on my face. "As long as you're okay with it, that's all that matters."

"You act like I'd kick you out of my wedding for a broken arm. Do you think so little of me?" She jokes, heading behind the curtain so the seamstress can help her into her dress for the final fitting. Two weeks from now we head to Vegas for the bachelorette party and her wedding is the weekend after that.

So many things are happening this summer. The good thing is, between the birth of Victoria and Lauren's wedding, it's been a nice distraction from losing my mom.

Stepping off the riser, I take a seat on the couch by one of Lauren's other bridesmaids named Holly. She works with Lauren. On her other side is Elizabeth, Anthony's sister. The wedding party is rounded out with two other friends—Kelsey and Sabrina whom she met through an art gallery she loves.

When Lauren steps out from behind the curtain, we all collectively gasp.

Lauren is stunning. Her dress is sleek and form fitting, modern and yet classic at the same time.

She grins at our reaction. "Isn't it beautiful?"

She went with only her mom to pick out her dress and ended up having something custom designed since nothing suited her taste, so it's the first time any of us are seeing it.

"You look stunning!" Holly cries.

"So beautiful." Elizabeth wipes a tear from her eye.

"You're an absolute looker," this is from Kelsey.

Sabrina adds, "Anthony is going to lose his mind when he sees you."

That leaves me for last. "You're beautiful, Lauren. You're a ... well, you're a bride."

She beams from ear to ear, clapping her hands together. She launches into a detailed description of what she has planned for her hair and makeup. I love hearing her so happy and excited for her wedding. Anthony's the perfect guy for her.

When the fitting appointment is over, we all head to brunch at one of Lauren's favorite restaurants in the city.

After our orders are placed, Lauren turns to me. "Tell me, how are things going with Caleb?"

"The usual, I guess."

Her eyes narrow and she picks up her mimosa, taking a sip. "You guess?"

I sigh, not really wanting to get into it, but Lauren is like a dog with a bone, and I know she won't let this go easily.

"It's just hard trying to figure out custody. Neither of us really wants to get a mediator involved, but with school getting ready to start I want her to live with me during the week and I'd like to have her some weekends too, but Caleb is arguing that her school is in Boston, and she's used to it so we shouldn't change her."

Lauren squeezes my hand sympathetically. "No offense to Caleb, but you're her mom. I don't just mean that in the DNA sense. You're the one who's stayed at home with her and all that. Besides, he works long hours. I don't think he can be as stable for her as he'd like to think he can be."

I pull my hair back into a ponytail, more from the need to busy my hands with something than an actual need to get my hair out of my face. "I think he assumed I'd move back to Boston and none of this would be a big deal, because even if I moved out of our place I'd still be in the city, but with me staying in Hawthorne Mills that puts us a few hours away."

"I know you probably won't like me saying this, but honey, he's being selfish. Seda needs to be with you, and he can have her some weekends."

She makes it all sound so simple, but there's *nothing* easy about sharing custody of your child. It doesn't matter how well things ended, it's a complicated situation.

"We'll figure it out," I say evasively.

"I'm not letting this go." She wags a finger. "If she's going to be with you, she has to get enrolled soon. You know this. Stop being a wimp and tell him like it is."

I pick up my mimosa with my good hand, downing it like a shot.

I think I'm going to have to be drunk to make it through the rest of the day.

***

I make it back home fairly early the next morning. It's Sunday, the street quiet. I let myself into the house, expecting to find Thayer still asleep but he's in the living room at his puzzle table, quietly putting together the Disney Princess puzzle Seda picked out for him. He promised to have it finished by the time she comes back since she's excited to see it.

"Hey." I wrap my arms around him from behind. "I missed you." I kiss his cheek.

"Mmm," he hums, "missed you too." His voice is still gruff and deeper than normal from sleep. His hair is a mess too, so I doubt he's been up long.

"I want some coffee. Have you had any yet?" I head out of the living room, toward the kitchen.

"Not yet," I hear him mutter.

I set the coffee to brew and make myself a bowl of cereal.

Thayer comes into the kitchen, Winnie and Binx on his heels. "I told you I could get you from the airport."

"I know, but it would've been silly to drag you out so early. The taxi was fine."

"We need to go to a dealership today."

"I know." I frown, my stomach rolling at the idea of the car buying process, but what's a girl to do? My car was declared totaled like I figured it would be, so it's time for a new one. "I don't even know what I want."

"That's what test drives are for. I've already researched some good options. I don't know your budget, so I picked a few different ones in different price ranges."

"Well, look at you," I say in amusement, grabbing a coffee mug from the cabinet, "doing all your research like a proper boy scout."

He eyes the cast on my arm. It's now adorned with all of the girls' signatures from the bridesmaid's party. Lauren signed hers with, *I licked it so it's mine*, above her name. I'd expect no less from her.

"I just want to keep you safe."

"I know, and I appreciate that." I pour coffee into my mug, then fill another for Thayer. "I wish you didn't worry so much."

He shrugs, fighting a smile. "Can't help it."

Sitting down at the table with my coffee and cereal, I say, "Show me these options."

***

A few hours later I find myself at a Toyota dealership.

"What do you think of this one?" The salesman shows me a white 4-Runner. It's beautiful, the paint a pearly finish with a beige interior.

I don't say anything, though, not wanting to indicate I like the looks of it. Thayer launches into a series of questions for the man who struggles to keep up.

There's something insanely hot about Thayer taking charge. He stands with his arms crossed over a gray t-shirt, a pair of athletic shorts hugging his toned backside.

I swear everything about this man turns me on.

Not that he complains.

Thayer has always made me feel safe to be myself with sex. I don't feel the need to downplay my desire and I know I can talk to him about what I like and don't like.

As a teenager I used to feel ashamed of my sexual urges, worried that it wasn't normal because of my past. Little did I know that being a teenager means almost all of you are raging hornballs whether you act on it or not.

"Let's take it for a drive."

"All right, sir. Let me grab the keys for this one," the young salesman replies, heading back to the dealership a short distance away.

"Do you like it?"

"It's pretty," I reply. "I don't know much about cars to be able to comment on anything else."

We've already been to three different dealerships, and I wasn't crazy in love with anything, so right now I'm feeling pretty neutral about the whole thing which is probably for the best anyway. That way I won't make any hasty decisions.

Thayer launches into different specifications about safety and handling, but finishes with, "This one is the Limited model, so it has an extra two seats."

I arch a brow. "And this is important because?" I try not to smile while I wait for his answer. Yes, I'm baiting him. Sue me.

He pulls me against his chest, lowering his head to rub his nose against mine. "We have to have room for all our future kids. Winnie and Binx need space too. They're important family members as well."

"How dare I forget the dog and the cat." I shake my head in mock shame and he clucks his tongue playfully.

"I've got the keys and the license plate." The salesman

returns, holding both up.

Thayer somehow manages to convince the salesman to stay behind while we take the SUV out for a spin. I roll the windows down, letting fresh air blow throughout. My hair whips around my shoulders and I can't stop smiling.

"I like this one."

Thayer laughs. "I had a feeling this might be the one."

I miss my old car, but there's no getting it back and I can't afford that kind of luxury vehicle on my own.

We return to the lot, and I let Thayer handle making the deal.

It takes forever, but two hours later I'm the proud new owner of a car.

Thayer walks out with me to the SUV. I hop inside the driver's seat and roll the window down so he can lean inside.

"Where do you want to go?" he asks. "I'll follow you."

There's only one answer. "Home."

His eyes light up. "I like the sound of that."

"Me too."

CHAPTER FORTY-TWO

Salem

The back room of A Checkered Past Antiques is full of a mixture of empty boxes and ones that are filled with random items that never made it out front.

This ... this is harder than the house.

This was my mom's love, her passion. This was the thing she made her own after my dad passed away. She worked so hard to make the store a reflection of herself. Filled with items that were beautiful but maybe a little broken, in need of some TLC and a little elbow grease.

I let myself cry instead of keeping the emotions bottled up.

Packing this up is like saying goodbye to the last substantial piece of my mom.

"What do you need me to do?" Thayer asks from across the room.

I know he's concerned about me, but he also knows I need to feel these things. I remind myself that every tear is filled with love. I didn't shed a single one for my father. There was no love in my heart for him. Now, my whole body weeps with this loss.

Sometimes I think if I close my eyes tight and think hard enough about it that I can conjure her image and bring her back to the living.

Is that how Thayer felt? That if he tried hard enough, he

could undo what happened?

"Just cut down the empty boxes for now and set them outside. Bring any full ones to me and I'll go through it."

"All right." He pulls a box cutter out of his pocket and gets to work.

I sort through the things, tagging some as I go. There's a flea market in town soon so I figure I can try to sell some of the smaller items that are in good shape.

I pick up the box with my candles, the one I brought back when my mom said someone already bought them. Only I have no idea who that was, and no one's ever tried to contact me about getting them.

I pull one out, looking at the label. It's peeling up on the right corner.

Just like baking, I stopped making candles.

When I left this town, so young and pregnant, I left behind pieces of me. It was like I was trying to forget the parts of myself that reminded me of Thayer.

"Hey, is something wrong?" He approaches me, gently settling his hand on my lower back.

"No." I set the box down. "It's just some of my old candles."

"I wondered where those were. I bought them forever ago and Allie was holding onto them for me."

I whip around, almost smacking my head into his chin. He takes a step back, putting out a hand to steady me.

"You're the one who bought these?"

"Yeah."

"Why?" I blurt out, surprised.

His brows furrow in confusion. "You really have to ask why?"

I nod. "I want to know."

"Because, you left and I had nothing but our memories, that ring," he points to my finger where the ring sits that he got me so long ago, "and a few candles. When I burned all those up and the house didn't smell like you anymore, I came here and bought more."

"They're all peony. I smell like peonies?"

"You do. And they're your favorite flower. I guess it had a two-fold purpose."

"So, you what, just bought up all the peony candles?"

"No, I bought them all."

"Yeah," I point at the box, "all the peony ones."

"No." He shakes his head, gripping my hips. "No, Sunshine. I bought all of them. Every last candle you made, and I've slowly gone through them over the years. This just happened to be what I was saving for last. I just never got it picked up. Your mom held onto all of them for me since it was a lot."

"You ... you got all of them? Thayer," I choke out a laugh. "There must have been at least two-hundred."

"At least," he agrees. "But I couldn't let anyone else have them."

"You ... I ..." I can't seem wrap my head around this.

He cups my cheek. "I lost you, for what I thought was forever. I wanted to hold onto you in any way that I could." He presses a gentle kiss to my lips. "Let's leave this for now. There's something I want to show you."

***

I'm surprised when we pull into the driveway of the house. "Why are we back home?"

Thayer puts his truck in park, shutting off the ignition.

"Because what I want to show you is here."

I rack my brain, trying to think about what he could possibly be referring to but nothing comes to mind.

Undoing my seatbelt, I climb out of the truck and follow him. He doesn't go inside like I expect, instead I follow him out back.

He leads me around the fenced in pool, following the pathway that leads to the greenhouse. I haven't ventured out here yet. I'm not even sure why.

Opening the door, he waits, letting me go in first.

My jaw drops. Spinning in circles, I take in the beautiful pink flowers. They're everywhere. The entire greenhouse is filled with peonies.

"This is where you've been getting the bouquets?" I ask, but I already know the answer. My hands go to my mouth.

"Yes," he answers softly, watching me spin in circles.

I blow out a breath, trying to wrap my head around this.

My favorite flower.

Thayer Holmes has lovingly grown my favorite flower in his greenhouse all this time just because it reminds him of me.

"I don't know what to say."

"You don't have to say anything."

"There's so many of them." The greenhouse isn't massive, but it is a decent size, and he's utilized every available inch to grow my favorite flower.

"What do you do with all of them?" I touch the stem of one, inhaling the scent.

"Before you came back?"

"Mhmm."

Surely he sells them or uses them in his landscaping business in some way.

"Nothing."

"Nothing?" I gasp, startled. "You just grow them? That's it?"

"Yeah." He says it so innocently. "The first time I ever cut one was for your first bouquet. Technically I cut them before that, but only when they died."

"You are ... You ... I ... I don't know what to say."

"You don't have to say anything."

I brush an errant tear off my cheek. Thayer Holmes loves me. He loves me more than I think anyone has ever loved another person before. And all this time, he stayed in the shadows, letting my life go on because he knew I was married. He did all this never thinking he'd get another chance with me.

I wrap my arms around his neck, his own arms go around my body. He holds me tight against his solid, warm chest.

"I love you," I whisper into the skin of his neck.

His lips press a soft kiss to the top of my head. "I love you, too, Sunshine. Thank you for loving me back."

That's one thing he doesn't need to thank me for.

Loving Thayer isn't a choice. It just is. Loving him is natural, automatic, just like my body's need to breathe air.

CHAPTER FORTY-THREE

Salem

"Dad! I'm here!" Seda runs into the house, dropping her bag on the floor.

I've been meeting Caleb halfway for pickups and drop-offs so one of us doesn't have to go the whole way, and I've finally gotten him to agree that it makes the most sense for Seda to live with me, which means I need to get her enrolled in the local elementary school as soon as possible.

"Hey, bunny." He comes around the corner just in time for her to launch herself at him. "Whoa. Someone missed me."

"I missed you guys."

"We missed you, too," I say, picking up her bag and carrying it to the steps.

"What's for dinner? I'm hungry."

"I'm making homemade pizza. You want to help?" Thayer asks her.

"Oh, yes!" She jumps up and down. "I love helping."

The two of them disappear into the kitchen so I carry her bag all the way up to her room. I unpack and put away her things, hanging the duffel bag on the closet door. I go ahead and set out a pair of her pajamas in the bathroom since it'll be time for bed soon. I know more than likely she won't like the pair I picked and will choose another, but oh well.

Downstairs, I smile when I find my two favorite people at the kitchen island. Seda sits on the counter, placing pepperonis onto one of the pizzas. There are three total, one for each of us.

Winnie paces on the floor, hoping to snag a bite of cheese or anything edible.

"What kind of pizza are you making?" I ask Seda, smacking a kiss on top of her head.

She giggles playfully trying to push me away. "Ew, mom. No kisses when I'm cooking." She holds up the stack of pepperonis she's holding. "I'm making a pepperoni pizza."

"And what kind are you having?" I poke Thayer's side, scooting behind him.

"Meat and veggies. Put whatever you want on yours and I'll pop these in the oven."

"All right."

I spoon some sauce onto the dough, add my cheese, and then top it with onions, green peppers, and olives.

"Those look gross, Mommy." Seda points at the olives. "They look like eyeballs."

"They're not eyeballs. They're olives," I explain. "I promise they taste good."

Seda crooks her finger at Thayer, urging him to bend lower to her level. When he does she cups her hands around her mouth like she's going to whisper, only at a normal level of volume she says, "I think she's lying. They must taste disgusting."

Thayer chuckles. "I don't like them."

Shaking my head, I cluck my tongue. "You two are ganging up on me."

Thayer puts a hand to his chest. "It's not my fault you like those things."

He sets all the pizzas in the oven, then turns to Seda. "Let me put you down."

"No, piggyback ride!"

"Seda," I warn.

"Please?" she adds.

Thayer turns around. "Hop on."

She does just that, giggling when he takes off running with her on his back. Winnie runs after them barking at his heels.

"Be careful you two," I plead.

They're going to be the end of me, I swear it. But I love it, love *them*, and the bond they've been able to form so quickly. I worried that even though Seda knew she had another dad that she'd struggle to connect with Thayer. But my worries were for nothing.

When our pizzas are finished baking, we sit on the back deck to eat our dinner.

"This is so yummy." Seda chews on a slice of her pizza. "Can we make this again?"

"Sure." Thayer smiles, pleased she likes it.

"I like this way more than delivery, Mommy."

"I guess we'll start making all our pizzas at home," I joke, tapping her nose.

She giggles, touching the spot my finger was at. "Did you get sauce on my nose?"

"Maybe."

"Ugh, Mom." She grabs a napkin, wiping frantically at her nose. "You made me dirty." Thayer watches us, amusement in his eyes. I can see how happy he is and it makes my heart soar. Setting her napkin back down, she asks, "After dinner can we watch a movie?"

"How about after you have a bath?"

She huffs. "Fine."

***

"Her favorite movie is *Hocus Pocus* too?" Thayer whispers in my ear.

Seda is fast asleep on the opposite side of the sectional couch with Winnie and Binx curled up beside her. She didn't even make it fifteen minutes into the movie.

"What can I say? I watched it a billion times while I was pregnant with her and when she was a baby. It must have rubbed off on her."

"She's not scared of the zombie dude?"

"Billy?"

"Yeah, that guy."

"No." I shake my head. "He's actually her favorite."

He shakes his head, tsking softly. "My girls are so weird."

I love the sound of that—not the weird part, but that we're his girls.

"You're one to talk, Mr. Lord-of-the-Rings."

"Those movies are amazing." He takes a handful of popcorn from the bowl. "The books too."

"You read the books?"

He looks at me like I'm insane. "Yes, I read the books."

"Aren't they like massive?"

"Not really. Did you think I couldn't read?"

"Of course, I didn't think that," I laugh softly. We're still whispering because of Seda. The last thing I want to do is wake her up when I know she needs her sleep.

"I guess I just didn't picture you sitting around and reading. I mean, you're already so busy and you have other hobbies and—" He shuts me up with a kiss. "What was that for?"

"Because you're adorable when you ramble."

"Oh."

He stares at me intensely and I wonder what he's thinking. Right about now I wish I had the power to read minds.

He leans forward, swiping a marker off the coffee table from when Seda was coloring.

I narrow my eyes, wondering what he's doing.

"You haven't let me sign your cast yet," he says in response to my questioning gaze.

"I didn't know you wanted to."

I hold my casted arm out to him. There's a lone bare spot left in the upper part of the cast near my elbow. He tugs my arm closer, lowering his head so I can't see what he's writing. It seems like he's writing out more than his name.

When he sits back up, he meets my gaze and holds it. Lowering my eyes, I look down at my cast.

My breath catches in my throat.

Marry me?

My eyes dart back up to his. "What?"

He shoves the blanket off his lap, kneeling on the rug in front of me. He takes my hands in his eyes.

"I wasn't going to ask you like this, but sitting here with you, with her," he glances over at Seda's sleeping form, "I thought what am I waiting for? You already know how I feel about you and I know you love me. We want to keep building our family and our life together, and so why not do that as husband and wife?"

There's nothing else for me to say but, "Yes."

He smiles, taking my cheeks in his hands he kisses me deeply. "Wait here." He gets up from his kneeling position on the floor, and heads upstairs. He comes back a minute or so later and opens a ring box. I can't help but gasp. The ring is emerald cut, with a thick silver band, and a pale pink diamond. It's unique and yet simple—the most beautiful ring I've ever seen. He slips it onto my ring finger and it's a perfect fit. "I saw this ring a few weeks ago and I had to buy it. I knew it was perfect for you."

"I love it. I love *you*."

He kisses me again, and Seda chooses that moment to wake up. "Why are you guys kissing? We're supposed to be watching the movie."

Thayer chuckles and I shake my head, beyond amused that she's oblivious to the fact that she's been sleeping.

"I asked your mom to marry me. Is that okay with you?"

She lights up, sitting up fully. Winnie gives a little whine at the change in position. "Does that mean I get to be a flower girl?"

Thayer and I exchange a look, both trying to hide our amusement. "Yes," we say in unison.

"Then it's definitely okay with me."

CHAPTER FORTY-FOUR

Salem

My toiletry bag sits half-packed on the edge of the bathroom sink. I stare at the handful of tampons sitting in the bottom of it from the last time I took a trip. I start counting up the days, realizing I'm almost a week late.

I'm supposed to be leaving for Las Vegas in only a few hours, but now...

"Thayer?" I call out from the bathroom. He's in the bedroom, getting ready for work, so he pokes his head in right away.

"Yeah?"

"I'm late."

He looks at his watch. "What? No, you're not. Your flight is still hours away."

"No, babe. My period. It's late."

"Oh fuck." His eyes widen. "You ... you're pregnant?"

I bite my lip, my hands unconsciously going to my stomach. "I think I could be. I'm going to run to the store and get a test."

"No, you stay and finish packing. I'll go buy it. I'll be back as fast I can." He finishes tugging his shirt on, the one with the Holmes Landscaping logo over the left side of the chest, and a bigger version of it on the back.

I pace the bathroom and bedroom while he's gone,

haphazardly throwing my things into my overnight bag. I'm only going to be in Vegas for two nights, so I'm definitely overpacking which isn't like me, but my head is all over the place.

I knew this would eventually be the outcome when I tossed my birth control, so it's not a surprise that I'm probably pregnant, but I know I'll feel unsure until I take the test.

I stand in front of the mirror, lifting my tank top to reveal my bare stomach. Obviously, there's no bump there, but I place my hand beneath my belly button, rubbing in small circles.

Is there a baby in there?

My feelings are vastly different than when I missed my period with Seda. Then, I was a terrified nineteen-year-old, panicked at the idea of an unplanned pregnancy and being a single mom.

This time around, I feel nothing but excitement at the idea of becoming a mom again.

It's crazy to think a few months ago I wasn't sure I'd ever have more kids. Deep down I knew I wouldn't want to have kids with anyone who wasn't Thayer.

I hear the front door open and nearly burst with nervous energy when Thayer strolls into the bedroom. He passes me the pharmacy bag and I remove the box. He splurged and got one that leaves absolutely no confusion that says either PREGNANT or NOT PREGNANT.

Hurrying into the bathroom, I close myself into the little room with the toilet while Thayer waits on the other side.

"It says it takes five minutes for results to appear," he says through the doorway.

I finish my business and pull up my shorts. Opening the door, Thayer moves out of my way. I cap the stick and lay it on the counter, washing my hands.

"How do you feel?" He wraps his arms around me, hugging me tight to his chest.

I bite my lip, leaning my head back to peer up at him. "Nervous. Excited. Happy. You?"

"Happy," he repeats with a grin, rubbing his thumbs over my cheeks. "So fucking happy."

"It might be negative," I remind him, though I'm convinced it won't be.

My period is never late, so the only logical conclusion is that I am pregnant. But there's always that small chance that I'm not, so I pace the length of the bathroom waiting for the five minutes to be up. Thayer watches me from the corner of the bathroom, his lips quirked in amusement. He doesn't say anything, just lets me get out my nervous energy.

"How long has it been?"

He looks down at his watch. "Another minute."

"Ugh!" I groan in frustration.

After the longest minute of my life, I pick up the pregnancy test. I stare at it in surprise. Thayer comes up behind me, looking over my shoulder.

NOT PREGNANT.

"Oh," I say softly, gently laying the stick back on the sink. "Oh," I say a bit louder this time. "I thought for sure I was pregnant. I..."

Devastation fills me.

I burst into uncontrollable sobs. It's stupid, I know, but I feel like I've failed at something. I know we haven't been trying long, and these things take time, but I guess I naively thought since I got pregnant with Seda while taking my birth control religiously that when I actually stopped it would just happen immediately.

So stupid of me.

On top it are the confusing emotions of grief for my mom that makes me extra emotional with everything these days.

"Hey," Thayer reaches for me, "it's okay."

"It's late, my period is late," I defend. "But I'm not..." I trail off, still in disbelief.

"Fuck, baby." He rests his chin on top of my head. "I'm sorry."

He's apologizing? Why? It's not his fault. It's not mine either. I know that, but I'm just sad. After so much devastation lately, I felt excited at the prospect of being pregnant.

"It's okay," I sniffle, pulling out of his hold. I grab a piece of toilet paper, using it to dry my blotchy face. "I'm just dealing with a lot right now." I fan my suddenly hot face with my hands. "It's no big deal."

I don't know whether I'm trying to convince him or myself.

"You're allowed to be upset."

"I-I know that." I hastily put the last few things in my toiletry bag and zip it up. "I need to go. I can't miss my flight."

"Salem—" He reaches for me, but I scoot out of his hold.

I add the small bag into my suitcase and zip it up. "I'm going to call an Uber." I look around for my phone, not able to remember where I last set it.

"Salem," he says my name again, sterner this time. "Maybe you shouldn't go."

I snort. "Not go? It's Lauren's bachelorette, I have to go. She's my best friend."

I'm not going to let this overshadow her weekend. That would be selfish.

"Please, just talk to me." He grips my arms, forcing me to

stop pacing around the room. "I'll drive you to the airport." I open my mouth to argue that he'll be late for work, but he beats me to it. "I'm the boss, I can be late if I want. I just want to know how you're feeling. I don't want you to keep this bottled inside. You do too much of that as it is."

I shake my head back and forth, biting my lip. "I don't want to talk about it."

"You need to," he insists.

But I don't want to voice my thoughts aloud. I know I'll sound selfish and whiny and that's not at all how I want to be as a person.

"Salem," he insists. "Please, talk to me. There's nothing you could say that would bother me."

"I don't want to complain."

"How is me *asking* you to talk about it, you complaining?"

I sit down on the edge of the bed. "Sometimes I think I'm being punished," I whisper the bad thought out loud. "That I'm not allowed to be happy."

His face falls. "Why would you think that?"

"My dad." I barely utter those two words. They taste like tar on my tongue. I don't like talking about him. Thayer kneels in front of me, his hands on my knees. "Maybe," I go on, "because of what he did to me, I'm supposed to suffer." This is a thought I've only ever shared with my therapist. It's one that hasn't haunted me in a long time, but when my mom's cancer came back terminal this time, that thought reared its ugly head again. I also had it when I had to leave Thayer. "It's like I can't catch a break. My mom got cancer, Forrest died, I lost you, the cancer came back, my mom died, and I just..." I let my head fall. "It's like every time I start to feel happy something happens to ruin it and maybe it's the universe saying I don't deserve that."

"Hey." I can hear the tears in his voice. He takes my cheeks in his hands, forcing me to look at him. "Don't think like that. It's not true. I don't believe it for a minute. What he did—*that's on him*. You did nothing wrong. Do you hear me, Salem? You. Did. Nothing. Wrong. You didn't ask for that to happen. He was an evil, disgusting man, and those choices are on him. He has to pay for them, not you. But sometimes," his cheeks are wet with tears, and it breaks my heart more, "things just happen. Life isn't perfect. It's not smooth sailing. There are good days and bad. Things happen that we don't understand, and we just have to keep going. I'll never understand why my son had to leave this earth before me, but I know I have to keep living for him even if he's not here to see it. Your mom getting cancer is a tragedy and it's awful, but it was just life and how things go. It wasn't to punish you. Please, don't think that. And neither is this," he tosses his thumb over his shoulder at the bathroom. "It's one negative test, and if it worries you, I'll pay whatever the fuck I have to for every test we both need to ease your mind. But I fucking hate that you, even for a second, think any of these things are your fault."

I swallow past the lump in my throat. I don't deserve this man, but I'm so thankful he's mine.

I wipe the tears from his cheeks. "I love you."

He kisses me softly, tenderly, and I still manage to feel it all the way to my toes. "I love you, too, Sunshine."

Taking a moment in the bathroom to splash my face with water and try to get myself looking like ... well, like I didn't just spend the last I don't know how many minutes crying which requires actually applying some makeup which I normally never bother wearing. When I come out of the bathroom, Thayer's sitting on the bed and my bag is gone. He holds a single peony in his hands.

He doesn't say a word. He merely stands up, hands me the flower, and leads me outside.

That's Thayer.

He doesn't need words to remind me he's got my back.

CHAPTER FORTY-FIVE

Thayer

I pull up to the airport drop off and park my truck. Salem seems to be feeling better, but the negative pregnancy test rattled her.

Hopping out, I grab her suitcase from behind my seat and wheel it around, stopping in front of her where she waits for me on the curb.

"Have fun," I tell her. "I mean it. Don't dwell on things. Just have a good time with the girls."

She smiles but I can tell it's a little forced. "I will." She stands on her tiptoes, pressing a quick kiss to my lips. Grabbing the handle of her suitcase, she tries to escape from me quickly.

"Wait." She stops, looking at me over her shoulder. "Call me if you need me. If you get upset, or need to vent, or just want to talk. Whatever it is, whenever, just call and I'll answer."

She tries to hide her tiny smile. "Even in the middle of the night?"

"Especially in the middle of the night."

There's only a few feet separating us and I close it in practically one stride. I give her a deeper, longer kiss, before I let her go. I stand by my truck, watching her disappear into the airport. I ache watching her leave me, especially like this. I'm worried about her.

When I can no longer see her, I hop back in the truck and

drive toward the first work site of the day that I need to check on.

Immediately the guys sense I'm distracted. No one says anything, but I feel the way they watch me.

By the time I make it to the second site, I'm a flustered mess.

"What's wrong, boss?" Aaron, one of my guys, asks.

He's been the first one brave enough to pose the question. "Nothing," I grumble.

"Ah, come on, Thayer—we're not blind. We can see something's up with you."

"It's my girl," I bite out. "She's upset."

"What'd you do?"

"I didn't do anything," I snap, leaning against the back of my truck. "There's just some shit going on that's upsetting her and I don't know how to make her feel better."

I'm not about to tell my employees the intimate details of our personal life, that we're trying to have a baby.

"When my girlfriend is mad at me I give her chocolate," Jake, another one of my guys, pipes in. "Chicks love chocolate."

"I don't think chocolate is going to make this better."

"Just go home, man," Aaron says, shooing his hand at me. "You're no good to any of us in your foul mood. Go talk to her and whatever."

"She's not home."

"Then go wherever she is. Is she working? Take her out to lunch."

I ponder his words. *Go to wherever she is.* The last thing I'm going to do is crash Lauren's bachelorette and ruin their girl trip, but I could go to Vegas and be nearby in case she needs me. It would make me feel better to be in close proximity to her.

I don't like that she got the bad news this morning and had to leave.

"You know what," I snap my fingers at Aaron, "I think you're on to something."

He chuckles, backing away with a shovel in hand. "That's why you're going to give me a raise, right boss?"

I toss the gloves from the back of my truck at him.

He barely dodges them, laughing as he goes. I scoop the gloves back up, finish what I need to at the work site, and go home. It doesn't take me long to book a flight, pack my shit, and head to the airport.

**

It's evening by the time I land in Vegas and make my way to the hotel. I managed to get a room at the same hotel Salem's at and I'm just praying I'm not on the same floor. I don't want to run into her and for her to think I'm stalking her.

I plan on taking a shower and ordering dinner in my room.

Salem and her friends are here tonight and tomorrow night, leaving in the afternoon on Sunday, so I booked a morning flight back on Sunday.

Hopefully Salem will be fine this weekend and not need me, but for my peace of mind, I'm glad I'm here.

The hotel bathroom is fancy, with a walk-in steam shower. I wash away today's worries and throw on a pair of sweatpants when I get out.

The hotel's room service menu is beside the bed. I pick it up, looking it over. The prices are ridiculous, but I'm hungry and not in the mood to go hunt down food. I put in an order for a burger and fries, just about the cheapest thing on the menu at thirty bucks.

Turning the TV on I log in to Netflix, putting on a random movie I come upon for background noise. I put in a quick call to Thelma to check in on Winnie and Binx. I asked Thelma and Cynthia if they'd be willing to watch the two animals and they were all too eager to help.

It takes my food nearly an hour to arrive and by the time it does I'm ready to eat my arm.

The guy that brings it looks at me expectantly for a tip. I nearly shut the door in his face because I just want to eat my food, but I remind myself that it's more than likely not his fault my food took so long, plus it's a big hotel. I hand him some cash and finally I'm left with the peace of my hotel room and my dinner.

Settling at the table, I unbox my burger and shove some fries into my mouth.

My phone lights up on the table beside me. It's a text from Salem.

Salem: Is everything okay there?

Me: Quiet. Just about to eat dinner.

See? I'm not lying.

Me: How are you feeling?

Salem: Lauren's keeping me distracted. She's freaking out over the ring. She's happy for us. We're getting ready to go to a show. I'll check in throughout the night even though you'll probably be asleep.

I smile at her paragraph long text.

Me: Just have fun.

I've only managed to scarf down about half of my burger when I get a FaceTime call from Caleb—well, not Caleb, but Seda.

Originally, we'd talked about Seda staying with me this weekend so we could have a chance to bond just the two of us. It ended up not working out, mostly because Salem and I noticed how uncomfortable it made Caleb and since I don't want to step on the guy's toes too much I backed off.

"Hey." I smile at my little girl's face. "Are you getting ready to go to bed?"

"Mhmm." She points at her pajamas with smiley faces on them. "Just had my bath too." This time she points at her wet head. "Daddy brushed my hair for me. I hate doing it. It gets all tangled and it hurts. But he uses this stuff. What's it called, Daddy?"

"Detangler," I hear Caleb say off screen.

"Detangler," Seda repeats. "That stuff helps."

I chuckle, amused by her rambling. "Are you going to read a book before bed?"

"Yes, I already picked it out. It's about a duck that lives in a purse."

"Is that so?"

"Well," her nose scrunches, reminding me of Salem, "I think so, but I can't remember. Where are you?" she asks, inspecting what she can view of the hotel behind me. I spot Caleb leaning into the camera, checking it out too, so I scoot the phone closer to me.

"I'm out," I answer vaguely.

"Oh, you went out to dinner. It's kind of late, Dad."

"You're right, it is kind of late. We better say goodnight so you can get some rest."

"Night, Dad. I love you."

"I love you, too, pumpkin."

She runs off, but the call doesn't end. Caleb picks up the phone.

"Where are you?" he asks in a bossy, demanding tone. His eyes are narrowed. "It looked like you were in a hotel room. I swear to fucking God if Salem is in Vegas and you're cheating on her I will personally hunt you down and slit your throat."

"That's very specific." I try not show my amusement. "Salem and I aren't together anymore, but I'll always care about her, and that means I don't want to see her hurt."

"I am in a hotel," I tell him, and he looks like he's going to jump through the phone and strangle me. "Settle down. I'm in Vegas. Don't say anything to Salem. She was ... it was a rough morning, okay?" I'm not giving him the intimate details of our life and I doubt he'd like it very much to know we're trying to have a kid when Salem didn't want to have a baby with him. "I decided to book a room in case she needs someone."

"Lauren's there."

"So? It's Lauren's bachelorette weekend. I think we both know Salem won't want to rain on her parade."

He sighs, running his fingers through the blond strands of his hair. "You're right."

"Don't say anything to Salem that I'm here. I only wanted to be close if she needs me."

"Fine. All right. I won't say anything." He looks like he's smelled something sour, so it surprises me when he says, "You really love her, don't you?"

"More than you can possibly comprehend."

I don't mean it as a slight at him, it's just the fucking truth. Sometimes I'm even shocked that it's possible to feel this much for another person.

"I won't tell her."

He ends the call and I exhale a sigh of relief.

I hope wherever Salem is, she's having a good time.

CHAPTER FORTY-SIX

Salem

Our first night in Vegas isn't so bad. We go to a Cirque Du Soleil performance and it's phenomenal, followed by a dinner out, with drinking and dancing at a club. Well, Lauren and her friends drink and dance. I mostly just sit there and cheer them on because it's not my kind of thing.

But the next night, I'm not feeling it. Not when I go into the bathroom and find the signs that my period has started.

Since my period still hadn't started, I'd held on to hope that maybe I had taken a test too soon. But that's clearly not the case. I'm not pregnant, just late, which might be from coming off my birth control and it effecting my cycle.

I send a text to Lauren, asking if she has any tampons with her since I idiotically didn't think to pack any after I unpacked the old ones from my bag. She texts right back that she'll be in my room in a few with some.

I clean up and wash my hands—which is awkward with the cast. I still haven't gotten used to showering and washing up. There's a knock on my door within a minute since her room is right across from mine.

"You didn't pack tampons?" She pushes her way inside, setting them on the counter. "It's not like you to forget something."

There's accusation in her tone. Lauren isn't stupid, she's probably figured something is going on.

"I took a pregnancy test before my flight."

She gasps in surprise. "You're not miscarrying, are you?"

I shake my head. "Just late."

"Wait." She shakes her hands back and forth in front of her face. "Are you glad your period started? Like was this an accidental scare or are you trying to get pregnant?"

I smile bashfully. "Trying."

"Salem!" She swats at my arm. "How could you not tell me this?"

I shrug. "It didn't seem like a big deal."

"You and Thayer have only been back together a few months and you're already talking about having a baby? That's a huge deal to share with your best friend. And engaged too." She reaches for my hand, looking at my pink engagement ring. "Listen, I'm not trying to be a bitch, just your friend, so please don't bite my head off, but do you think you're rushing things?"

I understand where she's coming from. If things were reversed, I have no doubt I'd be asking her the same question.

"Sure," I agree, "technically things are moving quickly, but you have to remember I loved him in secret for almost an entire year, and then I spent six years without him. In many ways, it's been too long and we're not rushing at all."

"When you put it like that, I understand." She looks down at the tampons on the counter. "I'm sorry."

"Thanks. You look amazing by the way."

She's dressed in a pale pink sequined mini dress that makes her already golden skin glow even more. Her dark brown hair is slicked back in a sleek low bun at the nape of her neck.

"Thank you." She strikes a pose, adjusting the sash around

her body that says BRIDE across it. "I'll leave you to your business. Let me know when you're done. I'm ready to get my dance on."

***

I've had a few drinks and find myself out on the dancefloor with all the other girls tonight. It feels nice to let go after feeling so heartbroken. Lauren takes my hands, spinning us in a circle. She's definitely drunk but having a blast. A couple of guys have been bold enough to hit on her despite her bride sash, maybe thinking she wants one last hook up before the big day, but she was quick to send them on their way.

I'm still not sure why she wanted to come to Vegas other than maybe the shows and dancing, but we could've done basically the same thing in Manhattan. Sometimes it gives me a headache trying to get inside her brain.

The music changes and I'm not feeling the song, so I head back to the bar, careful to let the girls know where I'm going first. Stranger danger is a real thing no matter how old you are—at least if you're female. I don't think men really have to worry about that kind of thing. At least not the way we do.

I order my drink and wait, leaning against the bar.

"Hey," a deep voice says to my right.

I turn, making eye contact with a hot guy. He's probably a few years younger than me, maybe twenty-two, with closely cropped brown hair and striking green eyes. With sharp cheekbones he looks like he could be a model.

"Hi," I say, practically yelling to be heard above the music.

"I'm Dylan," he says.

"Salem."

"Salem," he repeats, licking his lips. He looks me over, standing there in my silky orange dress. It covers more than probably anyone else's dress in this club, only showing a hint of cleavage and ending right at my knees. But the way he's looking at me makes me think I'm very much naked in his eyes. "Like the Salem Witch Trials?"

"The very one." I slide some cash to the bartender, taking my drink.

"I was going to pay for your drink," Dylan says with a pout.

"That's okay. I'm taken." I hold up my ring finger.

His smile grows, and he looks a tad high on something. I probably don't want to know what.

"I don't care. We can still have fun. Your man doesn't have to know."

"That's okay."

"Oh, come on," he grabs my wrist, "don't leave so soon."

"I'm okay, really." I try to move away but his hold tightens. "Let go."

"Fuck you." He releases me, moving on to another woman to annoy.

Rolling my eyes, I carry my drink back to the section where a few of the girls are sitting. Lauren is still out on the dancefloor along with Kelsey.

Sabrina eyes my drink. "Ooh, what's that? It looks yummy."

"I honestly don't know," I admit, stirring my drink up. "I just picked something random."

She stands, tugging down her dress. "I'm going to go get another. Be right back."

I sip happily at my drink, but my mood is soured when Sabrina returns with Dylan.

"This is Dylan," she introduces him to us. "We're going to

dance. Do you mind holding this for me?" She doesn't wait for a response, just shoves the drink at me. I don't complain, because I plan on staying right here anyway.

Dylan winks at me before she pulls him into the crowd. I flash my engagement ring again. I can't believe this dude actually thinks I care.

Checking my phone, I frown when I see nothing from Thayer.

I shouldn't text him, besides it's probably like ... I try to do the math in my head of what time it is back home. I can't seem to figure it out, so I text anyway.

Me: I miff zoo

Me: Huh

Me: Mizz too

Me: I MISS YOU

Me: R u tripping?

Me: Stripping?

Me: Zipping?

Me: Sleeping?

My phone rings in my hand and I jump like I've been scalded. Thayer's name lights up in the glow of the screen like a beacon.

"Hi," I answer.

"Are you drunk?" He doesn't sound accusatory, only

amused.

"Yes," I hiccup. "I started my period tonight, so I'm definitely not pregnant. I didn't drink at all yesterday, just in case." My lower lip trembles with the threat of tears. "I had to tell Lauren we're trying. I didn't have tampons, so I had to borrow some and I—"

"Sunshine," he says tenderly, and just with that one word I feel like I've been enveloped in a blanket of warmth. "Where are you?"

"Vegas."

He chuckles in amusement. "I know. But what club?"

"Uh ... hang on." I look at my texts from Lauren, scrolling back to where she mentioned what club we were going to tonight. I take a screenshot and send it to Thayer. "That one."

"I'm coming to get you. Stay put."

"How? You're in Massahootest. No, that's not right," I mumble to myself. "Damn, these drinks are strong."

"Just promise you'll stay there."

"I don't know. I really have to pee."

"You can go pee, Salem," he sounds like he's trying not to laugh. "I only meant don't leave the club."

"Oh. I got it. I won't leave, promise."

The call ends and I stare down at the screen. But wait, how is he supposed to get me if he's not even here?

I shake my head and go to find Lauren or at least one of the girls and let them know I'm going to pee. Elizabeth is quick to join me.

The bathrooms are packed, and we have to wait in line to finally make it to a stall. Thankfully I remembered to put some tampons in my clutch. I need to run by a drug store and get more before we go back to the hotel.

When I leave the restroom I run face first into a wall—well not a wall, but a person. For a moment I panic, thinking it's Dylan or another creep, but then the familiar scent of wood and pine and all things manly invades my senses.

I look up, up, up into Thayer's face. I drunkenly touch the heavy scruff on his cheeks.

"My lumberjack." His lips quirk. "I must be dreaming. What a weird dream, though." I look around at the club.

"You're not dreaming, Sunshine."

"You're really here? In Vegas?"

"I am."

"Why?" I ask, stunned.

"I thought you might need me." My jaw slackens. This man got on a plane and came to Vegas this weekend just in case I needed him? He must think because I'm silent that I'm mad, so he hastens to add, "I wasn't going to just show up and crash your weekend. If you were fine, I was going to be back in Massachusetts before you even left tomorrow, but I—"

Standing on my tiptoes I grab the back of his head and pull his mouth down to mine. He doesn't seem to care that I taste like alcohol. He kisses me back, his hands on my hips, pulling me impossibly closer.

"I love you," I murmur.

I say it because I mean it, I say it because I can. Our love is no secret anymore. It's the most beautiful thing and deserves to be celebrated.

When I finally stop kissing him, my cheeks redden in embarrassment when I find that Elizabeth has joined us from the restrooms. "Who's this?" she asks in amusement.

"Oh, um, Elizabeth this is my Thayer. My boyfriend. My fiancé. Yeah, that one. Thayer, this is Elizabeth. She's Anthony's sister."

He knows all about Anthony now and has been looking forward to meeting him at the wedding.

"It's nice to meet you." Thayer holds out his hand to Elizabeth.

"Likewise." She gives me a look that says she thinks I picked a good one. I can't help but laugh. Thayer's oblivious to the effect he has on women. He turns us all to mush.

We make our way through the club, finding the other girls, and I let them know I'm going back to the hotel with Thayer.

Lauren sends a smirk my way like she knows exactly what's about to go down. I roll my eyes. I'm on my period, in case she hasn't forgotten. I've never had sex on my period, and I doubt tonight will be any different

"If I had known our guys were invited, I would've told Anthony to tag along," she jokes, sipping on a pink-hued beverage.

"Ugh, no, I don't care if you're marrying him, my brother would rain on my parade."

"Yeah, sorry about this," Thayer says sheepishly. "I just—"

"Go on." She waves us away. "Have a good night. I'm going to call it quits soon anyway. I can't party like I used to. I like my sleep too much."

I give her a quick hug goodbye and let Thayer guide me through the throng of people to the exit.

We step out onto the street, and I eagerly breathe in the night air. Only, it's far from clean and filled with cigarette smoke and God knows what else.

"Do you want to walk?"

I shake my head. The hotel isn't far from here, but I don't feel like walking in my heels.

He quickly gets us a taxi, but the ride back takes forever thanks to traffic on The Strip. Walking might've been quicker but at least my feet aren't hurting.

The taxi finally reaches the hotel and Thayer pays for the ride. As we head inside, my stomach decides to grumble, reminding me I didn't eat much of my dinner, which is a shame because it was expensive.

"I'm hungry." Thayer glances down at me, his brows furrowed. "Stop frowning at me like that. You're going to get a wrinkle there." I reach up and smooth down said wrinkle.

"I'll order room service."

"Are you taking me back to your room then, Mr. Holmes?"

"Yep." He pushes the button to the elevator, trying not to show his amusement.

"Remember that concert? You were so mad you had to share a bed with me." I giggle at the memory.

"I remember." He says it in a way that makes me think he's thought about that night a lot.

"That's still one of the best nights of my life."

"That's only because you think the lead singer dude looked right at you."

I scoff, stepping onto the elevator. "Think? He very much did look at me. And don't act like you don't know his name."

"Mathias," he sighs. "I also remember you telling me that night after he looked at you that you were going to marry him."

"What can I say? I was overcome with lust." My heart gives a soft lurch, realizing that I was making that statement to my actual future husband. Wow. "Marry me," I blurt out, his eyes widening in surprise, "right now. We're in Vegas. That's what people do, right?"

"It might be, but we're not." He leans against the elevator, crossing his arms over the wall of his chest.

"Why not?" I pout, the doors sliding open on his floor. I follow him out and down the hall.

"Because, you're drunk right now and that's the only reason I need."

"I'm tipsy, not drunk."

"Salem," he looks at me over his shoulder, "do I need to pull up the string of unintelligible texts you sent me?"

"Okay, okay. Point taken. But I already agreed to marry you and I was perfectly sober then, so obviously I do want to marry you."

He sighs, coming to a stop in front of a room. He unlocks the door and holds it open for me. "You're not going to be able to convince me."

"I can be very persuasive."

"Sure." He shuts the door behind us. "What do you want to eat?"

"Something greasy."

He shakes his head, reaching for the room's phone to dial for room service.

"I'm going to shower." I start wiggling out of my dress.

His eyes watch me hungrily as the dress shimmies past my hips and lands on the floor. I'm not wearing a bra, and even though I don't have a lot going on when it comes to the size of my breasts, you wouldn't be able to tell that the way he's looking at me.

With a smirk, I close the bathroom door and lock it.

He really thinks I'm too drunk to know if I want to marry him or not?

I'm pretty sure I would've married him at eighteen. At almost twenty-six is no different, if anything the feeling is stronger. I want the world to know that man belongs to me.

I shower, washing away the sweat that has stuck to my body from the night of dancing.

I use the hotel's shampoo and conditioner to wash my hair. It feels gross and sticky from being in the club. I stay beneath the warm spray longer than necessary, but it feels so nice I don't want to get out.

When my fingers start to prune, I decide enough is enough. My casted arm aches too from holding it out of the shower. Stepping out, I wrap my body in a fluffy towel. I run my fingers through my hair since I don't have a hairbrush. It's the best I can do if I don't want it to tangle.

There's a robe hanging on the back of the door. Dropping my towel, I slip it on and step into the room. Thayer lays stretched out on the bed, his feet crossed.

He looks over at me, eyes zeroed in on my robe.

"I set a shirt out for you." He points at a white cotton shirt on the bed.

"Actually, it was nice meeting you and all, and thanks for letting me use your shower, but I'm going to head back to my room. I have pajamas there."

Those intense brown eyes narrow on me. "Nice joke, Sunshine. Get in the bed."

"Okay, but I don't need your shirt."

I let the robe drop, his jaw dropping along with it. I love that every time he sees me naked, he looks at me like it's the first time.

I slip beneath the covers, pulling them up to my chin.

"I don't think so," he growls, yanking the covers down to reveal my breasts. He hums in approval, reaching to cup them.

"No funny business. I started my period."

"I don't care." He lowers his head, flicking his tongue over first one nipple then the other.

It's on the tip of my tongue to say that I do care, but when he does that, it's impossible to speak.

My eyes close and I moan when he sucks on my breasts, my body arching up to meet his mouth. "Thayer," I pant his name. I don't know how it's possible, but I feel more turned on than ever before.

Unfortunately for me, we're interrupted when there's a knock on the door from room service. Thayer groans, his mouth leaving my breast. It's wet with his saliva and with the AC on it sends a shiver down my spine. He tosses the sheet over my body even though you can't see the bed from the door. He gets up, not at all bothered by his obvious erection and grabs the food.

I sit up, eager for my meal despite also being desperate for his touch.

He sets the tray of food down on the bed and swipes a bottle of water from the fridge, handing it to me.

"Eat up," he says lowly, "you're going to need it."

CHAPTER FORTY-SEVEN

Salem

I wake the next morning, smiling at the sleeping man at my side. He's on his stomach, his arms curled around the pillow beneath his head. The sheet barely covers his body and I take him in hungrily.

He starts to stir, feeling me staring at him.

He slowly blinks his eyes open. "What time is it?" he asks, stifling a yawn.

I sit up, looking at the clock on his side of the bed. "Seven."

We've only been asleep around two hours. I know that's going to suck later.

"Fuck." He rolls over onto his back. "I need to get to the airport."

"Or we could change our flights and go back together?"

"You want to change flights?" He yawns again.

"Duh."

He chuckles, reaching for his phone. "Let me see if I can make this work." It takes him a couple of minutes, but soon he declares, "Done. We fly out at eleven."

"Good." I roll over, laying my chin on his chest. "That means you can marry me today."

He looks at me in confusion. "You seriously want to get married in Vegas? What about Seda and—"

I cover his mouth with my hand. "I want to marry you today. I don't want to go another day without calling you my husband. We can have a ceremony later, but Thayer, I've waited a long time to marry you and I just don't want to wait anymore, even if that means marrying you in a drive-thru chapel."

"Are you sure this is what you want?"

"Completely."

***

I don't tell Lauren what we're up to. This was her weekend, and I don't want to make it about me. I'm sure she'll want to strangle me later on when she finds out I didn't tell her, but for now, what she doesn't know won't hurt her.

After getting some clothes from my room, Thayer and I go shopping since neither of us has something wedding appropriate, and I don't want to marry him in my usual shorts and tank top combo.

The white dress I find is a simple sundress with a corseted top and open in the back. It's not a wedding dress, but I wasn't looking for one anyway, just something a little nicer. I pay for the dress and change in a nearby restroom while Thayer does the same, changing into whatever he found.

When I walk out of the stall, I try to do something with my hair, but give up and leave it hanging down in its usual loose waves.

Walking out of the bathroom I'm met with Thayer leaning against the opposite wall in a pair of khaki-colored pants and a crisp blue button down. My eyes eat him up.

I get to love this man every day for the rest of my life.

If I could go back in time and tell my eighteen-year-old self that, I wonder what she'd think? She'd probably be cheering me on, to be honest.

Thayer looks me over in the white sundress. His tongue slides out, wetting his lips.

"You look..." He can't find the words.

"Back at you."

We already picked our wedding spot and called ahead for an appointment time. We head straight there since as soon as it's over—which shouldn't take long—we have to grab our stuff and head straight to the airport.

The venue is cheaply decorated with gaudy, stereotypical décor, but I don't care. As we stand in front of the officiant all that matters is the man at my side.

Thayer Holmes.

My asshole neighbor.

My boss.

My lover.

My child's father.

My *someone*.

And with the echoes of our vows, and the rings on our fingers, he finally becomes...

My husband.

CHAPTER FORTY-EIGHT

Thayer

The entire flight home I hold the hand of my *wife*. Did I think when I went to Vegas this weekend, I'd be marrying Salem? Absolutely not. Do I regret it? No.

I've waited a long time to marry this woman.

When the plane touches down, I can't wait to get home and just continue to live life with her.

It's fucking crazy, but with her, existing is enough. With her, I crave the little things—watching TV together, staying up late talking, even doing the dishes, which is just baffling.

But Salem Holmes is my best friend.

Salem Holmes. I love the sound of that so fucking much. Having her wear my last name is such a turn on. I would've been more than fine if she wanted to keep her maiden name, but she wanted my last name.

"Did you drive to the airport or take a taxi?"

"I parked my truck. It's this way." I wheel her suitcase behind me, my bag slung over my shoulder. It leaves one of my hands free to hold my wife's.

My wife—I grin to myself. I can't stop thinking about those two words.

"What are you smiling about?" she asks.

"You."

"Me?" She scoffs. "Oh no!" She starts to panic. "Do I have donut on my face?" She rubs at her mouth with the back of her free hand.

"No, your face is perfect."

"Then why do you have that goofy look?"

"This goofy look?" I let go of her suitcase long enough to point at my face. "That's called love, Sunshine, and it's all for you."

"Oh." Her cheeks turn the softest shade of pink.

We reach my truck in the parking garage, and I load our stuff into the backseat.

The weekend away was unplanned, but nice, just like our spontaneous decision to get married, but I'm going to be happy to get home.

"Oh my God." Salem looks at me with panic just as I start the engine.

"What?" I look around, thinking I did something wrong or forgot something or maybe something is wrong with the truck.

"Winnie and Binx! You didn't leave them alone, did you?"

"Of course not," I scoff. "They're in the very capable hands of Thelma and Cynthia."

"Oh no," she says softly.

"What?"

"There's no telling what Thelma has done to them."

She probably has a point.

***

I knock on the door of the house across the street, eager to get my pets back. It takes a moment for one of them to reach the door. It's Cynthia. She opens it with a smile.

"Come in, come in. Thelma is out back with Winnie. I think she wants one of them short squatty dogs now."

"A corgi?" I ask when Binx comes running out from some hidden corner, rubbing his body against my legs.

"If that's what they're called then, sure, that."

She opens the back door and yells for Thelma that I'm here. I scoop up Binx before I lose him again. He nuzzles his soft head into my neck. The cat and I have really taken to each other. I look him over and I—

"Is that nail polish on his nails?" I eye the hot pink glitter coating his nails. It definitely is, but I need to hear confirmation to believe my own two eyes.

"We had a spa night, boy," Thelma responds through the screened door, coming up the porch stairs. "And on spa night we pamper ourselves."

"And so you painted the cat's nails?"

Thelma shrugs. "He picked the color."

It takes me another fifteen minutes to get Winnie and Binx's things packed up, finish up talking to Thelma and Cynthia, before I finally can head back home.

Inside, there's a commotion coming from the kitchen. I set Binx down and take Winnie off her leash, both animals sprinting for the kitchen.

I follow along, more slowly, coming to a stop when I find Salem humming along to music, her hips swaying, as she stirs something in a bowl.

"Are you baking?" I try to hide the astonishment from my voice.

She whirls around, gracing me with a smile. She looks happy, and fuck if that doesn't make my chest puff up with pride because I know I'm part of the reason she feels that way.

"Yeah." A bit of pink flushes her cheeks. "I felt like it."

"I know you don't really bake anymore..." I trail off, eyeing the ingredients. "Cookie dough cupcakes?"

"I miss it," she admits with a shrug. "I stopped because..."

"Because why?" I prompt, needing to hear the answer.

She sets the bowl down, picking up cupcake liners and lining them up in a cupcake pan. "It reminded me of you too much. My candles too. But I have you again and now those things don't feel so painful anymore. I want to give it a try again. It was nice too, before my mom died, we made cupcakes a few times. She's pretty insistent when she wants—" She winces. "She was pretty insistent when she wanted something. I can't help thinking she wanted me to find my passion again."

"Your mom probably knew deep down you missed it."

"Probably." She smiles sadly, and I know her thoughts are now with her mom.

"I'll leave you to it, then." I head out back to my greenhouse. I want to cut a bouquet for my wife.

My wife. I can't help the stupid grin that overcomes me just thinking about it.

It doesn't take me long to trim enough flowers for a bouquet. When I come back inside from the back deck, Salem is sliding the cupcakes into the oven and she's spread the ingredients out for the icing.

"Caleb called. He's on his way to drop off Seda."

"All the way here?" I ask, since one or both of us usually meets him halfway. Besides, it's late.

"That's what he said. I assume he's going to spend the night at his parents or something. I didn't ask. I try not to pry into his business. I need to take Seda back-to-school shopping tomorrow and we need groceries." She starts naming off all the things she needs to do.

"All right. Let me know what I can help with." I grab a vase, adding some water into it and then her flowers. "These are for you."

She smiles. "They're beautiful." She turns her attention back to the frosting, her nose wrinkling in a way that I know she's thinking about something.

"What is it? You know you can talk to me about whatever is on your mind."

She sighs, powdered sugar smeared across her cheek. "It's just that, for so long I haven't known what I want to do with my life, what makes me happy. I didn't go to college, I didn't want to, and I've worked a few odd jobs just to bring in some income." She stares into the container of powdered sugar like maybe it holds the answer to everything she's searching for. "I want to find something that's just *mine*. Does that make sense?"

"It makes perfect sense. I want you to do whatever it is that makes you happy. I don't care. I'll support you no matter what."

"Thank you," she whispers almost shyly. "I want to keep my mom's store." I've suspected as much. She's far more attached to it than her mother's house, which we're hoping to put up for sale in a few weeks. "I'm just trying to figure out how. I can't keep it and not use it, you know."

"I'm sure you'll figure something out. I mean, you could always do this." I point at the spread of items for the cupcakes.

"Do what?" She sounds stunned. "Open a bakery? Thayer, I'm no professional."

"Lots of home bakers open their own business. You could do it too, Salem. I know you could."

Her nose crinkles as she thinks it over. "Hmm, maybe."

"What were you considering before?"

She shrugs. "Nothing I was crazy about, but cupcakes," she muses. "You might be on to something and I know it sounds crazy but I think my mom would be proud to know that I was making cupcakes in her shop."

"I think she would too."

"And maybe I could start making candles again—make ones in cupcake scents and sell them too." She's starting to glow now, getting excited over this idea.

She continues to ramble about what colors she'd paint the walls, what kind of décor she'd want. She might not realize it, but I do.

She's just found her passion.

***

It's fully dark when Caleb pulls into our driveway. Seda hops out from the back, running over to hug her mom and then me.

Caleb gets out, grabbing her bag and slowly approaches us on the porch.

"Seda, why don't you run inside and grab a cupcake?" Salem asks her.

"Really?" Her eyes light up. "You never let me have sweets before bed."

"Tonight is an exception."

"Yay!" Seda runs inside, the door slamming closed behind her.

When she's gone, Salem asks him, "You're not going all the way back to Boston tonight, are you?"

He shakes his head. "No, I was actually wondering ... well, I wanted to talk to you guys about something."

"Oh?" She arches a brow.

"Why don't we sit down?" He suggests, looking slightly uncomfortable.

Salem and I end up on the swing while Caleb pulls up one of the other chairs on the porch.

"Is everything okay?" Salem asks, genuine concern in her voice for her ex.

"Yeah, nothing's wrong." He runs his fingers through his hair.

"So, what is it?"

I narrow my eyes on the man across from me, watching him curiously.

With an inhale of breath, he says, "You're selling your mom's house, right?"

Salem's brows furrow. "Yeah." She crooks her head to the side. "Why?"

"And you're planning on living here? You won't be moving?"

Salem looks at me, a question in her eyes.

Do we tell him?

I nod. I'm not going to stop her from letting him know, and he's so involved in our lives he deserves to know.

"Thayer and I got married this weekend."

Caleb's eyes widen. "Oh, wow. Uh. Congratulations."

"Thanks." Salem tucks a piece of hair behind her ear. "To answer your question, yes, we plan on staying here. Thayer's updated this house and I love it. It feels right to stay."

"Good, good." He rubs his hands over the legs of his pants. "I want to buy your mom's house."

"What?" Salem blurts, stunned.

I narrow my eyes on the man across from me, wondering what his thought process is behind this.

"I want to buy it. Seda's going to be with you the majority

of the time and I know that makes the most sense with school and everything, and I like the idea of her growing up in my childhood hometown." Salem told me once that Caleb is descended from our town's founding family. "If I buy your mom's house that means I get to see her more often. I'm close, but I have my own space. I can fix it up and make it my own. I'd keep my place in Boston and I'd be there most of the time, but I could come here on the weekends. It might do me some good to get away from work and the city." He exhales heavily. "I want to be close to my little girl. I don't want our relationship to change. I promise you guys will hardly see me. I'll keep to myself. Whatever you and Georgia plan on selling the house for, I'll pay it."

Do I love the idea of Salem's ex living right next door?

Fuck no.

But at the same time, I understand his motivation and commend him. Not many men would go out of their way for a child that is biologically someone else's. I have my issues with Caleb—and if I'm honest with myself they all stem from jealousy—but he's a good man. He deserves to find his own happiness in this world, and I hope one day he does.

Salem and I exchange a look, a million words passing unsaid between us. It's a beautiful thing when you can talk to someone without even opening your mouth.

"All right," Salem says. "It's yours."

Caleb lets out a sigh of relief. "I thought you'd say no."

Salem shakes her head. "Honestly, I think it's a great idea for Seda. Perfect, really. But are *you* going to be okay with it?"

Caleb looks between us, his shoulders falling. "I am. A part of me will always love you, Salem. You were my first love, but seeing what you two have ... we never had that." He rubs a hand over his jaw. "I've been seeing someone. I don't know where it's going to go. We've only been on a few dates, but I thought you should know that."

Salem nods in thanks. Even though it isn't something she talks about with me, I know she worries about Caleb. He was her best friend, her first love too, and she wants him to be happy.

"The house is yours then."

NINE

CHAPTER FORTY-NINE

Thayer

We clear out the rest of Allison's house, Georgia and Salem both keeping only a minimal amount of their mom's stuff. I can tell it's hard for Salem, accepting that her mom is truly gone, but she's handling it better than I could've imagined.

"The relator is going to start the process this weekend while we're gone." She stuffs some socks in her bag. We're headed to the Hamptons for Lauren's wedding.

Despite us being a couple now, a married one at that, I didn't expect to get an invite to the wedding. I know Lauren's not my biggest fan, and I've accepted that. I appreciate it, even, because Salem is lucky to have a friend who cares so much.

My phone rings and I'm not surprised to see that it's my brother. I hold up my phone, letting Salem know I'm taking the call and step outside our bedroom. She's already added her touch, switching out my gray comforter for a white one, and changing the lamps beside the bed.

"Hello?"

"Hey, loser, how are you?"

I roll my eyes at my brother's greeting. "Fine. What's up?"

"Nothing much. Mom and Dad are bugging me about going to visit you."

"Why?" I ask curiously, leaning against the wall in the

hallway.

"Well, I'm guessing because you're married now with a kid that was a secret for years. They want to meet them both and they're old so need me to fly to them and drive them up there."

It's the middle of September now, the end of summer. The past few years I went to them for the holidays—Thanksgiving and Christmas—but maybe this year we should go back to our old tradition, and I'll have them here.

"What if I had Thanksgiving at my place again this year?"

Laith's quiet. "You would want that?"

I haven't hosted the holiday since Forrest passed. It felt too lonely. That's why going to see my parents was easier.

"Sure, why not? It's a few months away still, but I think it would be nice, all of us together. And it would probably be easier for Seda and Salem to meet them here where they're comfortable. Seda's young. I don't want to take her away from her home to meet strange people for the first time."

"I'm telling Mom and Dad you called them strange."

"You know what I meant," I grumble.

"No, I get it. It makes sense and that way I won't have to take too much extra time off work."

"I'll talk to them about it, and we can make plans."

"Cool. Talk to you later." He ends the call and I slide my phone back in my pocket.

When I come back from my phone call, Salem stands outside the closet, double checking her bridesmaid's dress.

"What's wrong?"

My stuff is already packed and by the front door along with a tux since apparently this wedding is black tie. Lauren knows a guy, so I was able to get one custom fitted. It cost a pretty penny, but I wasn't about to not do what the bride asked.

"It's just this stupid cast is going to stick out like a sore thumb." She pouts, holding up her arm.

"I'm sorry, babe. But it's on for a few more weeks. There's nothing we can do about it."

She sighs. "I know, and Lauren says it's no big deal, but I know it's going to stick out in photos."

"I think Lauren would rather you be alive and in a cast than worry about how it's going to look in photos."

"You're right," she agrees. "It's probably me that it bothers the most anyway. Showers are awkward and it itches."

"It'll be off before you know it. Do you have everything you need?"

She does one last check of her bag and nods. "Let's go."

***

The train ride is easy enough, and when we get off Lauren is waiting to pick us up. She hugs Salem, dissolving into a spiel about wedding details that sounds like gibberish to me.

She lets Salem go and surprises me when she opens her arms to me. "Come on, neither of us is going to melt from a hug. Besides, Salem is like my sister, which means you're practically like my brother-in-law." I accept her hug, not at all surprised when she whispers, "The threat still stands."

"Yeah, yeah, I know. You'll slit my throat. Pretty bloody if you ask me."

She lets me go, and turns back to Salem, launching back into wedding talk like she didn't just threaten to kill me.

Women are hostile—at least Lauren is. I wouldn't want to cross her. I have a feeling she knows how to hide a body and get away with it.

She leads us out to the parking lot and to a waiting SUV. We all climb in the back since there's a driver.

"Anthony insisted," Lauren explains of the driver. "He was worried about my road rage if I drove."

Salem laughs, her eyes shining in amusement. "The man just knows you suck at driving."

"Do not." She sticks her tongue out. "I'm an excellent driver."

"Tell that to your twenty plus speeding tickets."

"It's not that many. You're exaggerating."

The girls talk the entire way from the train station to her fiancé's parent's place. That's where we'll be staying since supposedly the place is huge.

We pull up to a gate that slowly opens to reveal...

Fuck, she wasn't lying. This place isn't just huge, it's a whole fucking compound.

We're let out at the front of the house, with the driver grabbing our bags.

"The guest house is this way," Lauren says, motioning with her hand for us to follow.

Salem shoots me a look, thinking the same thing I am, that there's a whole separate house for guests?

"This is where you all will be staying." Lauren lets us into a cottage-like building on the property. "Rehearsal dinner is at six o' clock out back. Don't be late. I'll leave you two to it for now." She waves over her shoulder, taking a pathway toward the main house.

"This place is insane." Salem spins around in a circle, taking it all in. "I can't believe people live like this. This isn't even their house. It's for *guests*," she hisses the last part under her breath like she's afraid someone is going to pop out from behind the potted plant in the corner.

I take our bags into the bedroom, Salem trailing behind me.

We get ready for the dinner, and I dress up in a pair of gray slacks and a white button down. I'm rolling up my sleeves when Salem steps out of the bathroom. She takes my breath away in a blue dress, her hair curled and cascading down her back. Her eyes rake over me, and I look down at myself.

"This is all right, isn't it? I know Lauren is particular. I have another shirt—"

"My husband is hot."

I grin. "You think so?"

"Oh, yeah."

"Stop looking at me like that or we'll never make it to the dinner."

"I wouldn't mind ... but Lauren would."

She straightens my collar, smoothing her hand down my chest to rub out any wrinkles—at least I think that's what she's doing.

She takes a step back, her eyes zeroing in on the simple black band around my finger. "I wish my mom was still here. I think she'd be happy for us."

"She would be." I cup Salem's cheek in one hand. She leans into my touch with a sigh. "She knew how much you meant to me."

"She wanted this, didn't she? Us together?"

"I think she wanted whatever would make you happy."

Salem steps back, fanning her face. "I can't cry. I don't want to ruin my makeup."

"By the way," I say, leaning against the wall, "I was thinking my parents could come up to our place for Thanksgiving."

She smiles, swiping a tissue to dab at the remaining moisture in her eyes. "I think that's a great idea. I'd love to finally be able to meet them in person."

Salem and Seda have been getting to know my parents through FaceTime calls for the past few months. It works fine, but it's not the same as getting to know someone in person.

"They can be a bit much," I warn, resting my hands on her hips. "I know they're going to want to spoil Seda silly and probably tell you way too many embarrassing stories about me."

"Family is important," she reminds me. "Not everyone has a great one. My father was trash. They're good people. I want them to come. Stop worrying over nothing." She smooths out my brow with her thumb.

I smile. "I'll try."

"Good." She takes a step back. "Let's go to dinner. I'm starving."

***

I haven't seen Salem in hours. She left early in the morning to get ready with Lauren and the other bridesmaids. I take my seat, waiting for the ceremony to get underway and more than eager to see my wife.

While I've been waiting, I called my parents this morning and cemented the plans for them to come for Thanksgiving. I could tell they weren't happy about the wait but understood where I was coming from when I laid it all out. We can't take Seda out of school right now for a long trip, and besides I think it would be a bit much for her since she doesn't really know them yet.

I also texted Laith to let him know everything was a go

and all he did was reply with a one-word text of: Good.

Little dipshit. We're adults and he's still driving me crazy.

The wedding planner points me in the direction of my seat, and I head over there, giving a head nod to the group of people I'm seated with but don't know. Most of these people seem familiar with one another, while I'm the odd man out. But that doesn't bother me.

The music changes, signaling the bridal party is going to begin coming out.

I hold my breath, waiting for Salem to appear. When she finally does, she takes my breath away, and it makes me glad we decided to have a ceremony one day, because fuck, I want to see her walk down the aisle to me.

Her eyes search the aisles, stopping when they land on me. A smile takes over her face and she winks.

I don't want to take my eyes off her.

I had resolved myself to a lonely fate, one where I lived out my days alone, and I didn't get the girl. It's what I thought I deserved. I was the villain of my own story in my eyes. When Forrest died, I thought I didn't deserve to live either, and I'm sure if it wasn't for my brother and therapist I probably wouldn't be alive today.

Salem told me once, that she wanted to have the confidence of wildflowers. She wanted to grow and thrive no matter what life tossed her way. And she's done just that.

But if she had the confidence of wildflowers, then I was the resurrection of wildflowers. My soul withered with the death of my son. I was lost, and that version of myself was gone forever. But I came back—I came back and now I'll grow and thrive alongside her.

When Lauren comes out, on the arm of her father, I get

choked up because I realize one day I'll be walking Seda down the aisle to whomever she chooses to give her heart to. And while I won't get to experience the same for Forrest, I know he's always with me, because the love in my heart for my son has never dwindled. If anything, it has grown stronger.

As I watch Lauren start down the aisle, I swear I can feel Forrest's small hand in mine. Like he's reminding that my beliefs aren't crazy, that he's right here.

Our loved ones never really leave us—not as long as we remember. Even when it hurts, even when the pain is unbearable, we have to remember.

CHAPTER FIFTY

Salem

The last of summer comes to an end, the final days of warm weather bleeding into the crisp cold weather of October. Caleb moves into my mom's house, spending most weekends there and his weekdays in Boston. It's an adjustment at first, having him right next door, but it turns out to be the right thing all the way around for us and for Seda.

The door to my mom's shop opens—*my* shop now, I remind myself. I set down the paint roller, smiling when Thayer walks in with our daughter. She sets her rainbow backpack down and runs over to me, giving me a hug.

"I got an A on my spelling test, Mommy. Mrs. Lowell says she thinks I should be in the spelling bee."

"Wow, that's amazing." I tap her nose. "Do you have homework?"

She pouts, muttering, "Yes."

"Go get started on it while your dad and I paint. If you need help just yell for us."

"Fine." She grabs her backpack, running into the back where a commercial kitchen is almost finished being put in. It feels far too fancy for me, and I question whether I'll even be able to make a go of all this, but the only true failure is in not trying.

"Here, I got you something."

I narrow my eyes curiously on my husband. "And what is it?"

From behind his back, he holds out a Diet Coke. "For you."

I put a hand to my chest, then take the soda. "My hero." I stand on my tiptoes, kissing his scruffy cheek.

"I like this color." Thayer picks up another roller, dipping it in the pan.

"You do?" I'm a tad surprised he likes the burnt orange color. That's only the base color, and then I'm having someone come in to paint a mural of retro style flowers. It seems like a lot of bakeries go the pastel route, and there's nothing wrong with that, but I wanted to do something different. A little quirky. Something that was ... *me*.

"I do. With the flowers it's going to look great."

I take a sip of the Diet Coke, looking around at the transformed space. Jen has already been by to congratulate me. It'll be a while before we open, but what matters is that I'm doing this, and I think my mom would be proud of me. I think she'd be happy knowing that this space will continue to exist with a new life. I even kept some of the vintage pieces for wall décor and there's a green colored couch from the 70s that will sit beneath the big window in the front.

Thayer and I work together, mostly in silence since we can get more done that way, and manage to finish the second coat on one whole wall. It's progress, so I'm not going to complain.

"Are you done with your homework?" I ask Seda, poking my head in the back.

"Yeah. Mostly."

"What does mostly mean?"

"I need some help with a few questions when we get home.

You were busy so I didn't want to ask."

"Sweetie, I told you if you needed help, we would."

"I know." She shoulders her backpack. "But I wanted you to paint so you can open this place and I can have cupcakes anytime I want."

I sigh in amusement. "Sound logic."

"You have paint on your nose," she tells me, brushing by me into the main shop space.

That's my kid, always keeping me humble.

Thayer's truck is parked outside, and I make sure Seda's secure in her seat, then get in myself.

"There's somewhere I want to take you ladies before we go home."

"And where's that?" I ask as he pull away from the curb.

"You'll see."

A few minutes later we're parked outside the cemetery. I send him a questioning glance, but he only motions with his hand for me to follow him out of the truck.

"Are we visiting Grandma and brother?"

"Yeah," Thayer takes her hand, "we are."

"But we didn't bring flowers." She frowns, seeming highly distraught by this fact. "Wait." She pulls her hand from Thayer's and takes off running for the field beside the cemetery. She plucks a handful of wildflowers, smiling at her bouquet. The flowers are dry and brittle, practically dead since the weather has been getting cold, but she smiles at them like they're the most beautiful thing she has ever seen.

She runs back over to us, taking each of our hands and somehow managing to keep ahold of the flowers too. Thayer looks down at her, then up to me, and I wonder if he feels it too. How despite the tragedies we've both had to face in our lifetimes, that our lives are still beautiful, still filled with love, and though some might think we're extremely unlucky, I'd argue the opposite. We've come out on the other side scarred, but beautiful. Life has tested us in some of the cruelest ways, but we're both still standing here. We're smiling. We're thriving. That's the true test of a person—the beauty they're able to find in the simple things.

In the wildflowers that bloom and blossom freely.

In the bees that pollinate our earth.

In the sound of the wind rustling the leaves.

Those are the things that matter.

This. Us.

Thayer leads us through and around. He has the path memorized. My mom isn't beside Forrest, but they are near, so as we approach, I notice something new, something different.

"What's that?" I ask.

"It's a bench, Mom," Seda says like she can't believe I don't know what one looks like.

She lets go of our hands, running ahead and to her brother's grave first.

"Did the cemetery put a bench in or something?" I search his brown eyes for an answer.

He shakes his head, tugging a beanie down over his ears more. "No."

"Then why? I ... I don't understand."

We get closer and I start to take in the detail of it. It has my mom's name carved into it. Forrest's too. My hand flies to my mouth, tears stinging my eyes. Damn him for making me cry.

"I made it," he says softly. "We're here often enough and I spoke with the caretaker. I was able to buy an empty plot almost exactly between them, so that way we can sit here and we'll be close to both of them."

I gape at him. "You bought a whole grave plot just to put a bench on it?"

"Yes."

One word. So simple. But it speaks volumes about the kind of man Thayer is.

He put a whole gym in his basement and now he bought an entire grave just to put a bench on it so we can be with our family.

"You ... you're amazing." I throw my hands around his neck, my feet lifting off the ground with his height. His arms wrap around me, his face burrowing into the crook of my neck.

"I'm really not."

"And that's even more of a reason why you are." I take his face in my hands. "You do these things from the goodness of your heart. Because you want to. You're not asking for credit, but you deserve it anyway."

This man deserves *everything*, and I hope I'm the one who can give it to him.

I take a seat on the bench, and he joins me.

Closing my eyes, I lay my head on his shoulder.

I feel at peace. Despite the chaos of our lives, the turmoil, the ups and downs, and everything it took to get us to this point, I feel thankful in a strange way. Thankful that we're here, together, and didn't let the bad things break us.

We sit there, together, as the sun sets, watching Seda speak to her grandma and brother, leaving her flowers trailing behind her, our hands clasped together.

I get a flash of what Thayer spoke about one time, of sitting on the front porch swing one day, watching our grandchildren run around the yard.

And I smile.

CHAPTER FIFTY-ONE

Salem

It's a strange thing, hosting Thayer's family for the Thanksgiving holiday. Of course I know Laith, not well but enough, but I don't know his parents at all. Not really, in my opinion. We've been FaceTiming with them weekly since Thayer first broke the news to them of our relationship, past, and Seda, but it's been awkward getting to know them that way, and I fear they won't like me. After all, I kept their grandchild a secret for six years. I could understand if there was animosity. But when the car shows up, Laith driving since he flew all the way to their house in Florida just to drive them here, Thayer's mom is all too eager to get out of the car and hug me.

She smells of freesia and her hug feels like home.

"Elaine," I hug her tighter, "it's so nice to meet you."

She pulls away slightly, taking me in. "It's nice to meet you too, sweetheart. My Thayer is different. He's happy again. You made him smile again—his real smile. I can never thank you enough for that."

Her words touch my heart. Over her shoulder, Thayer meets my eyes with a small, almost shy smile. He's been nervous about this, I think because he knew I was feeling that way. Meeting the parents is always an awkward affair.

Seda is next door at Caleb's house. The three of us decided

it would be best for her to meet her grandparents and uncle tomorrow. Seda is smart, kind, and understanding but this is overwhelming for a girl her age so while we explained they were coming to her, and how they're related, we figured we'd let everyone get settled tonight and introduce her tomorrow.

It's been surprisingly easy, adjusting to parenting with three of us, and it's actually been nice, and good for Seda, having Caleb next door most weekends.

I thought things might get weird, but they haven't, and while things haven't worked out with the one woman Caleb was seeing, he's been dating and is happy. That's all I want for him.

"Come inside," I tell Elaine. "I'm sure you guys want to rest, and dinner is almost ready."

"That would be nice. Laith drives like a maniac. He shaved five years off whatever is left of my life."

"Mom!" Laith yells, having heard her. "Don't say that. I did no such thing."

She purses her lips, shaking her head. "He did. Too much time with that motorcycle of his and now he doesn't know how to drive a proper car."

"A proper car?" He argues, coming up the porch stairs. "That is a minivan. Tell me why you and Dad need a minivan."

"Well, son," their dad says, walking up to join us, "there's more room in the back if you catch what I'm saying."

Behind him, Thayer shakes his head, trying not to laugh. Laith's eyes widen in horror and he gags.

"Fuck, Dad, don't say that shit around me. Gross."

Ignoring Laith, their dad, Douglas, comes up to me, opening his arms for a hug. "Hi, Salem. It's so nice to meet you."

"It's nice to meet you as well."

We lead everybody inside and let them get settled in the

guest bedrooms. While they're resting up, Thayer and I finish dinner. We decided to make lasagna since that was simple enough and put it in the oven earlier. He turns the oven light on, checking on the progress.

"It should be ready in about thirty minutes."

"Perfect." I put the finishing touches on the homemade garlic bread we'll pop in the oven just before the lasagna is finished cooking.

Thayer pushes a button, turning on the music speaker. A Taylor Swift song comes on from my playlist.

"What are you doing?" I ask, fighting a smile as he closes the distance between us.

"I want to dance with my wife. Can't I do that?"

I don't answer him, not with words anyway. I let him take me into his arms, slowly twirling me through the kitchen. As a little girl, I used to wonder if true love existed between a man and woman. My parents certainly weren't a good example. My father craved power, control. He didn't love my mom, or care about her. To him, she, and by extension my sister and me, were a part of an image he wanted to cultivate in the public of being a family man.

It was all a lie.

Behind closed doors he was a monster in more ways than one.

To this day, I'm glad he's gone.

I've never shed a single tear for him, but I have shed tears for the little girl I was, who should've had a dad who loved and cared for her. Who protected her and showed her how a man treats a woman. Sometimes, that little girl doesn't even feel like me. To survive what I did, I had to separate myself mentally from my past. I don't know if that's how it is for everyone, but that was my coping mechanism.

I feel blessed, that as a teenager, I met Caleb. He was kind, caring—my best friend. He treated me the way every guy should treat a girl. Then I met Thayer too.

I've had two good men in my life to prove to me that they're not all like my father.

I know not everyone's story plays out like mine.

Thayer continues to sway us to the song, and I lay my head against his chest, listening to the steady pounding of his heart against my ear.

I love this man.

And I'm thankful every day the universe sent him my way.

He turns us again and I find his parents standing in the entry way to the kitchen, watching us. Each has a wistful expression. I'm sure after Thayer's divorce, and Forrest's passing, their worry for their son was beyond what I can imagine.

Sometimes, when you're in the midst of tragedy—of heartbreak—it can be impossible to see the other side. It's like you're drowning beneath the weight of your emotions, memories, your very thoughts, but if you just keep going, keep swimming, then eventually you make it to shore. You're tired, but stronger, and look at yourself in a new light. I think it's our tendency to doubt ourselves, to think we're weaker than what we are, but there's more in all of us than we realize.

I rest my chin on Thayer's chest, looking up at him with all the love I used to think I would never be capable of. Closing my eyes, I rest my head on his chest once more.

I made it.

***

"My son," Elaine begins, whispering quietly so Thayer won't hear. "He's different with you. It's beautiful to see."

"He is?" I ask, taking the macaroni and cheese out of the oven.

She nods, smiling over at him. He stands with Caleb, his brother, Dad, and Seda. His hands are on her shoulders, and she's looking up admiring him. It stirs something in me, seeing Seda look at him like that. Their bond has grown naturally, and I know Seda loves him as much as she does Caleb and me.

Thelma and Cynthia sit at the table, watching everything with keen eyes. The two little gossips. We wanted to invite them over, though, because they've sort of turned into extended family.

"You make him happy." She sets out the green bean casserole. We're lining everything up on the counter buffet style so people can plate themselves and sit in the dining room.

"He makes me happy."

"I've only ever wanted my boys to be happy. When ... well, when Forrest died, I worried I'd lose Thayer. A parent's grief has to be unimaginable, and I worried he might take his own life. I'm thankful that he's still here, that he's doing as well as he is, that he's found love. Seda too, she's such a blessing. An amazing girl. You've done well."

"You don't ... you don't hate me for keeping her a secret?"

Elaine gives me a soft, motherly smile. "Us mothers will do whatever it takes to protect our babies, so I understand you were only doing what you thought was right. But the past is the past. Let's not dwell on it. Not when we have such a beautiful life to live."

We finish setting out all the dishes and call everyone over. Winnie and Binx toddle over as well, hoping to snag some scraps from the floor. Once everyone has their plates, we sit down to eat.

Caleb ends up on my left with Thayer on my right. Seda opts to sit by Laith who I think has quickly become her new favorite person, probably due to the fact that he's basically an adult man child and has no problem playing with her.

Thayer clears his throat. "I ... uh ... I wanted to say some things before we start eating." Everyone quiets, and Laith sets down his fork, trying to pretend that he doesn't have a mouthful of turkey at the moment. "I'm really glad that we're all here together. It means a lot to be sitting down with all of you. I'm thankful to Salem," he squeezes my hand beneath the table, "for giving me a second chance and for becoming my wife. I'm thankful to you, Caleb, for ... well, for a lot, actually, which probably sounds so strange to you, but ... yeah." He trails off, clearing his throat. "Mom and Dad, you two have always been a strong presence in my life, showing me how to be a strong, kind-hearted person. Laith ... you suck. Thelma and Cynthia, thank you for joining us for dinner and always being willing to lend a helping hand. And Seda, I'm so proud to be your father. You're the brightest little girl I know. I'm so lucky." He looks around at all of us. "So lucky."

"Since I suck and all, I'm going to be the one to say it, you've turned into a sappy fuck."

"No cussing in front of my kid," Thayer growls at his brother.

Seda just giggles, not at all fazed by it.

Thayer shakes his head, his eyes meeting mine.

I look from him to all the people gathered around us. Our family might be unconventional to some, but for us, it's perfect.

CHAPTER FIFTY-TWO

Salem

The New Year comes and passes. In a blink it's March and the opening of my bakery. To say I'm nervous is an understatement. But as I stand outside looking at the building that was once my mother's antique shop, I can't help but feel a little proud. I think she would be proud of me too. She worked hard to make this place her own, and I've done the same to make it mine.

"There's one last thing it needs," Thayer says from beside me.

We're due to open at noon, and more than a few townspeople have already stopped by to wish me luck and give me flowers.

"What is it?"

"Hold on," he says, jogging over to his truck.

He returns with a metal sign. It's carved with the name of my shop. In an elegant script font, it says: Sunshine Cupcakes.

I gasp. "It's beautiful. Did you make this?"

He sets it down, going back to grab a ladder. He's thought of everything.

"I did, with help from one of my guys. He does welding on the side as a hobby so I asked him to help me out with this."

He grabs the rest of his tools and gets to work securing the sign where my mom's once was. The spot was bare since I hadn't found a sign I liked yet. Leave it to Thayer to fix that problem.

When the sign is secure, he climbs back down and we stand on the sidewalk, taking it in.

"You did it, Sunshine." The pride shines in his eyes. "You found your calling."

I did. I guess, ironically, I found it a long time ago and I didn't want to see it.

Maybe all along, my mom knew what I was meant to do. Perhaps that's why she kept asking me to bake with her. In those final weeks, I would have given her anything that she wanted, even if it meant setting foot in the kitchen and baking cupcakes again. Mothers have a way of always knowing what we need before we do. I suppose in a way this was her final gift to me. And maybe she hoped too that I would keep the shop.

I hope wherever she is, she's happy. I hope she's looking down on us, smiling at me right now. More than anything, I hope she's proud. I miss her so much every day. Even after I moved away, we talked on the phone multiple times a day. I always knew that no matter what, my mom had my back. She was strong even when she thought she was weak. And I know she didn't think that she was worth admiring, but I always looked up to her.

"You did this," Thayer says, wrapping an arm around my shoulders. He rubs up and down over my jacket, trying to stave off the chill. But with the ice and snow, there's no way to stay warm out here. It's March, but in Hawthorne Mills that just means winter isn't done with us yet.

"It wasn't just me."

He shakes his head. "You did this." Maybe he thinks if he says it enough it'll sink in for me. "I'm so proud of you, babe."

He puts his tools back in the truck and we head inside

where it's warm and the smell of baked goods permeates the air. I only plan on selling cupcakes for now, a few set flavors with one specialty flavor that changes every day. In the future I might add more baked goods, but I've always enjoyed cupcakes the most and figured it was easier to start with one thing and go from there.

Balloons and streamers are set up for my grand opening this afternoon, but there's another reason as well. I talked it over with Thayer and decided I wanted to open the shop for the first time on Forrest's birthday. It felt like a way to celebrate him. He would've loved this. We set up a table in the corner with birthday cupcakes and a donation jar for a local program that teaches babies and young kids how to swim. People underestimate the dangers of water. They think drowning is loud, chaotic, but it's the complete opposite. It's silent and often it's too late to do something when you realize there's a problem.

To think Forrest would be fourteen today.

My stomach aches that he's not here with us.

Sometimes I dream about him, what he'd be like now, how he'd be with Seda.

It's always painful when I wake up and realize it wasn't real.

In the kitchen, the two women I hired are hard at work finishing up more batches of cupcakes. I've already been here since early this morning to get a head start, but they shooed me out since I was getting too stressed.

"Is everything going okay?" I ask, peering at what they've gotten done.

"Yes, we're fine. You worry too much," Hannah says. She's young, barely out of high school, but she demonstrated a love for baking and has a talent with her icing work that I could learn a thing or two from.

"It's coming along great. Go take a break. We mean it," says Susanne.

She's in her forties and is actually Hannah's aunt. Hiring the two of them to help out has been the best thing I ever did. Not only did they pick up on all the recipes without a hitch, but they've pitched in and helped in other ways to get the store ready for this day.

Leaving them to it, I rejoin Thayer who's straightening the candle display. There aren't that many since I haven't had time to make a big batch, not with everything else that has been involved with opening my own store, but the shed behind the store is still there and I fully plan to make candles more of a priority. More for me than anything else. Making candles was my creative outlet and I still need one. I think every person benefits from working with their hands and finding something that allows them to be artistic. It's just like Thayer with his sewing—which is still the cutest thing I've ever seen. He's even started teaching Seda.

"They're fine, Thayer. Leave them be."

He takes a step back from the display, looking it over again. He adjusts one candle and nods to himself. "Now, it's perfect."

"I think you might be more nervous than I am."

He rubs a hand over his jaw. "You might be right, but only because I want today to be perfect for you." His eyes drift over to Forrest's table. "He'd almost be a high schooler."

My lips press into a flat line. "Yeah, he would be. Wow. That's crazy to think about."

Thinking about where he'd be in life is difficult to picture at times because I still see him as that sweet six-year-old boy who stole my heart just like his dad did.

He glances down at his watch. "I'm going to pick up Seda from school and then it's showtime."

We agreed to pick her up early because we wanted her to be a part of the grand opening. I still can't believe she turned six last month. I think that was tough for Thayer, though he didn't talk about it

"Okay, I'll be ... here ... trying not to overthink or throw up."

He laughs. "You're not going to do either."

"You have too much faith in me."

I watch him leave, and the desire to throw up becomes stronger when a line begins to form. I'm not surprised Thelma and Cynthia are at the very front of it.

I wipe my sweaty palms down the front of my shirt. Closing my eyes, I say a little prayer and ask my mom to send me strength.

I knew this day would be nerve-wracking, but I didn't think I'd be this much of a wreck.

Straightening things up that are already in order, I wait for Thayer to get back with Seda. My sister, Michael, and their kids are supposed to be here for the opening as well but haven't shown up yet.

I send her a text, asking where they are.

Georgia: Running a tad behind. Ms. Victoria decided to have a poop explosion.

Me: Oh no. Poor baby.

Georgia: We'll be there, don't worry.

My niece is the cutest thing, it makes me that much more excited to have another, but so far it just hasn't happened yet. I'm trying not to worry about it too much.

Hannah carries a tray of cupcakes out, adding them to the case. It's full now and ready to go, with more waiting in the back.

"Take a deep breath," she tells me, sensing my worry. "Enjoy today. You're going to want to remember it."

I know she's right. "Thanks."

Georgia and Michael arrive with the kids, and I let them inside. "This girl is giving me a run for my money," Georgia says, setting down the carrier. Michael is wrangling the two boys, telling them they can't run around the store. "Where's Thayer?" She looks around, not finding him.

"He should be here any minute. He was picking up Seda."

"The store opens in ten minutes."

Does she think I don't know that?

"It'll be fine." I don't know who I'm trying to assure—her or me.

With only two minutes to spare, they arrive. Seda runs up to me with a bouquet of peonies. "These are for you, Mommy."

I crouch down to her height. "Thank you, baby." I take them, kissing her cheek.

"They're from Dad, and me too."

Thayer grins that crooked smile I love so much. "And this too." He hands me a Diet Coke and I laugh. "I have to keep you sane."

"Thank you." I look around at my family gathered. "All of you—thank you. I couldn't have done this, any of it, without you."

Georgia points a warning finger at me. "Don't get sappy

on me now. I did my makeup and that's rare. I can't have it smeared all over my face."

I laugh, looking up at Thayer. The clock hits noon.

He bends down, whispering in my ear, "Show time."

***

"I did it, I actually did it." I jump up and down, still on a high from the grand opening. It's evening and everyone else has left. Caleb even showed up, which was nice of him, and Seda went home with him since she was tired of being at the store.

"I knew you could." Thayer finishes counting the cash in the register. "I wish you believed in yourself as much as I do—as much as everyone around you does."

I lower my head. "I'm working on it."

Sometimes it's difficult for me to understand that I'm capable of anything I set my mind to. I spent a long time lost, not knowing what I wanted or who I wanted to be, and that confusion led me to believe that maybe I wasn't good enough or smart enough. I guess, you could say, I'm my own worst critic.

Thayer tilts my chin up with the soft touch of his finger. "I know you are, or you wouldn't have done this." He looks around the shop. "But you did."

We finish cleaning up the shop and lock up for the night. I have to be back early in the morning to get started on fresh cupcakes for the day.

Thayer's truck is parked out back near the shed I make my candles in.

The sun has long since set, the sky dark with the moon and stars bright in the sky.

It's cold out and I shiver despite my coat.

"What are you doing?" Thayer asks, locking up the shop. "I started the truck. It should be warm. You don't have to stand out here."

"I know. But the stars are so beautiful tonight. They seem extra bright for some reason."

Thayer stops beside me, looking up as well. "Hmm," he hums. "They do look brighter." A soft smile touches his lips.

"How do you feel?" I ask.

His gaze lowers to mine, immediately knowing I'm asking since it's Forrest's birthday. "It's always a bittersweet day."

"I'm sorry."

"I'll see him again one day. I feel it. Somehow, someway, I will. I have to believe that."

We stand in the cold for a minute longer, taking in the night sky before we get in the truck and drive home.

Home.

The house I used to sneak over to, is my home now, but that's also just a shell. It's framework and drywall, while the man at my side is my real home.

As long as I have him, I'll have a place I belong.

The house is dark and quiet since Seda is with Caleb. Winnie and Binx watch us from the couch with annoyed expressions for disturbing their beauty sleep.

"We should eat something," Thayer says as I follow him into the kitchen.

"We probably should," I agree, biting my lip, "but..."

"But?" He turns around, looking me up and down.

"I want you."

He doesn't hesitate. His mouth is on mine in an instant. I melt beneath his touch. He lifts me up, legs going around his waist. He carries me up the stairs and straight back to our room.

My back hits the mattress and he undresses me slowly, kissing every part of my skin as he exposes it. I try to reach for his shirt, but he steps away from me. "Not yet."

"Not yet?" I whine.

He shakes his head, his eyes dark with desire. He loops his arms around my legs, pulling me to the edge of the mattress. Dropping to his knees, he wastes no time. He licks my pussy like he's been waiting all day to taste me.

"Thayer," I pant his name.

He licks and sucks, drawing out every moan and curse word he can from me.

He brings me right to the edge and stops. "Thayer!" I cry out his name in a pleading tone. "I need—"

"I know what you need," he says in a voice that tells me not to argue with him. "The delayed gratification will be worth it. You'll see."

He hooks his thumbs in the back of his shirt, yanking it off and letting it drop to the floor. My core pulses with need and desire as I watch him undress the rest of the way.

He palms his cock, his eyes heated. He looks at me lying on the bed, naked and wanting for him.

"You're mine, Sunshine," he growls in a way that is somehow both possessive and needy all at once.

"Yours."

I belonged to Thayer Holmes the summer of my eighteenth year. Neither of us knew it, but when he moved in next door, it was about to change both of our lives.

He pushes his way inside me, and we both moan from the pleasure of it.

"Do you feel that?" he asks, his voice huskier than normal. "Do you feel the way your pussy grips my cock? Your pussy was made for me and only me."

He fucks me hard and fast, like he can't get enough of me.

"Fuck, I love you," he growls into the skin of my neck. I push him over, and he obliges, lying on his back so I can ride him. I roll my hips, my head falling back.

My hands lay flat on his chest for balance. He looks up at me like I'm a fucking goddess and dammit if I don't feel powerful.

His thumb finds my clit and I gasp. "That, right there, don't stop," I beg, desperate for an orgasm after he denied me my first one.

He listens, though, and he was right, because when the orgasm overtakes me, I feel it through my entire body. I've never felt anything so powerful and intense.

My legs shake, threatening to give out and he switches our positions easily. His fingers dig into my hair, pulling at the strands.

I cry out again, another orgasm ripping through my body. "Thayer, oh God. Don't stop."

He fucks me so hard I know I'm going to feel it in my entire body tomorrow. But I don't care. I love the reminder that I'm his.

He pulls my body up, until we're sitting, rocking against each other. He's looking right into my eyes. It's intense, romantic, sexy. I wrap my arms around his neck, his chest hair tickling my bare skin. I kiss him, our tongues meeting just like our bodies.

"I think ... I think ... *oh my God.*" It feels impossible that my body can hit that peak a third time, and so close together, but it does.

Then he's coming too, shouting my name.

We collapse onto the bed, our skin damp with sweat. He wraps his big arm around my torso, tucking me against him.

We both lay there, marveling at the intensity of our love.

I don't care that this man is more than a decade older than me. It used to worry me, falling for someone so much older than me, what people might think. But fuck them. They don't know us, they don't know our love, our life, how hard we've fought to get here. I wouldn't take back loving this man. Not for a thing.

CHAPTER FIFTY-THREE

Thayer

"Babe." I knock on the door for what feels like the hundredth time. "Let me in."

"No. I have the stomach flu and I don't want you to get it." I hear her heave over the toilet. "Has Caleb gotten in from Boston yet?"

"No, not yet."

I hear her throw up again. "I'm going to take Seda and run to the store. You need some Gatorade to keep your electrolytes up."

She gags when I say Gatorade. "No Gatorade. Please."

"Well, I'm getting something. There's water in here on the nightstand. Try to drink it while I'm gone."

I hate leaving her when she's sick, but if she's this bad off, then I need to get some things.

Downstairs, Seda sits at the kitchen table with her coloring book. "Hey." I ruffle her hair, and she looks up at me with a beaming smile. "We need to run to the store to get your mom a few things."

"Okay. Can I get ice cream?"

This kid. She always knows how to sucker me. "Sure."

She closes her coloring book, putting her crayons away. We drive into town to the pharmacy. I grab a bottle of Gatorade despite Salem's protests, and some Pedialyte. Sure, it's for kids, but what could it hurt? Seda trails along with me as I go down the next aisle, searching for some medicine that might help her kick this flu.

That's when I stop dead in my tracks in the family planning aisle.

"Ow." Seda rubs her forehead from where she bumped into the side of me. "Dad, why did you stop?"

Salem hasn't bothered to take a pregnancy test for at least three months since it was constantly negative.

But it's possible what she thinks is the stomach flu is ... more.

A baby.

I swipe a pregnancy test and add it to the basket.

"What's that?" Seda asks me.

"Well, you know how your mommy and me have been trying to have a baby?"

"Yeah." She nods vigorously. "I want a sister."

I chuckle. "We don't have any choice in whether the baby is a boy or girl, but we'll love them no matter what, right?"

"Mhmm," she hums, running her finger along the goods that are lined up as I continue through the store. I'm still going to grab some flu medicine while I'm here, just in case I'm wrong. "But I still want a sister."

My shoulders shake with barely contained laughter.

Once I've gotten the medicine, I check out and drop by the local ice cream shop before heading back home. Seda licks happily at her vanilla ice cream the whole way.

Caleb isn't in yet—Salem had me call him to see if he'd come up so Seda could stay with him and not catch the flu.

The flu.

I chuckle to myself.

I don't think what Salem has is contagious. But it's cute of her to think so.

Putting a movie on for Seda, Winnie and Binx jump up on the couch to join her. "I'm going to check on Mommy."

"Okay," she replies, completely unbothered.

Grabbing the bag of goods, I jog upstairs and into the bedroom. Salem's not in the bedroom, so I try the bathroom. The door is locked.

Giving a knock, I say, "Salem, let me in."

There's a groan on the other side of the door. "I can't give you medicine if you don't unlock the door."

"I'm contagious," she whines. "I don't want you to get sick."

"Sunshine," I say through the door, "my tongue has been inside your pussy. Your sick germs are the least of my concern."

She squeaks from the other side, the door finally opening. "That was unnecessary," she mutters, her hair mussed around her face.

"It got you to open the door, didn't it?"

She rolls her eyes, holding her bathrobe tighter around her. She watches me with narrowed eyes as I set everything out on the counter. The pregnancy test is the last thing I put there. She snorts when she sees it.

"I'm not pregnant," she scoffs.

"Are you sure?"

"Are you seriously asking me if I'm sure?"

I hand her the test. "Humor me."

"I don't have to pee. Besides, you're supposed to do it in the morning."

"That's never stopped you before."

She huffs out a breath, snagging the box from my hands.

"Fine. But I can't wait to say I told you so."

She closes herself off in the separate space with the toilet. While I wait, I clean up the bathroom as best I can in just a few minutes.

The door opens and she sets the test down, washing her hands. Her nose wrinkles at the Gatorade on the counter. "I told you I didn't want that."

"And I didn't listen."

"This isn't morning sickness. In case you didn't realize, I've been sick all day long for two days now."

I clear my throat, hesitant to bring up my ex. "When Krista was pregnant with Forrest, she was sick all day the first trimester. She lost a lot of weight because of it. It was bad."

Salem exhales unsteadily. "I'm not pregnant."

I know why she's so insistent. After so many negative tests in the past I don't know how many months, she's scared to get her hopes up. I know she's been devastated time and again. I don't want to be wrong this time, for her sake, and I don't think I am. But we need that confirmation.

Salem turns a light shade of green and lunges back for the toilet.

"Sunshine," I murmur, pulling her hair back. Her body lurches.

"Go away. You shouldn't see me like this." She tries to shove me back, but her attempt is weak.

I massage the back of her neck. "In sickness, and in health, right?"

She dry heaves, gagging. "Fuck off."

I grin to myself. I love it when she gets feisty with me.

When she settles, no longer heaving, I ask, "Can I go look now?"

She slumps against the floor, shooing me away with her hand. "Knock yourself out."

I walk over to where she left the stick. My heart jolts, speeding up at the positive test.

"Salem?" I only get a groan in reply. "You're pregnant."

Her eyes widen. "No, I'm not. Don't lie." She starts to cry. "Don't lie. Not about this."

I crouch down in front of her, cupping her cheek in my hand. "I'm not lying, Sunshine. We're going to have another baby."

She sobs, and I sit down on the floor beside her, gathering her into my arms and just holding her, because that's what she needs

***

"Right there," the doctor points to the screen at a tiny little blip that doesn't even look like anything yet. "That's your baby."

Salem's hand hovers over her mouth, her eyes glued to the black and white image displayed on the screen.

I pick up her other hand, kissing her knuckles.

"That's our baby, Sunshine. Look at them."

I think to myself that this is how things should've happened with Seda, but life had other plans for us. We needed to be apart to grow into the people we've become. Our love is stronger for the trials we've endured, and both of us knows how precious life is, how important it is to cherish every moment. At the end of the day, it isn't the expensive things, or the big things you remember. It's the people you love and the simple moments— dancing in the kitchen together, sitting down and having a meal together, just *existing*.

Life is not an infinite source—it's finite, and the best thing we could all learn, is to treat it as such, because each breath in our lungs is a precious gift we shouldn't waste.

CHAPTER FIFTY-FOUR

Salem

It's beneath the treehouse, the entire structure covered in the peonies Thayer has lovingly grown for me, and a bouquet of them in my hands, just two months after finding out we're having our second baby, that we're having our official wedding ceremony in front of our loved ones.

Ironically, it was this same day a year ago that I returned to Hawthorne Mills, and now I never plan to leave this small town. We didn't plan for it to work out that way. Thayer just wanted to finally have a real ceremony, and to make good on our promise to Seda that she could be the flower girl.

The backyard is covered in peonies and white twinkle lights. It looks like something out of a dream.

I walk down our makeshift aisle on my own.

I don't need someone to give me away. I'm not an object to be given to another. I'm my own person, and I chose to be Thayer's partner, his equal, a long time ago.

My bare feet brush over the grass mixed with the petals Seda scattered. She stands at Thayer's side, smiling like a sweet little fool. Her blonde hair is curled in ringlets, hanging down her back, with a floral headband sitting like a crown on top of her head.

She's so beautiful and so grown up.

I haven't even made it to Thayer and I'm already going to cry.

The people we have here with us are an eclectic mix. Thayer's parents and brother, my sister and her family, Caleb, Cynthia and Thelma, Lauren and her husband Anthony, Hannah and Susanne from my cupcake shop, and even Jen who owns the shop in town and who has become a good friend. At the end with Thayer and Seda sits Binx and Winnie. Binx looks dapper with a bowtie and Winnie is sporting a tutu, both made by Thayer.

I finally reach the end, stopping beside my husband.

There's no officiant since our marriage is already official, this is just the icing on the cake, I guess.

Thayer's eyes crinkle at the corners. There's more gray at his temples now than a year ago, but I love it. I love *him*.

We're going to be exchanging our own vows today, new rings as well, since before we just got whatever we could in Vegas and it was nothing special or meaningful.

Thayer looks down, at the small swell of my belly pushing against the white satin of my slip dress. You can barely tell I'm pregnant yet, but soon enough my belly will pop. We've decided not to find out the gender. We thought it would be more special to wait until the birth. The anticipation might kill me, but I know it'll be worth it.

Thayer clears his throat. "I'll go first." He takes each of my hands in his. "When you came into my life almost eight years ago, I should've known from the get go that you were going to shake up my life. With your blond hair, long legs, and beautiful smile you were the most gorgeous thing I'd ever seen but also the most confounding. It drove me crazy when I realized you were running so early in the mornings, and the way you'd sit on your roof nearly gave me a heart attack." I laugh, shaking my head. I think I worried everybody but myself with my love of sitting on the roof. "I fell for you slowly, accidentally, and suddenly you became my whole world. Our journey to this moment wasn't a straight line. We've had a lot of ups and downs, but they've made us who we are, and I love you, I love us, and I love the life we've built together despite everything stacked between us."

I pull one of my hands from his, wiping beneath my eyes. "You made me cry."

Chuckles sound around us, and Thayer smiles down at me.

I give myself a moment to catch my breath before I start.

"Thayer, Thayer, Thayer," I cluck my tongue. "Do you remember the first thing you ever said to me?" He smiles, knowing where I'm going with this. He certainly didn't smile at me that day. Oh, no, all this man did for the longest time was glare and grunt at me like some prehistoric caveman. "You said, and I quote, 'You're trespassing.'" I make my voice deeper when I say it, ringing out laughs from everyone. "And *now* you're marrying that trespasser in the exact spot you were that day. How about that?" His smile grows bigger. "You said it best when you said our path wasn't linear. There's been a lot of trials and tribulations thrown our way, but somehow, we've come out stronger in the end. Thank you for letting me love you. Thank you for choosing me. I love you. Today. Tomorrow. All my days."

I sound like such a sap, but I'm pregnant so I'm allowed to be.

Cupping my cheeks, he leans forward and brushes his nose against mine, our lips a breath apart. "I love you, too, Sunshine."

His lips meet mine, kissing me with a promise.

When we break apart, Lauren passes me his new ring and

Laith hands Thayer mine.

I slip the thick black band onto his finger. The inside is gold, so he'll always have the sun close to his heart.

He takes my left hand, smiling as he slips the ring in place. It's gold with suns carved into it all the way around. It's perfect and I love that we had similar thoughts with our choices.

He kisses me again, his hand on my stomach.

A year ago, I was still angry at him.

A year ago, I was terrified to face him.

A year ago, I never could've imagined us standing in this spot.

But a lot can happen in twelve months. That's three-hundred and sixty-five days of change.

Each one leading you a step closer to your destination, whatever that might be.

I thought our story was over when I left town seven years ago, but sometimes what you think is the end, is only the beginning.

EPILOGUE

Salem

Thayer's head presses against mine, tears coating his cheeks. Our baby isn't even here yet and he's already having trouble keeping it together.

"You can do it, Sunshine. You're almost there. We're going to meet our baby."

I feel like I've waited forever to meet this little one and grow our family.

Seda's going to be a big sister, and Forrest is going to be a big brother again.

"One more big push, Salem," my doctor coaches.

I squeeze Thayer's hand, giving it my all. I'm so tired, but I just want to see my baby. To hold him or her and shower them in kisses.

And then, with a cry, our second baby comes into the world.

The doctor holds the baby up for Thayer to see—we told her ahead of time that we wanted him to tell me the gender.

Crying, he kisses me and murmurs, "We have another little girl."

I cry with him as they lay her onto my chest. I count her tiny toes and fingers. There's a light dusting of sandy brown hair on her head. Thayer's hair color.

"Hi, little baby." She curls her finger around mine. "I'm your mommy."

Thayer kisses the top of my head, then hers, then back again. "My girls." He places his hand on her back. "My little sun." He touches her cheek. "Welcome to the world, Soleil."

She cries out like she approves of the name. At least, I hope that's what she's saying.

"She's perfect." I hold her tight to my chest, not wanting to let go, but know they'll soon take her from me to do their checks.

"So are you," Thayer murmurs. "I have the three most perfect girls a man could ask for."

"You're definitely outnumbered now."

"No such thing." I know he means it too.

They take her from me then, getting her weight, height, and everything else they need.

Hours later, when things have calmed and Soleil has taken to breastfeeding, I finally get to watch Thayer have his moment with her. He sits in the chair, his shirt off, with her tiny little body resting in his arms against his chest for skin to skin. She looks so tiny in his arms, the little wrinkles in the back of her neck the cutest thing I've seen in a long time.

He starts to sing to her, and tears spring to my eyes.

"*You are my sunshine. My only sunshine.*"

We struggled to come up with a name for a long time, knowing we wanted to go with something that was special to us and could be gender neutral.

I don't even know when or where we heard Soleil, but we knew instantly it was perfect, because when the sun doesn't shine, we have our own little sun now.

THE RESURRECTION OF WILDFLOWERS

ACKNOWLEDGMENTS

This duet has been one of my greatest joys and greatest challenges to write. Salem and Thayer go through a lot, but their love is beautiful, and I hope you love their happy ending as much as I do.

A huge thank you to Emily Wittig for creating the two most stunning covers I've ever seen. But mostly for being the best friend I could ever ask for. You are the most supportive, kindest person I've ever met and I'm so lucky to have you on my side. I believe fate made sure our paths crossed.

Kellen—thank you for being my constant cheerleader. You came into my life at a very challenging time for me and your friendship has meant everything. Let's go get cheesecake now.

Cheyenne and KatieGwen, I can't thank you both enough for taking a chance on my books (and my crazy self) and ordering my books for your Barnes and Noble. You guys are so great and your passion for books (the spicier the better) is unparalleled. Please keep entertaining all of us with the best reels and tiktoks.

Thank you to Melanie for being so patient and fitting me in last minute for edits on this. You're the real MVP and I appreciate it so much. Truly.

To all the bookstagrammers, bloggers, tiktokers, and readers who have spoken so passionately about this duet. Thank you. From the bottom of my heart, thank you. Your love for Salem and Thayer has been a beautiful thing to see. Thank you for loving them like I do.

ABOUT THE AUTHOR

Micalea Smeltzer is an author from Northern Virginia. Her two dogs, Ollie and Remy, are her constant companions. As a kidney transplant recipient she's dedicated to raising awareness around the effects of kidney disease, dialysis, and transplant as well as educating people on living donation. When she's not writing you can catch her with her nose buried in a book.

Coming Soon

The Endurance of Wildflowers
Fall 2023